THE EYE IN THE DOOR

In this second volume of the trilogy which opened with *Regeneration*, the year is now 1918. The setting has shifted from Scotland and Craigl~~...~~ ~~an~~ ~~England~~ ~~suffering~~ shorta~~ges, grey bread and meagre clothes. In~~ this climate of exhaustion and hysteria amidst which the war grinds wearily to its close, pressures to fall into line for both military and civilians alike become fierce and take ugly forms. Prior is now based in London, working as an Intelligence Officer in a department run by those too old to fight at the front or who have been invalided out. His concern in this volume is the enemy within—though a clear definition of who exactly is the enemy is harder to come by than he might have expected.

THE EYE IN THE DOOR

Pat Barker

CHIVERS PRESS
BATH

First published 1993
by
Viking
This Large Print edition published by
Chivers Press
by arrangement with
The Penguin Group
1997

ISBN 0 7451 3804 7

British Library Cataloguing in Publication Data available

Photoset, printed and bound in Great Britain by
REDWOOD BOOKS, Trowbridge, Wiltshire

For David

It was on the moral side, and in my own person, that I learned to recognize the thorough and primitive duality of man; I saw that, of the two natures that contended in the field of my consciousness, even if I could rightly be said to be either, it was only because I was radically both . . .

The Strange Case of Dr Jekyll and Mr Hyde
                                    —*R. L. Stevenson*

PART ONE

CHAPTER ONE

In formal beds beside the Serpentine, early tulips stood in tight-lipped rows. Billy Prior spent several moments setting up an enfilade, then, releasing his companion's arm, seized an imaginary machine-gun and blasted the heads off the whole bloody lot of them.

Myra stared in amazement. 'You barmy bugger.'

He shook his head sadly. 'Five months in a loony bin last year.'

'Go on.'

She didn't believe him, of course. Smiling, he came back and offered her his arm. They had been wandering along beside the lake for an hour, but now the afternoon was waning. A coppery light, more like autumn than spring, slanted across the grass, turning the thorned twigs of rose bushes into strips of live electric filament that glowed, reddish, in the dusk.

Prior, always self-conscious, was aware of approving glances following them as they passed. They made a romantic picture, he supposed. The girl, young and pretty, clinging to the arm of a man in uniform, a man, moreover, wearing a greatcoat so grotesquely stained and battered it had obviously seen a good deal of active service. As indeed it had, and was about to see more, if only he could persuade the silly bitch to lie on it.

'You're cold,' he said tenderly, unbuttoning the greatcoat. 'Put your hand in here. You know, we'd be warmer under the trees. We'd be out of the wind.'

She paused, doubtfully, for by the lake it was still light, whereas the avenue of trees he was pointing to smoked darkness. 'All right,' she said at last.

They set off across the grass, their shadows stretching ahead of them, black, attenuated figures that reached the trees and began to climb before they were anywhere near. In the darkness they leant against the trunk of one of the trees and started to kiss. After a while she moaned, and her thighs slackened, and he pressed her back against the fissured bark. His open greatcoat shielded them both. Her hands slid round him, underneath his tunic, and grasped his buttocks, pulling him hard against her. She was tugging at his waistband and buttons and he helped her unfasten them, giving her free play with his cock and balls. His hands were slowly inching up her skirt. Already he'd found the place where the rough stockings gave way to smooth skin. 'Shall we lie down?'

Her hands came up to form a barrier. 'What, in this?'

'You'll be warm enough.'

'I bloody won't. I'm nithered now.' To emphasize the point she pressed her hands into her armpits and rocked herself.

'All right,' he said, his voice hardening. 'Let's go back to the flat.' He'd wanted to avoid doing that, because he knew his landlady would be in, and watching.

She didn't look at him. 'No, I think I'd better be getting back.'

'I'll take you.'

'No, I'd rather say goodbye here, if you don't mind. Me mother-in-law lives five doors down.'

'You were keen enough the other night.'

4

Myra smiled placatingly. 'Look, I had a woman come nosying round. The voluntary police, you know? They can come into your house, or anything, they don't have to ask. And this one's a right old cow. I knew her before the war. She was all for women's rights. I says, "What about my rights? Aren't I a woman?" But there's no point arguing with 'em. They can get your money stopped. And anyway it isn't right, is it? With Eddie at the Front?'

Prior said in a clipped, authoritative voice, 'He was at the Front on Friday night.' He heard the note of self-righteousness, and saw himself, fumbling with the fly buttons of middle-class morality. Good God, *no*. He'd rather tie a knot in it than have to live with that image. 'Come on,' he said. 'I'll walk you to the station.'

He strode towards Lancaster Gate, not caring if she followed or not. She came trotting breathlessly along beside him. 'We can still be friends, can't we?'

He felt her gaze on his face.

'Can't we?'

He stopped and turned to face her. 'Myra, you're the sort of girl who ends up in a ditch with her stockings round her neck.'

He walked on more slowly. After a while, her hand came creeping through his arm, and, after a moment's hesitation, he left it there.

'Have you got a girl?' she said.

A brief struggle. 'Yes.'

She nodded, satisfied. 'Thought you had. Lying little git, aren't you? Friday night, you said you hadn't.'

'We both said a bellyful on Friday night.'

At the underground station he bought her ticket, and she reached up and kissed his cheek as if nothing

5

had happened. Well, he thought, nothing had happened. On the other side of the barrier she turned, and looked as if she might be regretting the evening they'd planned, but then she gave a little wave, stepped out on to the moving staircase and was carried smoothly away.

Outside the station he hesitated. The rest of the evening stretched in front of him and he didn't know what to do. He thought about going for a drink, but rejected the idea. If he started drinking as early as this and in this mood, he'd end up drunk, and he couldn't afford to do that; he had to be clear-headed for the prison tomorrow. He drifted aimlessly along.

It was just beginning to be busy, people hurrying to restaurants and bars, doing their best to forget the shortages, the skimped clothes, the grey bread. All winter, it seemed to Prior, an increasingly frenetic quality had been creeping into London life. Easily justified, of course. Soldiers home on leave had to be given a good time; they mustn't be allowed to remember what they were going back to, and this gave everybody else a magnificent excuse for never thinking about it at all.

Though this week it had been difficult to avoid thinking. Haig's April 13th Order of the Day had appeared in full in every newspaper. He knew it off by heart. Everybody did.

There is no other course open to us but to fight it out. Every position must be held to the last man: there must be no retirement. With our backs to the wall, and believing in the justice of our cause, each one of us must fight on to the end.

Whatever effect the Order had on the morale of the

army, it had produced panic among civilians. Some women, apparently, were planning in all seriousness how they should kill themselves and their children when the Germans arrived. Those atrocity stories from the first months of the war had done the trick. Rather too well. Nuns with their breasts cut off. Priests hung upside-down and used as clappers to ring their own bells. Not that there hadn't been atrocities, but prisoners of war were always the main victims, and the guilt was more evenly distributed than the press liked to think.

There were times—and tonight was one of them—when Prior was made physically sick by the sight and sound and smell of civilians. He remembered the stench that comes off a battalion of men marching back from the line, the thick yellow stench, and he thought how preferable it was to this. He knew he had to get off the streets, away from the chattering crowds and the whiffs of perfume that assaulted his nostrils whenever a woman walked past.

Back in the park, under the trees, he began to relax. Perhaps it was his own need that coloured his perceptions, but it seemed to him that the park on this spring evening was alive with desire. Silhouetted against the sunset, a soldier and his girl meandered along, leaning against each other so heavily that if either had withdrawn the other would have fallen. It made him think of himself and Sarah on the beach in Scotland, and he turned away sharply. No point thinking about that. It would be six weeks at least before he could hope to see her again. Further along towards Marble Arch the figures were solitary. Army boots tramped and slurred along the paths or, in the deepest shadow, jetted sparks.

He sat on a bench and lit a cigarette, still trying to

decide what to do with the stump of his evening. He needed sex, and he needed it badly. Tossing off was no use, because ... because it was no use. Prostitutes were out because he didn't pay. He remembered telling Rivers, who'd been his doctor at Craiglockhart War Hospital, the 'loony bin' where he'd spent five months of the previous year, about a brothel in Amiens, how the men, the private soldiers, queued out on to the pavement and were allowed two minutes each. 'How long do officers get?' Rivers had asked. 'I don't know,' Prior had said. 'Longer than that.' And then, spitting the words, '*I don't pay.*' No doubt Rivers had thought it rather silly, a young man's ridiculous pride in his sexual prowess, his ability to 'get it' free. But it was nothing to do with that. Prior didn't pay because once, some years ago, he had been paid, and he knew exactly how the payer looks to the one he's paying.

'Got a light?'

Automatically, Prior began tapping his pockets. At first he hardly registered the existence of the speaker, except as an unwelcome interruption to his thoughts, but then, as he produced the matches, some unconsciously registered nervousness in the other man's voice made him look up. He had been going to offer the box, but now he changed his mind, took out a match and struck it himself. The rasp and flare sounded very loud. He cupped his hands to shield the flame, and held it out as the other bent towards it. An officer's peaked cap, dark eyes, a thin moustache defining a full mouth, the face rounded, though not fat. Prior was sure he knew him, though he couldn't remember where he'd seen him before. When the cigarette was lit, he didn't immediately move off, but sat further along the bench, looking vaguely around

8

him, the rather prominent Adam's apple jerking in his throat. His left leg was stretched out awkwardly in front of him, presumably the explanation of the wound stripe on his sleeve.

Prior could see the problem. This wasn't exactly the right area, though it bordered upon it, and his own behaviour, though interesting, had not been definitely inviting. He was tempted to tease. Instead he moved closer and said, 'Have you anywhere to go?'

'Yes.' The man looked up. 'It's not far.'

*   *   *

The square contained tall, narrow, dark houses, ranged round a fenced-off lawn with spindly trees. The lawn and the surrounding flowerbeds were rank with weeds. Further along, on the right, a bomb had knocked out three houses and partially demolished a fourth, leaving a huge gap. They walked along, not talking much. As they approached the gap, the pavement became gritty beneath their feet, pallid with the white dust that flowed so copiously from stricken houses and never seemed to clear, no matter how carefully the ruin was fenced off. Prior was aware of a distinct sideways pull towards the breach. He'd felt this before, walking past other bombed sites. He had no idea whether this sideways tug was felt by everybody, or whether it was peculiar to him, some affinity with places where the established order has been violently assailed.

They stopped in front of No. 27. The windows were shuttered. A cat, hunched and defensive, crouched on the basement steps, growling over something it had found.

Prior's companion was having trouble with the lock. 'Part of the damage,' he said over his shoulder, pulling a face. He jabbed the door with his shoulder, then seized the knob and pulled it towards him. 'It works if you pull, I keep forgetting that.'

'Not *too* often, I hope,' said Prior.

His companion turned and smiled, and for a moment there was a renewed pull of sexual tension between them. He took off his cap and greatcoat, and held out his hand for Prior's. 'The family's in the country. I'm staying at my club.' He hesitated. 'I suppose I'd better introduce myself. Charles Manning.'

'Billy Prior.'

Covertly, they examined each other. Manning had a very round head, emphasized by thick, sleek dark hair which he wore brushed back with no parting. His eyes were alert. He resembled some kind of animal, Prior thought, an otter perhaps. Manning saw a thin, fair-haired man, twenty-three or four, with a blunt-nosed, high-cheekboned face and a general air of picking his way delicately through life. Manning pushed open a door on the left, and a breath of dead air came into the hall. 'Why don't you go in? I won't be a minute.'

Prior entered. Tall windows shuttered, furniture shrouded in white sheets. A heavy smell of soot from the empty grate. Everything was under dust-sheets except the tall mirror that reflected, through the open door, the mirror in the hall. Prior found himself staring down a long corridor of Priors, some with their backs to him, none more obviously real than the rest. He moved away.

'Would you like a drink?' Manning asked from the door.

'Yes, please.'

'Whisky all right?'

'Fine.'

Alone, Prior walked across to the grand piano, lifted the edge of the dust-sheet and found himself looking at a photograph of a woman with two small boys, one of them clutching a sailing boat to his chest.

When Manning came back, carrying a whisky bottle, a jug and two glasses, Prior was staring at a crack above the door. 'That looks a bit ominous,' he said.

'Yes, doesn't it? I don't know what I'm supposed to do about it, really. One can't get workmen, so I just come in and look at it now and then.' He held up the jug. 'Water?'

'Just a dash.'

They moved across to the fireside chairs. Manning pulled off the sheets, and Prior settled back against the stiff brocade. It didn't give at all, but held him tensely upright. They started making the sort of conversation they might have made if they'd been introduced in the mess. Prior watched Manning carefully, noting the MC ribbon, the wound stripe, the twitches, the signs of tension, the occasional stammer. He was in a state, though it was difficult to tell how much of his nervousness was due to the situation. Which *was* dragging on a bit. If this went on they'd demolish the whole bloody bottle and still be swapping regimental chit-chat at midnight. All very nice, Prior thought, but not what I came for. He noticed that Manning's eyes, though they roamed all over the place, always returned to the stars on Prior's sleeve. *Well, you knew I was an officer*, he said silently. He was beginning to suspect Manning might be one of those who cannot—simply cannot—let go

11

sexually with a social equal. Prior sighed, and stood up. 'Do you mind if I take this off?' he said. 'I'm quite warm.'

He wasn't warm. In fact, to coin a phrase, he was bloody nithered. However. He took off his tie, tunic and shirt, and threw them over the back of a chair. Manning said nothing, simply watched. Prior ran his fingers through his cropped hair till it stood up in spikes, lit a cigarette, rolled it in a particular way along his bottom lip, and smiled. He'd transformed himself into the sort of working-class boy Manning would think it was all right to fuck. A sort of seminal spittoon. And it worked. Manning's eyes grew dark as his pupils flared. Bending over him, Prior put his hand between his legs, thinking he'd probably never felt a spurt of purer class antagonism than he felt at that moment. He roughened his accent. 'A' right?'

'Yes. Let's go upstairs.'

Prior followed him. On the first floor a door stood open, leading into a large bedroom with a double bed. Manning pulled the door shut. Prior smiled faintly. 'E would not take Oi into the bed where 'e 'ad deflowered 'is broide. Instead 'e went up and up and bloody up. To what were obviously the *servants'* quarters. Manning pushed open a door at the end of the corridor, handed Prior the lamp and said, 'I won't be a minute.'

Prior went in. A double bed with a brass bedstead almost filled the tiny room. He sat on the edge and bounced up and down. It was quite possibly the noisiest bed he'd ever encountered. Thank God the house was empty. Apart from the bed there was a washstand with a jug and bowl, a table with a looking-glass, and a small closet curtained off. He got up and pulled the curtain back. Two housemaids' uniforms hung there, looking almost like the maids themselves, the sleeves and caps had been so neatly arranged. A smell came from the closet: lavender and sweat, a sad smell. Prior's mother had started her life in service in just such a house as this. He looked round the room, the freezing little box of a room, with its view of roofs, and, on a sudden impulse, got one of the uniforms out and buried his face in the armpit, inhaling the smell of sweat. This impulse had nothing to do with sex, though it came from a layer of personality every bit as deep. Manning came back into the room just as Prior raised his head. Seeing Prior with the uniform held against him, Manning looked, it had to be said, daunted. Prior smiled, and put the uniform back on the peg.

Manning set a small jar down on the table by the bed. The click of glass on wood brought them into a closer, tenser relationship than anything they'd so far managed to achieve. Prior finished undressing and lay down on the bed. Manning's leg was bad. Very bad. Prior leant forward to examine the knee, and for a moment they might have been boys in the playground again, examining each other's scabs.

'It looks as if you're out of it.'

'Probably. The tendons've shortened, you see. They think I've got about as much movement as I'm going to get. But then who knows? The way things are going, is anybody out of it?'

Prior straightened up, and, since he was in the neighbourhood, began to rub his face across the hair in Manning's groin. Manning's cock stirred and rose and Prior took it into his mouth, but even then, for a long time, he simply played, flicking his tongue round and round the glistening dome. Manning's thighs tautened. After a while his hand came up and

13

caressed Prior's cropped hair, his thumb massaging the nape of his neck. Prior raised his head and saw that Manning looked nervous, rightly, since in this situation it was a gesture of tenderness that would precipitate violence, if anything did. And Manning was in no state to cope with that. He went back to his sucking, clasping Manning's buttocks in his two hands and moving his mouth rapidly up and down the shaft. Manning pushed him gently away and got into bed. They lay stretched out for a moment side by side. Prior rolled on to his elbow and started to stroke Manning's chest, belly and thighs. He was thinking how impossible it is to sum up sex in terms of who stuffs what into where. This movement of his hand had in it lust; resentment, of Manning's use of the room among other things; sympathy, for the wound; envy, because Manning was *honourably* out of it ... And a growing awareness that while he had been looking at Manning, Manning had also been looking at him. Prior's expression hardened. He thought, Well, at least I don't twitch as much as you do. The stroking hand stopped at Manning's waist, and he tried to turn him over, but Manning resisted. 'No,' he said. 'Like this.'

Athletic sod. Prior unscrewed the jar, greased his cock with a mixture of vaseline and spit, and wiped the residue on Manning's arse. He guided Manning's legs up his chest, being exceedingly careful not to jerk the knee. He was too eager, and the position was hopeless for control, he was fighting himself before he'd got an inch in, and then Manning yelped and tried to pull away. Prior started to withdraw, then suddenly realized that Manning needed to be hurt. 'Keep still,' he said, and went on fucking. It was a dangerous game. Prior was capable of real sadism,

14

and knew it, and the knee was only a inch or so away from his hand. He came quickly, with deep shuddering groans, a feeling of being pulled out of himself that started in his throat. Carefully, he lowered Manning's legs and sucked him off. He was so primed he was clutching Prior's head and gasping almost before he'd started. 'I needed that,' he said, when it was over. 'I needed a good fucking.'

You all do, Prior thought. Manning went to the bathroom. Prior reached out and turned the looking-glass towards him. Into this glass they had looked, half past five every morning, winter and summer, yawning, bleary-eyed, checking to see their caps were on straight and their hair tucked away. He remembered his mother telling him that, in the house where she'd worked, if a maid met a member of the family in the corridor she had to stand with her face turned to the wall.

Manning came back carrying the whisky bottle and glasses. He was limping badly. Despite Prior's efforts the position couldn't have done the knee any good.

'Where d'you get it?' Prior asked, nodding at the wound.

'Passchendaele.'

'Oh, yes. Your lot were in the assault on the ridge?'

'That's right.' Manning poured the whisky and sat at the end of the bed, propping himself up against the bedstead, and stretching his left leg out in front of him. 'Great fun.'

Prior said, 'I've just had a Board.' He didn't want to talk about his condition, but he was incapable of leaving the subject alone. Manning's silence on the subject, when a question would have been so much more natural, had begun to irritate him.

15

'What did they say?' Manning asked.

'They haven't said anything yet. I'm supposed to be Permanent Home Service, but with things the way they are...'

Manning hesitated, then asked, 'It *is* neurasthenia, isn't it?'

No, Prior wanted to say, it's raging homicidal mania, with a particular predilection for dismembering toffee-nosed gits with wonky knees. 'No, it's asthma,' he said. 'I *was* neurasthenic, but then I had two asthmatic attacks in the hospital, so that confused things a bit.'

'Which hospital were you in?'

'Craiglockhart. It's up in—'

'Ah, then you know Rivers.'

Prior stared. 'He was my doctor. Still is. He's ... he's in London now.'

'Yes, I know.'

It was Prior's turn not to ask the obvious question.

'Are you still on sick leave?' Manning asked, after a pause.

'No, I'm at the Ministry of Munitions. In the...' He looked at Manning. 'And *that's* where I've seen you. I *knew* I had.'

Manning smiled, but he was very obviously not pleased. 'Just as well I didn't call myself "Smith". I thought about it.'

'If you're going to do that I'd remove the letters from the hall table first. They aren't addressed to "Smith".' Prior looked down into his glass, and gave up the struggle. 'How do you know Rivers?'

Manning smiled. 'He's my doctor, too.'

'Shell-shock?'

'No. Not exactly. I ... er ... I was picked up by the police. About two months ago. Not quite caught in

16

the act, but ... The young man disappeared as soon as we got to the police station. Anyway.'

'What happened?'

'Oh, we all sat around. Nobody did anything unpleasant. I sent for my solicitor, and eventually he arrived, and they let me go. Wound helped. Medal helped.' He looked directly at Prior. '*Connections* helped. You mustn't despise me too easily, you know. I'm not a fool. And then I went home and waited. My solicitor seemed to think if it went to court I'd get two years, but they probably wouldn't give me hard labour because of the leg.'

'That's big of them.'

'Yes. Isn't it? Then somebody said the thing to do was to go to a psychologist and get treatment and and ... and that would help. So I went to Dr Head, who has quite a reputation in this field—I was actually told in so many words "Henry Head can cure sodomites"—and he said he couldn't do me, he was snowed under, and he recommended Rivers. So I went to him, and he said he'd take me on.'

'Do you *want* to be cured?'

'No.'

'What does he do?'

'Talks. Or rather, *I* talk. He listens.'

'About sex?'

'No, not very often. The war, mainly. You see that's where the confusion comes in because he took one look at me and decided I was neurasthenic. I mean, I can see his point. I was in quite a state when I came out of hospital. A lot worse than I realized at the time. One night at dinner I just picked up a vase and smashed it against the wall. It was quite a large party, about twelve people, and there was this awful ... silence. And I couldn't explain why I'd done it.

17

Except the vase was hideous. But then my wife said,
"So is your Aunt Dorothea. Where is that sort of
thinking going to lead?"' He smiled. 'I can't talk to
anybody else, so I talk to him.'

Prior put his hand on Manning's arm. 'Are you
going to be all right? I mean, are they going to leave
you alone?'

'I don't know. I think if they were going to bring
charges they'd've brought them by now.' His voice
deepened. '"*At that moment there was a knock on the
door* ..."'

Prior was thinking. 'All the same, it's rather
convenient, isn't it? That you're neurasthenic?'

'Not particularly.'

'I meant for Rivers. He doesn't have to talk
abou—'

'I don't know what Rivers thinks. Anyway, it's the
war I need to talk about. And even with him, you
know, there are some things I couldn't—'

'You will.'

They lay and looked at each other. Manning said,
'You were going to say which part of the ministry—'

'Yes, so I was. Intelligence.'

'With Major Lode?'

'Yes. With Major Lode. And you?'

'I'm on the fifth floor.'

Evidently the location was the answer. Manning
turned and threw his arm across Prior's chest. 'Do
you fancy a bit of turn and turn about? Or don't you
do that?'

Prior smiled. 'I do anything.'

18

CHAPTER TWO

Charles Manning left the Ministry of Munitions two hours earlier than usual and went to his house, where he'd arranged to meet a builder who'd promised to repair the bomb damage. It was mid-afternoon. A surprisingly sticky day for spring, warm and damp. When the sun shone, as it did fitfully, emerging from banks of black cloud, the young leaves on the trees glowed a vivid, almost virulent green.

He was walking abstractedly past the bombed site, when the crunch of grit and the smell of charred brick made him pause, and peer through a gap in the fence. The demolished houses had left an outline of themselves on either side of the gap, like after-images on the retina. He saw the looped and trellised bedroom wallpaper that once only the family and its servants would have seen, exposed now to wind and rain and the gaze of casual passers-by. Nothing moved in that wilderness, but, somewhere out of sight, dust leaked steadily from the unstaunchable wound.

Suddenly a cat appeared, a skinny cat, one of the abandoned pets that hung around the square. It began picking its way among the rubble, sharply black and sleek, a silhouette at once angular and sinuous. It stopped, and Manning was aware of baleful yellow eyes turned in his direction, of a cleft pink nose raised to sift the air. Then it continued on its way, the soft pads of its feet finding spaces between shards of glittering glass. Manning watched till it was

19

out of sight. Then, thinking he must get a move on, he swung his stiff leg up the steps to his house and inserted his key in the lock, remembering, with a faint smile, that he must *pull* and not push.

There was an envelope in the post-box. He took it out and carried it through into the drawing-room, his eyes gradually becoming accustomed to the darkness. A heavy smell of soot. There must have been another fall: chimney-sweeping was another job one couldn't get done. He looked down at the envelope. Typewritten. Tradesman, probably. His family and friends all knew he was staying at his club. He put the letter down on the dust-sheet that covered the sofa and walked to the other end of the room, where he opened the shutters, letting in a flood of sickly yellow light.

He went to look at the crack above the door. Is it a load-bearing wall? the builder had asked. Manning thumped with his clenched fist. It didn't sound hollow or feel flimsy, but then these houses were very solidly built. He crossed to the front wall, banged again and thought perhaps he *could* detect a difference. Not much in it, though. He went back to the crack and noticed that the whole surround of the door had been loosened. In fact the more closely one examined it the worse it appeared. That looks ominous, Prior had said, smiling slightly. Odd lad. Even as he felt himself begin to stir at the recollection of the evening, Manning's mind was at work, categorizing. At first, noting Prior's flattened vowels, he'd thought, oh yes. Temporary gentleman. A nasty, snobbish little phrase, but everybody used it, though obviously one tried not to use it in connection with people one liked. But the amazing thing was how persistent one's awareness of class distinction

20

was. The mind seemed capable of making these minute social assessments in almost any circumstances. He remembered the Somme, how the Northumberlands and Durhams had lain, where the machine-guns had caught them, in neat swathes, like harvested wheat. Later that night, crashing along a trench in pitch-blackness, trying desperately to work out where the frontage he was responsible for ended, he'd stumbled into a Northumberlands' officer, very obviously shaken by the carnage inflicted on his battalion. And who could blame him? God knows how many they'd lost. Manning, sympathizing, steadying, well aware that his own nerves had not yet been tested, had none the less found time to notice that the Northumberlands' officer dropped his aitches. He'd been jarred by it. Horrified by the reaction, but jarred nevertheless. And the odd thing was he knew if the man had been a private, he would not have been jarred, he would have handled the situation much better.

As the evening with Prior had gone on, the description 'temporary gentleman' had come to seem less and less appropriate. It suggested one of those dreadful people—well, they *were* dreadful—who aped their betters, anxious to get everything 'right', and became, in the process, pallid, morally etiolated and thoroughly nauseating. Prior was saved from that not because he didn't imitate—he did—but because he wasn't anxious. Once or twice one might almost have thought one detected a glint of amusement. A hint of parody, even. All the same, the basic truth was the man was neither fish nor fowl nor good red herring. *Socially*. Sexually too, of course, though this was a less comfortable reflection. He had a girl in the north, he said, but then they all said that.

21

Manning had suggested they should meet again, and Prior had agreed, but politely, without much enthusiasm. Probably he wouldn't come, and probably it would be just as well. His working at the Ministry brought the whole thing rather too close to ... well. Too close.

Manning looked at his watch. Ten minutes before the builder was due. He walked across to the piano, lifted the dust-sheet and brought out the photograph of Jane and the boys. Taken last summer. What a little podge Robert had been. Still was. He'd always be a round-cheeked, nondescript sort of child. He was clutching the boat as if he suspected somebody was planning to take it away from him. No doubt James had been. He's like me, Manning thought, looking at Robert. He felt an almost painful love for his elder son, and sometimes he heard himself speaking too sharply to the boy, but it was only because he could see so much of himself. He knew the areas of vulnerability, and that made him afraid, because in the end one cannot protect one's children. Everybody—Robert too, probably, that was the sad thing—assumed James was his favourite. It wasn't true. His love for James was an altogether sunnier, less complicated emotion. He had more *fun* with James, because he could see James was resilient. He had his mother's dark, clearly defined brows, her cheekbones, her jaw, the same amused, direct look. The photograph didn't do her justice; somehow the sunlight had bleached the strength out of her face. Probably she looked prettier because of it, but she also looked a good deal less like Jane. 'It was *hideous*.' The vase he'd thrown at the wall. 'So is your Aunt Dorothea. Where is that sort of thinking going to lead?' Typical Jane. It sounded unsympathetic, but

22

it wasn't. Not really. She was a woman who could have faced any amount of physical danger without flinching, but the shadows in the mind terrified her.

Manning moved across to the fireplace. On the way he noticed the letter and picked it up again, wondering once more who would have written to this address. There were no outstanding bills. Everybody knew he was at the club. He began to open it, thinking he should probably ask the builder to do something about the dent in the wall where the vase had struck. Inside the envelope, instead of the expected sheet of paper, was a newspaper cutting. He turned it the right way up and read:

THE CULT OF THE CLITORIS

To be a member of Maud Allen's private performance in Oscar Wilde's *Salome* one has to apply to a Miss Valetta, of 9 Duke Street, Adelphi, WC. If Scotland Yard were to seize the list of these members I have no doubt they would secure the names of several thousand of the first 47,000.

He'd seen the paragraph before. It had been reproduced—usually without the heading—in several respectable newspapers, though it had originated in the *Vigilante*, Pemberton Billing's dreadful rag. Maud Allan—they hadn't even spelt her name right—was suing Pemberton Billing for libel. A grave mistake, in Manning's view, because once in the witness-box Pemberton Billing could accuse anybody with complete impunity. He would be immune from prosecution. The people he named would not. Of course you could see it from Maud Allan's point of view. She would be ruined if she didn't sue. She was probably ruined anyway.

23

The question was, why had it been sent to him, and by whom? The postmark told him nothing useful. There was no covering letter. Manning dropped the cutting on the sofa, then picked it up again, holding the flimsy yellowing page between his thumb and forefinger. He wiped his upper lip on the back of his hand. Then he turned to the mirror as if to consult himself and, because he'd left the drawing-room door open, found himself looking into a labyrinth of repeated figures. His name was on that list. He was going to *Salome*, and not simply as an ordinary member of the public, but in the company of Robert Ross who, as Oscar Wilde's literary executor, had authorized the performance.

Immediately he began to ask himself whether there was an honourable way out, but then he thought, no, that's no use. To back out now would simply reveal the extent of his fear to to to ... to whoever was watching. For obviously somebody was. Somebody had known to send the cutting here.

Prior worked in the Intelligence Unit with Major Lode. Perhaps that had something to do with it? He didn't know. He didn't know anything, that was the devil of it.

The bell rang. Still holding the page, Manning went to the door. A thin, spry, greying man, with rheumy blue eyes and 'a top o' the morning to you, sorr' expression, stood on the step.

'Captain Manning?' He took off his cap. 'O'Brien, sir. I've come about the repairs.'

Manning became aware that he was gaping. He swallowed, pushed the cutting into his tunic pocket, and said, 'Yes, of course. Come in.'

He showed O'Brien the crack in the wall, feeling almost too dazed to follow what he was saying. He

24

made himself concentrate. It was a load-bearing wall.

'How long do you think it'll take?'

O'Brien pursed his lips. 'Three days. *Normally.* Trouble is, you see, sir, you can't get the lads. Williams now.' O'Brien shook his head sadly. 'Good worker in his day. The nipper. Willing lad. Not forward for his age. Samuels.' O'Brien tapped his chest. 'Dust gets on his lungs.'

'How long?'

'Fortnight? Three weeks?'

'When can you start?'

'Any time, sir. Would Monday suit you?'

It had to be said O'Brien was a man who inspired instant mistrust. I hope I'm doing the right thing, Manning thought, showing him to the door. He went back to look at the crack again. In the course of exploring its load-bearing properties O'Brien had dislodged a great quantity of plaster. Manning looked down at the grey dust. He was beginning to suspect O'Brien's real talent might be for demolition. Oh, what does it matter, he thought. His fingers closed round the cutting and he brought it out again. He'd remembered that, a couple of months ago, when the article about the Black Book and the 47,000 had first appeared, Robert Ross had been sent a copy. Just like this. Anonymously. No covering letter. He walked to the window and looked into the garden. There was a curious tension about this yellow light, as if there might be thunder in the offing. And the bushes—all overgrown, there'd been no proper pruning done for years—were motionless, except for the very tips of their branches that twitched ominously, like cats' tails. A few drops of rain began to fall, splashing on to the dusty terrace. A memory struggled to surface. Of sitting somewhere in the dust

25

and rain beginning to fall. Drops had splashed on to his face and hands and he'd started to cry, but tentatively, not sure if this was the right response. And then a nursery maid came running and swept him up.

He'd ask Ross tonight whether he'd received a cutting, or knew of anybody else who had. Not that it would be reassuring. Ross was a dangerous person to know, and would become more dangerous as the hysteria over the Pemberton Billing case mounted. The prudent thing would be to drop him altogether. Somehow, articulating this clearly for the first time helped enormously. Of course he wasn't going to drop Ross. Of course he was going to *Salome*. It was a question of courage in the end.

Why to the house? Anybody who knew him well enough to know his name would be on the list of subscribers must also know he was staying at his club. But then perhaps they also knew he visited the house regularly, to check that everything was all right, and ... other things.

He mustn't fall into the trap of overestimating what they knew. At the moment he was doing their job for them.

Opening the letter like this in his own home was in some ways a worse experience than opening it at the club would have been. His damaged house leaked memories of Jane and the children, and of himself too, as he had been before the war, memories so vivid in comparison with his present depleted self that he found himself moving between pieces of shrouded furniture like his own ghost.

There was nothing to be gained by brooding like this. He made sure the fallen plaster was caught on the dust-sheet and had not seeped underneath to be

26

trodden into the carpet, shuttered the windows, replaced the photograph beneath the dust-sheet, and let himself out.

Rain was falling. As he left the square and started to walk briskly down the Bayswater Road, reflections of buildings and shadows of people shone fuzzily in the pavements, as if another city lay trapped beneath the patina of water and grease. He kept his head down, thinking he would go to see Ross tonight, and remembering too that he was due to see Rivers next week. He passed the Lancaster Gate underground with its breath of warm air, and walked on.

In Oxford Street a horse had fallen between the shafts of a van and was struggling feebly to get to its feet. The usual knot of bystanders had gathered. He was going to be *all right*. He was...

Suddenly, the full force of the intrusion into his home struck at him, and he was cowering on the pavement of Oxford Street as if a seventy-hour bombardment were going on. He pretended to look in a shop window, but he didn't see anything. The sensation was extraordinary, one of the worst attacks he'd ever had. Like being naked, high up on a ledge, somewhere, in full light, with beneath him only jeering voices and millions of eyes.

CHAPTER THREE

Prior sat in the visitors' waiting-room at Aylesbury Prison, right foot resting on his left knee, hands clasping his ankle, and stared around him. The shabbiness of this room was in marked contrast to the brutal but impressive blood-and-bandages façade of the prison, though the shabbiness too was designed to intimidate. Everything—the chipped green paint, the scuffed no-colour floor, the nailed-down chairs—implied that those who visited criminals were probably criminals themselves. A notice on the wall informed them of the conditions under which they might be searched.

Prior looked down at his greatcoat and flicked away an imaginary speck of dust. This was not the battered and stained garment that Myra had so foolishly refused to lie on, but an altogether superior version which had cost two months' salary. In these circumstances, it was worth every penny.

The door opened and the wardress came in. With very slightly exaggerated courtesy, Prior rose to his feet. Sad but true, that nothing puts a woman in her place more effectively than a chivalrous gesture performed in a certain manner.

'Yes, well, it does seem to be in order,' she said.

He nodded. 'Good.'

'If you'd like to come this way.'

He reached the door first and held it open. He wasn't inclined to waste sympathy on her, this middle-aged, doughy-skinned woman. She had her own power, after all, more absolute than any *he* possessed. If she were humiliated now, no doubt some clapped-out old whore would be made to pay.

He followed her down the corridor and out into the yard.

'That's the women's block,' she said, pointing.

A gloomy, massive building. Six rows of windows, small and close together, like little piggy eyes. Prior looked at the yard. 'But surely the men can see the women when they exercise?'

'Oh, no,' she said. 'They can't see out of the windows. They're too high up for that.'

He asked her one or two questions about the way the prison was run, how the shift system worked, whether transport to the prison was provided. It had occurred to him that it might not be some anonymous whore who paid for his victory, but the woman he had come to see, and he was anxious to avoid that. 'Shift working must be quite difficult,' he said. 'Particularly for women.'

They stood in the cold yard while he got the story of her ailing mother. Then he held the door of the women's block open for her, and this time she blushed instead of bridling, since the gesture was being offered in a different spirit. Or she thought it was.

Another corridor. 'I know this is terribly irregular,' he said. 'A man seeing a female prisoner alone. But you do understand, don't you? It *is* a matter of *security...*'

'Oh, yes, yes. The only reason I questioned it was her being confined to the cell. We know all about security. We've had a leader of the Irish rebellion in *here.*' An internal struggle, then she burst out, 'She was a *countess.*'

29

Her face lit up with all the awe and deference of which the English working class is capable. Oh dear oh dear.

'Roper's a different kettle of fish,' she went on. 'Common as muck.'

They went through another set of doors and into a large hall. Prior would have liked some warning of this. He'd expected another corridor, another room. Instead he found himself standing at the bottom of what felt like a pit. The high walls were ringed with three tiers of iron landings, studded by iron doors, linked by iron staircases. In the centre of the pit sat a wardress who, simply by looking up, could observe every door. Prior's escort went across and spoke to her colleague.

Prior looked around him, wondering what sort of women needed to be kept in a place like this. Prostitutes, thieves, girls who 'overlaid' their babies, abortionists who stuck their knitting needles into something vital—did they really need to be here? A bell rang. Behind him the doors opened and a dozen or so women trudged into the room, diverging into two lines as they reached the stairs to the first landing. They wore identical grey smocks that covered them from neck to ankle and blended with the iron grey of the landings, so that the women looked like columns of moving metal. Evidently they were not allowed to speak, and for a while there was no sound except for the clatter of their boots on the stairs, and a chorus of coughs.

Then a youngish woman turned her head and noticed him. Instantly, a stir of excitement ran along the lines, like the rise of hair along a dog's spine. They broke ranks and came crowding to the railings, shouting down comments on what they could see, and speculations on the size of what they couldn't. Somebody suggested he might like to settle the matter by getting it out. Then a short square-headed woman jostled her way to the front and lifted her smock to her shoulders, high enough for it to become apparent that His Majesty's bounty did not extend to the provision of knickers. She jabbed her finger repeatedly towards the mound of thinning hair. Then a whistle blew, wardresses came running, and the women were hustled back into line. The tramp of feet started again, and soon the landings were empty and silent, except for the banging of doors and the rattle of keys in locks. The entire incident had taken less than three minutes.

Prior's wardress came back. 'That's a relief,' he said. 'I was beginning to feel like a pork chop in a famine.'

This did not go down well. 'Roper's on the top landing,' she said.

Their boots clanged on the stairs. Looking down now at the empty landings, Prior was puzzled by a sense of familiarity that he couldn't place. Then he remembered. It was like the trenches. No Man's Land seen through a periscope, an apparently empty landscape which in fact held thousands of men. That misleading emptiness had always struck him as uncanny. Even now, as he tramped along the third landing, he felt the prickle of hair in the nape of his neck.

The wardress stopped outside No. 39. She bent and peered through the peephole before unlocking the door. 'Here you are,' she said. 'I'm afraid I'll have to lock you in. When you're finished just bang on the door. I'll be along at the end. Good loud bang, mind.' She hesitated. 'She's been on hunger strike. You'll

31

find her quite weak.'

He followed the wardress into the room. It seemed very dark, though a small, high, barred window set into the far wall let in a shaft of light. The reflection of the bars was black on the floor, then suddenly faded, as a wisp of cloud drifted across the sun. As his eyes became accustomed to the dark, he saw a grey figure huddled on the plank bed, one skinny arm thrown across its face. Apart from the bed, the only other furnishing was a bucket, smelling powerfully of urine and faeces.

'Roper?'

The figure on the bed neither moved nor spoke.

'This is Lieutenant Prior. He's come to talk to you.'

Still no response. For a moment he thought she was dead, and he'd arrived too late. He said, 'I'm from the Ministry of Munitions.'

Her face remained hidden. 'Then you'd better bugger off back there, then, hadn't you?'

The wardress clicked her tongue. 'I'll leave you to it,' she said. She glanced round the bare cell. 'Do you want a chair?'

'No, I can manage.'

'He'll not be stopping long enough to need a chair.'

The door banged shut. He listened for the sound of retreating footsteps. He walked closer to the bed. 'You know, if you co-operate, there could be a chance of remission.'

Silence.

'That's if you give us the information we need.'

Her eyes stayed shut. 'I've told *you* once already. Bugger off back to London you greasy, arse-licking little sod.'

At last he heard the clump of boots on the landing.

'Prison hasn't done much for your language has it, Beattie?'

Her eyes opened. He moved so that the light from the window fell directly on to his face.

'Billy?'

He went closer. She looked him up and down, even touched his sleeve, while a whole army of conflicting emotions fought for possession of her face. She settled for the simplest. Hatred of the uniform. 'Your dad must be turning in his grave.'

'Well, I expect he would be if he was *in* it. He isn't, he's alive and kicking. My mother, mainly.' She'd never liked him to talk about his father's treatment of his mother. Now, with that remark, they were back in Tite Street, in the room behind the shop, beef stew and dumplings simmering on the stove, Hettie peering into the mirror above the mantelpiece, tweaking curls on to her forehead. Before the sense of intimacy could be lost, he went and sat on the end of her bed, and she shifted a little to make room for him. 'You'll never guess what *I've* just seen,' he said in the same gossipy tone, and lifted an imaginary smock above his head.

Her face lit up with amusement. 'Mad Mary,' she said. 'Eeh, dear me, everybody sees that, chaplain, governor. I says, "Put it away, Mary, it's going bald." But you can't reason with her, she's away to the woods is that one, but you'd be surprised how many are. There's women in here should *never*'ve been sent to prison. They need help. Hey, and we've had a countess, an Irish rebel, I met her in the yard. She says, "You're the woman who tried to kill Lloyd George. Let me shake your hand." I says, "Well, it's very kind of you, love, but I didn't."'

'Didn't you?'

'Course I bloody didn't.' She stared at him. 'Did I try to kill Lloyd George by sticking a curare-tipped blowdart in his arse? No. I. did. not. Now if you're asking, "Suppose you *had* a curare-tipped blowdart and Lloyd George's arse was just here, would you stick it in?" 'course I bloody would, because there'll be no peace while that bugger's in power.'

Prior shook his head. 'You can't fasten it on to *one* person like that.'

'Can't you? *I* can.'

'I don't see how you can derive that from a Marxist analysis.'

'Bugger Marxist analysis, I hate the sod.'

He waited. 'Enough to kill him?'

'Yes, enough to kill him! And I wouldn't feel guilty about it either. Any more than he feels guilty about the millions and millions of young lives he's chucked away.' She fell back, her mouth working. 'I'm not your milk-and-water, creeping Jesus sort of pacifist.'

'It might've been better if you hadn't said all that in court.'

'I told the *truth* in court. The truth, the whole truth, and nothing but the truth.' She laughed. 'Bloody fatal, that was. Do you know, Billy, I've seen the time I could con anybody into anything, when I was a young woman. Now they ask me a simple question and the truth pours out.' She shook her head. 'It's mixing with bloody Quakers, that's what's done it. Good Christian company's been the ruin of me.'

'So you didn't plan to kill him?'

'The poison was for the dogs.'

She hitched herself up the bed and propped her head against the wall. It was possible in this position to see how emaciated she was, how waxy her skin. Her hair, which had been brown the last time he saw her, was now almost entirely white. Thin strands escaped from the bun at the back of her head and straggled about her neck. He started to speak, but she interrupted him. 'What are you here for, Billy?'

'To help you.'

She smiled. 'So what was all that about information?'

'I had to say that. She was listening.'

'But you *are* from the Ministry of Munitions?'

''Course I am. How do you think I got in? Doesn't mean I'm here for information, does it?' He leant forward. 'Think about it, Beattie. What information have you *got*?'

She bridled. 'You'd be surprised. People coming in and out.' Then she pulled a face. 'Actually, there's not that many politicals in here. They're all on about their fannies. You lose patience.'

'I want you to tell me what happened.'

'You mean you don't know?'

'I haven't got a transcript of the trial.'

'Haven't you? You do surprise me. Why don't you go and talk to Spragge?'

'I will. I want your version first, because I haven't heard your version.' He waited. 'Look, Beattie, whatever damage was done was done at the trial. I'm not asking you to name any names that didn't come out then.'

She brooded for a moment. 'You know Tommy Blenkinsop's dead?'

'Tommy—'

'The deserter I had stopping with me. Hettie had gone away to live, you know, she was teaching over at Middleton, so I had this spare room, and I said I'd put Tommy up. Eeh, poor little Tommy, eleven kids, and do you know to look at him you wouldn't've

35

thought he had a fuck in him? He says to me, "You know, Beattie, I only joined up for a bit of peace." Poor lad. Anyway, that night we were sat over the fire, Tommy and me, and there was this knock on the door, and I says to Tommy, "You go on upstairs, love." I answered it and there was...' She sighed, looking into the distance. 'Spragge. Rain pouring off him, it was a terrible night. And he said he had a letter from Mac, so of course I asked him to come in. I've had time to think since then. It was *Mac* he was after. *He* was the big fish, we just got caught in the net. And the letter was genuine enough, he'd took Mac in as well as me, so he must've been convincing, mustn't he? Anyway, he explained he was on his way to Liverpool, and he says, "Can you put me up?" and I says, "Well, no, not really." And then I thought, we-ell, and I says, "Unless you don't mind sharing a bed," and I told him about Tommy. "Is he of the homogenic persuasion?" he says. Well, I just looked at him. I says, "No, I shouldn't think so, he's got eleven kids, do you want the bed or not?" So he decided he was stopping and we sat down round the table, and after a while he notices the photograph of our William on the mantelpiece. I don't know whether he knew about our William, I think he must've done, though, because he kept bringing the conversation round, and saying what a fine lad he was and all that. And you know I was worried sick about our William, because I knew what was going on, you see, he'd managed to get a letter smuggled out.'

'What *was* going on?'

'Well. You see, William didn't get exemption. He ... Partly he was unlucky with the Board, but you know they don't like *moral* objectors anyway. If

36

you're religious—doesn't matter how batty it is— you can say you've got the Holy Spirit in a jamjar on the mantelpiece—that's all right, that's *fine*. If you say, "I think it's morally wrong for young men to be sent out to slaughter each other," God help you. The Chairman of the Board actually said to our William, "You can't be a *conscientious* objector because you don't believe in God, and people who don't believe in God don't have consciences." That was the level of it. Anyway, if you're refused exemption you get handed over to the army. The military police show up and take you off to the barracks and you get given your first order, generally, "Get stripped off and put the uniform on." And of course the lads refuse, and then it's the detention centre. Our William was sent to Wandsworth, and it was really tough. He was stripped and put in a cell with a stone floor and no glass in the window—this is *January*, mind—and then, he says, they just put a uniform beside you and they wait to see how long it'll take you to give in. Of course I was worried sick, I thought he was going to get pneumonia, but actually he said in his letter it wasn't the cold that bothered him, it was being *watched* all the time. The eye in the door.' She laughed. 'I didn't know what he meant.'

She looked past Prior's shoulder, and he turned to follow her gaze. He found himself looking at an elaborately painted eye. The peephole formed the pupil, but around this someone had taken the time and trouble to paint a veined iris, an eyewhite, eyelashes and a lid. This eye, where no eye should have been, was deeply disturbing to Prior. For a moment he was back in France, looking at Towers's eyeball in the palm of his hand. He blinked the image away. 'That's horrible,' he said, turning back to

Beattie.

''S not so bad long as it stays in the door.' She tapped the side of her head. 'You start worrying when it gets in here.'

'Anyway, go on. He was talking about William.'

'Yes, he kept bringing the conversation round, and of course I was worried, and out it all came. It wasn't just our William that was bothering me, it was all of them.'

'All the conchies?'

'You know I don't mean that.'

No, he thought. She was one of those who felt every death. She'd never learnt to read the casualty lists over breakfast and then go off and have a perfectly pleasant day, as the vast majority of civilians did. If she had learnt to do that, she mightn't have been here. 'Go on,' he said.

'He could see I was getting upset and he says, "Why don't we have a drink?" Well, money was a bit tight, you know, with feeding Tommy as well, but he says, "Don't you worry, love, this one's on me." And he went into the scullery and came back with two bloody great big jugs, and off he went. Eeh, special brew. Well, you know me, Billy, two glasses of that, he was me long-lost brother, and I did, I *talked*, I played me mouth. I cussed Lloyd George, I cussed the King, I don't know what bugger I didn't cuss, but I was *lonely*, Billy. I'd had nobody to talk to except Tommy for months, and *he* was no company, poor little bugger, his nerves were gone. And of course at the trial it all got twisted. He said I kept dropping hints Lloyd George was going to die. I can remember exactly what I said. I says, "That bloody, buggering bastard Lloyd George, he's got a head on him like a forty-shilling pisspot, but you mark my words he'll

38

come to rue." There. That was it. That was *the death threat.*' She shook her head. 'It was nowt of the sort. Anyway we were half way down the second jug—or I was—and he says, "Can I trust you?" I says, "Well, you're in a pretty pickle if you can't." And then he starts telling me about this detention centre where the regime was very bad. Worse than Wandsworth. And you know all the stuff he was telling me was stuff *I'*d told *him*, about being naked in the cells and all that, but I was too daft to see it. And then he says, him and some of his mates had found a way to get the lads out. They had a contact inside the centre, one of the guards it was supposed to be. But, he says, the problem was the dogs. They had these dogs patrolling the perimeter fence. I says, "Well, *poison.*" He says, well, yes, but there was a problem about that. It had to look like an outside job because of the guard. You see, they didn't want the detention centre to twig about *him*. So I says, "Curare."'

'Fired through the fence in a blowdart?'

'Yes.'

'Fired *at the dogs*?'

'Yes.'

'Of course,' Prior said, 'you do realize, don't you, a lot of people wouldn't know about curare?'

For the first time she looked uneasy. 'Yes, well, I read about it in a book on South America, and then I happened to mention it to Alf—our Winnie's husband—and he says, "Oh, yes, we've got some of that in the lab." That's the only way I knew about it.'

'No previous thoughts of killing Lloyd George? They said at the trial you'd plotted to kill him before, when you were in the suffragettes.'

'The suffragettes *never* threatened human life. That was a point of honour: property, not life. It just

39

shows Spragge's ignorance, does that. Couldn't even think up a convincing lie.'

'He seems to have convinced the jury.'

'You know what was going on there as well as I do. You put a pacifist—any pacifist—in the dock—could be Jesus Christ—and the biggest rogue unhung in the witness-box, and who do you think they're gunna believe?'

'What did he say when you mentioned curare?'

'He says, yes, but how on earth was he going to get his hands on that? I says I knew where to get it, but it was too risky. And then he says if I helped him, he'd help me. He'd get little Tommy across to Ireland, and that clinched it for me, because you know Tommy was getting really weird. I mean, to be honest, I thought if I didn't get him out I was gunna have a loony on me hands, like Lily Braithwaite's husband. You know what a state *he* was in when he come back.'

'So you agreed to get the curare?'

'Yes, he give me an address and told me to write to him when I got it. I wrote to our Winnie's Alf, and he mentioned dogs in his letter back to me, but that letter was never produced, I think it slipped down a crack in the pavement. And Alf said, yes, he'd get it. He works in a big medical laboratory, and he had to sign for the poison. But he wasn't worried, see, because the dogs'd be dying at the other end of the country and nobody would make the connection. But can you imagine him signing his name like that if he'd thought it was for Lloyd George?'

'Then what?'

'I waited. The post seemed to take such a long time, but of course unbeknownst to us all the letters were being opened. The parcel was opened. And then when it was finally delivered the police were on the

40

doorstep in a matter of minutes. And I was charged with conspiracy to murder Lloyd George, *and others*. That's the other thing they dropped. It wasn't just Lloyd George they were on about. To begin with it was *hundreds* of people I was supposed to be plotting to kill. And, of course, all I could say was, "The poison was for the dogs," but I couldn't prove it, it was Spragge's word against mine, and *he* was working for the bloody Ministry of Munitions. Oh, and the trial. You know he read all the letters out in court?'

'Smith did?'

'Yeh, Smith. The Attorney-General. Oh, I was honoured, they wheeled out all the big guns. And he read me letters out in court, about Winnie's period being late and all that. And you know he read the words the way I'd wrote them. Just to get a laugh out of me, because I can't spell, I never have been able to. But I wonder how good *his* spelling'd be, if he'd left school when he was eight?'

'He shouldn't've done that.'

'I was fair game. Language too. He couldn't get over the language, this dreadful, coarse, lewd, vulgar, low woman who kept using all these words his dear little wifie didn't even know. *I'll bet.*'

Prior sat back against the wall. He was finding the eye in the door difficult to cope with. Facing it was intolerable, because you could never be sure if there were a human eye at the centre of the painted eye. Sitting with his back to it was worse, since there's nothing more alarming than being watched from behind. And when he sat sideways, he had the irritating impression of somebody perpetually trying to attract his attention. It tired him, and if it tired *him* after less than an hour, what must it have done to

41

Beattie, who'd had to endure it for over a year? He noticed that the latrine bucket had been placed where it could be seen from the door. 'Why's the bucket there?' he asked.

'Because some poor bloody cow drowned herself in her own piss.'

'My God.' He stared at her. 'You're not as bad as that, are you?'

'No, I keep going. Trouble is, you're punished if you go on hunger strike, so I can't have any visitors. I haven't seen our Hettie for ... oh, I don't know, it must be two months.'

'I'll see what I can do.'

'That's what Spragge said. When I told him about not being able to get Tommy across to Ireland, he says, "I'll see what I can do."'

'The difference is I'm not asking for anything back.'

She touched his sleeve. 'We were close once, Billy. You were like a son to me.' She waited. 'I'm not going to ask whose side you're on because you mightn't tell me the truth, and if you did, I wouldn't believe you. But just tell me this. Do you *know* whose side you're on?'

He looked at her and smiled, but didn't reply.

CHAPTER FOUR

The Ministry of Munitions was housed in the Hotel Metropole. The reception desk, now guarded by armed police, had once been manned by smooth-faced young men, trained not to look surprised when the sixth couple in succession turned out to be called Smith, or when prosperous-looking gentlemen, entertaining their curiously unprosperous-looking nephews, requested a double room. No such innocent frolics now, Prior thought, crossing the foyer. Goodness how the moral tone had declined.

On the third floor he tapped on Major Lode's door. Lode looked up from the file he was reading, dabbing, as he always did when confronted by a new situation, at the outer corners of his large, silky, red-gold moustache. In defiance of biology, Prior saw this moustache as a *feminine* adornment: perhaps because it seemed to require so much protection from the outside world.

'How did it go?' Lode asked.

'Quite well, I think. She was ... fairly hostile to begin with, but I think towards the end she was starting to open up.'

'Did you mention MacDowell?'

'Only in passing. I thought it better not to ... focus on him.'

'Hmm, yes, quite right. So what's the next step?'

'I'd like to see Hettie Roper. The younger daughter. You remember she was walking out with MacDowell?'

43

Lode smiled. 'Walking out? Yes. I was just thinking, what a quaint expression. But I thought that was over? That's what she told the police.'

'I don't believe it. They were too close.'

'Yes, well, do what you need to do. Good.'

And now, Prior thought, closing the door quietly behind him, you can fumigate your fucking office. 'What a quaint expression.' *I could buy and sell you*, he told the closed door. Lode had *no idea*. He'd spent his entire adult life—boyhood too, for that matter—in uniformed, disciplined, hierarchical institutions, and he simply couldn't conceive of the possibility that other people might function differently. It was all a great big chessboard to him. This rag-bag collection of Quakers, socialists, anarchists, suffragettes, syndicalists, Seventh Day Adventists and God knows who else was merely an elaborate disguise, behind which lurked the real anti-war movement, a secret, disciplined, highly efficient organization dedicated to the overthrow of the state as surely and simply as Lode was dedicated to its preservation. And on the other side of the board, at the head of the opposing army, elusive, tenacious, dangerous: the Black King himself, Patrick MacDowell. It wasn't complete nonsense, of course. Mac was certainly a more effective opponent of the war than most, if only because he was not in love with suffering. Poor Mac, he'd had enough of that by the time he was ten.

Prior walked down the corridor to his own room, tiny in comparison with Lode's, hardly more than a cupboard. Evidently, in pre-war days this room had been reserved for those obliged to sin on a budget. He felt dirty, physically dirty, after the long train journey, and when he looked into the small glass

44

above the washbasin he saw that his face was covered in smuts. He washed as much of himself as he could reach without undressing, and then began searching through the filing cabinet. He'd made a list of a number of files that contained reports from Lionel Spragge, and it took him only a few moments to gather them together and dump them on his desk. He had an hour to read through them before Spragge arrived. Spragge had been reluctant to come to the Ministry at all, suggesting they should meet outside, at some pub or other, but Prior had wanted this first meeting to be on his own ground.

He'd read the reports several times already, so it was merely a matter of refreshing his memory. When he came to Beattie's file, to Spragge's reports on the Roper affair and then to his deposition, he read more slowly. After a while he looked up, puzzled by the sense of something unfamiliar in the room. He stared round him, but could see nothing different, and then he realized that the change was in himself. He had not been angry until now.

LIONEL ARTHUR MORTIMER SPRAGGE
on his oath saith as follows:

2 February 1917. I am employed at the Ministry of Munitions. I entered the employ of the Ministry on 1 July 1916. I have been engaged making certain inquiries concerning various organizations amongst others the Independent Labour Party and the No Conscription fellowship. I reported to Major Lode. He was the officer from whom I chiefly got my directions.

Between October and December 1916 I was sent to Liverpool to make inquiries concerning one Patrick MacDowell. He had been the leading
45

organizer of the Sheffield strike in the Munitions factories. I told MacDowell I wanted to go to the Manchester area. MacDowell gave me a letter to give to Mrs Beatrice Roper. On the night of I think the 23rd December I went to Mrs Roper's shop, at 11 Tite Street, Salford, and gave her the letter. After reading the letter Mrs Roper agreed that I could stay with her and we shook hands very heartily indeed. She sat at one end of the table, and I sat next to her. There was another man staying in the house at the time who was introduced to me as Tommy Blenkinsop, a deserter. He did not come downstairs until later. Mrs Roper asked me about myself. I told her I had been refused exemption and that I had been on the run since September as a moral objector. I told her about being locked up in a detention centre and I think I told her something of the treatment I had received there. At that she said, 'That is just like my William,' and she got up and fetched a photograph from the dresser. It was a small photograph of her son, William Roper. As she was showing me the photograph she told me that before the war she had been active in the suffragettes and that she had burnt down a church. I think her exact words were, 'You know about St Michael's? We were nearly copped, but we bloody well did it.' She laughed and said, 'You should have seen the flames go up.' She then said, 'And that was not all we did.' She told me she had been party to a plan to kill Mr Lloyd George, by inserting a curare-tipped nail through the sole of his boot in such a way that it would pierce the skin when he put his weight on the foot, causing instant lassitude followed by seizures. They had been planning to do this on the Isle of Wight where Mr

46

Lloyd George was staying at that time. There was a waiter in his hotel sympathetic to the suffragette cause. I do not recollect the name of the hotel, or of the waiter. I asked her why the attempt had not succeeded. She replied, 'The bloody, shitting, buggering old sod pissed off to France, didn't he?' Mrs Roper's language was fairly good most of the time but when she spoke of Mr Lloyd George she used bad language. I then made diligent inquiries as to the nature of Mrs Roper's attitude to Mr Lloyd George. She several times expressed the opinion that he ought to be killed. I then asked her whether there was anybody else who ought to be killed and she replied, 'Yes, the other George, that poncing old git in the Palace, he'd not be missed.'

I then asked her whether this was all talk or whether some plan was afoot. She replied, 'Can I trust you?' I think I said something to the effect that she was in a pretty pickle if she could not. She then said that she knew where to get curare and that Walton Heath Golf-course would be a good place to get Mr Lloyd George with an air-gun. She said she knew three good lads in London who would do the job. She then asked me if I wanted to be in on it and I considered it my duty to reply in the affirmative in order to procure further information. I passed that night at Mrs Roper's house, and the following morning I reported back to Major Lode's department in code.

Spragge was a big, fleshy, floridly handsome man, with thick brows and startling blue-green eyes that slanted down at the outer corners. His neck and jowls had thickened, and rose from his broad shoulders in a single column. Hair sprouted from his ears, his nostrils, the cuffs of his shirt. He was as unmistakably and crudely potent as a goat. Beattie would have gone for him, Prior thought, as he stood up to shake hands. He wondered how he knew that, and why he should mind as much as he did.

'I asked you to come in,' Prior said, after Spragge had settled into his chair, 'because we're thinking of employing you again.' He watched the flare of hope. Spragge was less well turned out than he appeared to be at first sight. His suit was shiny with wear, his shirt cuffs frayed. 'You'll have gathered from the papers there's a lot of unrest in the munitions industry at the moment. Particularly in the north, where you spent a good deal of time, didn't you? In '16.'

'Yes, I—'

'With MacDowell. Who'd just come out of a detention centre, I believe?'

'Yes, he's a deserter. Conchie. You should see the size of him, for God's sake. Built like a brick shithouse. See some of the scraggy little buggers that get sent to France.' Spragge was looking distinctly nervous. 'I don't think I could approach him again. I mean, he knows me.'

'He knows you from the Roper case, doesn't he?'

'Before that.'

'You might be able to give advice, though. Obviously we'd need to keep you away from the areas you were working in before.'

Spragge looked relieved.

'You met MacDowell in the summer of '16? In Sheffield?'

'Yes, I was making inquiries into the shop stewards' movement.'

Prior made a show of consulting his notes. 'You stayed with Edward Carpenter?'

48

'I did.' Spragge leant forward, his florid face shining with sweat, and said in a sinister whisper, 'Carpenter is of the homogenic persuasion.'

'So I believe.' That phrase again. It had stuck in Beattie's memory, and no wonder. It was transparently obvious that Spragge's natural turn of phrase would have been something like 'fucking brown 'atter'. 'Of the homogenic persuasion' was Major Lode. Who had once told Prior in, of all places, the Café Royal, 'This country is being brought to its knees. *Not* by Germany'—here he'd thumped the table so hard that plates and cutlery had leapt into the air—'NOT BY GERMANY, but by an unholy alliance of socialists, sodomites and shop stewards.' Prior had felt scarcely able to comment, never having been a shop steward. 'Do you think that's relevant?'

'It was relevant to *me*. There was no lock on the door.'

'He *is* eighty, isn't he?' said Prior.

Spragge shifted inside his jacket. 'A vigorous eighty.'

'You went to a meeting, next day? Addressed by Carpenter.'

'I went with Carpenter.'

'And in the course of his speech he quoted a number of . . . well, what would you call them? Songs? Poems? In praise of homogenic love.'

'He did. In public.'

'Well, it was a public meeting, wasn't it? And then after the meeting you went into a smaller room, and there you were introduced to a number of people, including the author of these songs?'

'Yes.'

'Walt Whitman.'

49

'Yes.'

'Walt Whitman is an American poet.' Prior waited for Spragge's mouth to open. 'A *dead* American poet.'

'He didn't look well.'

'1819 to 1892.'

Spragge jerked his head. 'Yeh, well, it's the money, innit?'

'Is it?'

'I'll say it is. Two pound ten a week I was promised. Mind you, he says the information's got to be good and you've got to keep it coming.' Spragge sat back and snorted. 'Didn't matter how good it was, I never had two pound ten in my hand, not regular, just like that. Bonuses, yes. But what use are dribs and drabs like that to me? I'm a family man.'

'You got bonuses, did you?'

'Now and then.'

'That would be if you turned up something special?'

Spragge hesitated. 'Yes.'

'How big a bonus did you get for Beattie Roper?'

Spragge hesitated again, then clearly decided he had nothing to lose. 'Not big enough.'

'But you got one?'

'Yes.'

'All in one go?'

'Half on arrest, half on conviction.'

'You got a *bonus* if she was *convicted*?'

'Look, I know what you're after. You're saying I lied under oath. Well, I didn't. Do you think I'm gunna risk—what is it, five years—for a measly fifty quid? 'Course I'm bloody not. I'd have to be mad, wouldn't I?'

'Or in debt.'

50

Spragge blinked. 'Just because I lied about Walt Whitman doesn't mean I was lying all the time. That was the first report I wrote, I was desperate to get enough in.'

'You never talked about dogs to Mrs Roper?'

Spragge made an impatient gesture. 'What dogs? There weren't any fucking dogs. They're not *used* in detention centres. You might not know that, but she does. She's talked to men who've been in every detention centre in England. She *knows* there aren't any dogs.' He stared at Prior. 'Have you been talking to her?'

'I've interviewed her, yes.'

Spragge snorted. 'Well, all I can say is the old bitch's got you properly conned.'

'I haven't said I *believed* her.'

'She was *convicted*. It doesn't matter what you believe.'

'It matters a great deal, from the point of view of your job prospects.' Prior gave this time to sink in. 'The letter that came with the poison. From Mrs Roper's son-in-law.' He drew the file towards him. '"If you get close enough to the poor brutes, I pity them. Dead in twenty seconds".'

'All that proves is that the *son-in-law* thought it was for the dogs. Well, she'd have to tell him something, wouldn't she?'

'You still say she plotted to kill Lloyd George?'

'Yes.'

'And that the suggestion came from her, and not from you?'

'*Yes*. She didn't need any bloody encouragement!'

'Even to the details? Even to suggesting Walton Heath Golf-course as a good place to do it?'

'That's right.'

'How would she know that? She's spent her entire life in the back streets of Salford, how would *she* know where Lloyd George plays golf?'

Spragge shrugged. 'Read it in the paper? I don't suppose it's a state secret.' He leant forward. 'You know, you want to be careful. If you're saying I acted as an *agent provocateur*—and that *is* what you're saying, isn't it?—then you're also saying that Major Lode *employed* an *agent provocateur*. Either knowingly, in which case he's a rogue, or unknowingly, in which case he's a fool. Either way, it's not gunna do *his* career much good, is it? You watch yourself. You might find out it's your head on the chopping-block.'

Prior spread his hands. 'Who's talking about chopping-blocks? I'm interviewing a new agent— new to *me*. And I've made it clear—at least I *hope* I've made it clear—that any little flight of fancy—Walt Whitman rising from the dead—and I'll be on to it. If there *aren't* any flights of fancy, well then . . . no need to worry.' With the air of a man getting to the real purpose of the meeting at last, Prior drew another file towards him. 'Now tell me what you know about MacDowell.'

After he'd finished milking Spragge of information, all of which he knew already, and had sent him home to await the summons, Prior sat motionless for a while, his chin propped on his hands.

'The poison was for the dogs.'

'There weren't any fucking dogs. You might not know that, but she does.'

Was it possible Beattie had tried to reach out from her corner shop in Tite Street and kill the Prime Minister? The Beattie he'd known before the war would not have done that, but then that Beattie had

52

been rooted in a communal life. Oh, she'd been considered odd—any woman in Tite Street who worked for the suffragettes was odd. But she hadn't been isolated. That came with the war.

Shortly after the outbreak of war, Miss Burton's little dog had gone missing. Miss Burton was a spinster who haunted the parish church, arranged flowers, sorted jumble, cherished a hopeless love for the vicar—how hopeless probably only Prior knew. He'd been at home at the time, waiting for orders to join his regiment, and he'd helped her search for the dog. They found it tied by a wire to the railway fence, in a buzzing cloud of black flies, disembowelled. It was a dachshund. One of the enemy.

In that climate Beattie had found the courage to be a pacifist. People stopped going to the shop. If it hadn't been for the allotment, the family would have starved. So many bricks came through the window they gave up having it mended and lived behind boards. Shit—canine and human—regularly plopped through the letter-box on to the carpet. In that isolation, in that semi-darkness, Beattie had sheltered deserters and later, after the passing of the Conscription Act, conscientious objectors who'd been refused exemption. Until one day, carrying a letter from Mac, Spragge had knocked on her door and uncovered a plot to assassinate the Prime Minister. Or so he said.

Could she have plotted to kill Lloyd George? Prior thought he understood how the powerless might begin to fancy themselves omnipotent. The badges of hopeless drudgery, the brush and the cooking-pot, become the flying broomstick and the cauldron, *and not only in the minds of the persecutors*. At first there would be only wild and flailing words, prophecies

53

that Lloyd George would come to a dreadful end and then, nudged along by Spragge—because whatever Beattie's part in this, Spragge had not been innocent—the sudden determination to act out the fantasy: to destroy the man she blamed for prolonging the war and causing millions of deaths.

Lode would have had no difficulty in believing Spragge. The poison plot fitted in very neatly with his preconceptions about the anti-war movement. Not much grasp of reality in all this, Prior thought, on either side. He was used to thinking of politics in terms of conflicting interests, but what seemed to have happened here was less a conflict of interests than a disastrous meshing together of fantasies.

He began putting away the files. It was a situation where you had to hang on to the few certainties, and he was certain that Spragge had lied under oath, and since Spragge had been the only witness, this of itself meant the conviction was unsafe.

He locked the filing cabinet and the door of his room, and walked along to the end of the corridor. The lift was stuck on the fifth floor. He decided not to wait and ran downstairs, coming out on to the mezzanine landing where he paused and looked down into the foyer, as he often did, liking to imagine the hotel as it must have been before the war, before this drabness of black and khaki set in.

The shape of a head caught his attention. *Charles Manning*, waiting for the lift, and with him—good God—Winston Churchill and Edward Marsh. Prior watched. Manning, though obviously junior, seemed perfectly at ease in their company. Certainly he was not merely dancing attendance; there was a good deal of shared laughter, and, as they moved into the lift, Marsh's hand rested briefly on his shoulder. Well,

well, well, Prior thought, continuing on his way downstairs. 'Connections' indeed!

* * *

Prior lived in a seedy basement flat in Bayswater. He could have afforded better, but he preferred to spend his money on properly tailored uniforms, and these did not come cheap. His bedroom had french windows that opened on to a small high-walled yard, so dark that he had never been tempted to sit out, though his landlady had made an effort. The walls were painted cream to a height of about ten feet, and there were a number of thin, straggly plants dying in a great variety of containers.

The room was small and L-shaped. His bed lay along the upright of the L, facing the window, with a desk and hard chair at the foot. The baseline of the L contained a wardrobe, with an oval mirror set into the door. There was space for nothing else.

The bathroom was next door. He had a tepid bath, and then, wrapped in his dressing-gown, lay on the bed and lit a cigarette. He was too tired to think constructively, and yet his mind whirred on. This was the frame of mind that led to a bad night, and it irritated him, almost to the point of tears, that he could do nothing about it.

He thought of Beattie in her cell. Eighteen months since Lionel Spragge knocked on her door. Eighteen months ago he'd been in France. Eighteen months ago William Roper had been in Wandsworth Detention Centre. An image of William began to form in Prior's mind, tiny but powerful, like the initial letter of a gospel. William, naked in his cell, watched constantly through the eye in the door, and beside him, on the stone floor, the uniform he'd refused to put on. A small, high, barred window, lit with a bluish glow from the snow outside.

He found himself resenting the power of this image. The claim it made on his sympathy. Deliberately, he entered the cell and then let himself drift out of the window, between the bars, into the falling snow. He was in France now, lying out in the open with his platoon. The trenches had been blown flat, there was no shelter from the icy wind, no hope of getting the wounded back. And no water, because the water in the water-bottles had frozen. Once a hawk flew over, its shadow black against the snow. The only movement, the only life, in a landscape dead as the moon. Hour after hour of silence, and the snow falling. Then, abruptly, Sanderson's convulsed and screaming face, as they cut the puttees away from his frost-bitten legs.

This was no use. Prior sat up and started reading *The Times*, but the print blurred and Beattie's face took its place, the white hair straggling round her neck. He closed his eyes. The bell of the shop in Tite Street rang as he pushed the door open. How old? Four? Five? A smell of cat pee and tarred string from the bundles of firewood in the corner. Beattie's cat had never been able to resist marking those bundles. Mrs Thorpe plonked their Alfie on the counter while she paid her bill. Alfie swung his short legs in their sturdy boots, puffing away at a fag end, though he was only three. Between drags, he sucked his mother's breast, puffing and sucking alternately, peering round the white curve at Prior, who was a Big Boy and therefore an object of interest and suspicion. It was late in the afternoon. Mrs Thorpe would be far gone. Jugs of best bitter were her favourite, chased down by sips of something medicinal that she kept in a flask fastened to her thigh with a home-made elastic garter. Whisky for the heart, brandy for the lungs, gin for the bladder. Alfie, guzzling away at his mother's milk, looked contented, and well he might, since it could hardly have been less than 70% proof.

The past is a palimpsest, Prior thought. Early memories are always obscured by accumulations of later knowledge. He made himself walk to the counter again, this time remembering nothing but the moment, push his sweaty coin across the cool marble, and ask, 'What can I have for a ha'penny?'

There was a white apron round Beattie's waist with two pockets, stained black from the coins inside them. These coins smelled very strong when she emptied them on to the table to count them, a dark, dank, heavy smell.

'What can I have for a ha'penny?'

Beattie's voice, patient as if she hadn't said all this a million times before, reeled off the list: aniseed ball, sherbert delight, liquorice stick, a packet of thousand-and-ones, and finally—his favourite because it lasted so long—a gob-stopper.

Towers's eye lay in the palm of his hand. 'What am I supposed to do with this gob-stopper?' Logan's hand reached out, grasped his shaking wrist, and tipped the eye into the bag.

Don't think about it, he told himself. It was too late in the day to risk thinking about that.

He had no memory of Beattie's face. She'd been an object then, a mountain, the side of a house, vast, taken for granted, not a person to whom you could attach adjectives. Though he could attach them readily enough now: lively, opinionated, intelligent, uneducated, foul-mouthed, impulsive, generous,

57

quick-tempered, kind. Prior's mother, his gentle and, it had to be said, *genteel* mother, hated Beattie Roper, though, when his mother became ill with suspected tuberculosis, it was to Beattie he'd been sent. That must have been his father's decision.

For almost a year, when he was five or six years old, he'd lived with Beattie and played with her two daughters, Winnie, who was now in Leeds Prison, and Hettie, who'd been charged with conspiracy to murder, but acquitted. He'd been the baby, when they played houses; the customer, when they played shops; the pupil, when they played schools; the patient, when they played nurses; and all these roles had been extremely boring, except, now and then, the role of patient.

They'd played under the big table in the kitchen, because its green tasselled cloth hanging down all round them made a separate world. Particularly on wash days, when the house was invaded by smells of soda, Dolly Blue and wet wool, and the wind blew grit in from the yard, the table was their refuge. Between the green tassels they looked out at adult boots coming and going, and felt a pleasant sense of power.

Mr Carker's boots. Mr Carker was secretary of the Independent Labour Party, and sometimes he and Beattie sat together at the table, discussing politics. These discussions had been, in every sense, above Prior's head, though he remembered one remark of Mr Carker's to the effect that the suffragettes simply exploited working-class women like Beattie. 'It's all very well, talking about sisterhood, but when *they* go home at night and drop their knickers, it's somebody else's job to pick them up.'

Probably it was the reference to dropping knickers

that had made that particular remark stick in his mind. Perhaps it excited Mr Carker too, for shortly afterwards his boot crept along the floor and brushed against Beattie's foot. She moved her foot. The boot followed, accompanied this time by a hand on her knee, a hand that just lifted the green tassels. Prior looked round and saw Hettie's stricken face. It was a house with no father, and all the children, but particularly Hettie, were passionate in defence of their mother. For the first time in his life, perhaps, Prior was aware of another's pain. Stealthily, he reached out and tied Mr Carker's boot laces together, so that when, finally, he got up to go, he tripped and measured his full length on the floor.

The disciplining of children must have been the only subject on which Beattie held no advanced views. She'd hauled him out of his hiding place, tipped him over her knee and tanned his arse; and he'd clenched his teeth, divided between a blaze of joy that he was suffering for Hettie's sake, and regret that the suffering should not have taken a more dignified form.

Major Lode, interviewing him for his present post, had leant across the table and said, 'You see, you *know* these people, don't you?'

Prior took a last drag of his cigarette, leant over the edge of the bed and stubbed it out in the ashtray. *Yes*.

He drew the curtains and got inside the sheets. He was afraid to go to sleep, but he had learnt, from long experience, that to keep himself awake at night only to fall asleep shortly before dawn made for the worst nightmares of all. He lay and stared at the ceiling, unblinking, until his eyelids prickled, then rolled over on to his side and brought his knees up to his chin.

He was back in the winter landscape, with a sound

59

like wind blowing, only it was not the wind, but the sound of emptiness. A hawk flew over and he watched its shadow on the snow. They were marching back. His boot went through thin ice into freezing mud. The ice meshed out round his foot, white opaque lines radiating out so that he stood at the centre of a frozen web.

The cold half woke him. He found his leg outside the covers and brought it back inside, but now his whole body was cold. He was lying naked on a stone floor. Because his sleep was light, he knew he was dreaming, and he knew also that he had to wake up before something worse happened. He turned and saw the eye watching him, an eye not painted but very much alive. The white glittered in the moonlight. The same noise of emptiness he'd heard in France had followed him into the cell. He stared at the eye, and then, by a supreme effort of will, forced himself to sit up.

Sweating and clammy, he reached down for his cigarettes, and remembered he'd left them on the desk. He got up and felt his way along, not wanting to switch on the light because the horror of the nightmare was heavy on him, and he was afraid of what the glare might reveal. He was standing by the desk, in the half-darkness, dabbing his hands among his papers, searching for the cigarette packet, when he heard a chuckle and spun round. The eye was watching him from the door. He shrank back against the table, his hands groping behind him for the paper-knife. His fingers closed round the hilt and he sprang at the door, stabbing the eye again and again, his naked body spattered with blood and some thick whitish fluid that did not drip but clung to his belly, and quickly chilled. Then, exhausted, he slipped to the floor and lay there, sobbing, and the sound of his sobbing woke him up.

At first he simply stared at the door. Only when he was sure there was no eye did he start to relax and take in the strangeness of his position. The fingertips of his right hand patted the cold oilcloth, as if by touching it he could make it turn into a mattress and sheets. No, he was out of bed, lying on the floor. Nightmare, he thought, drawing a deep breath. He started to pull himself up, feeling a wetness in his groin, and, as he did so, his splayed fingers touched the knife. So that had been real. With a spasm of revulsion, he struck out at it and sent it skittering across the floor.

CHAPTER FIVE

The aerodrome consisted of two runways and a straggle of low buildings set in one corner of a field.

Rivers and Dundas got out of the car and stood looking at the sky: clear, except for one bank of dark cloud away on the horizon.

'Good weather for it, anyway,' Dundas said.

It was possible to tell he was frightened, but only because Rivers had been observing him closely for weeks. Dundas suffered from abnormal reactions in the air. Where healthy pilots experienced no sensation at all, Dundas reported feeling his head squashed into his body, or a loss of movement in his legs. He suffered from nausea. More seriously still, he had more than once experienced the preliminary stages of a faint. After every physiological test possible had proved negative, he had been handed over to Rivers for psychological observation. Unfortunately, Rivers was making no progress. Dundas seemed to be exactly the sort of cheerful, likable, slightly irresponsible young man he'd grown accustomed to dealing with in the Royal Flying Corps. Apart from flying, his main interests were amateur dramatics, music and girls, not necessarily in that order. He appeared, in fact, to be entirely normal. Until he got into an aeroplane. And they were here to do just that.

'We seem to have arrived a bit early,' Dundas said. 'Would you like a cup of tea?'

The canteen was empty, except for a group of

62

young fliers gathered round a table in the far corner, most of them in their twenties, one ginger-haired lad noticeably younger. Dundas went off to get the tea, and Rivers sat down at a table whose entire surface was covered with interlocking rings of tea stains. The young men were reading newspapers, chatting in a desultory fashion about the events of the day: the massive German advance, Maud Allan's libel action against Pemberton Billing, the cult of the clitoris. A dark-haired young man held up a photograph of Maud Allan. 'If she ever fancies anything bigger she's welcome to knock on my door.'

'She'd not notice the difference,' somebody said.

A good-natured scuffle. Then a new voice: 'Did you hear the one about Lord Albemarle? Went into the Turf, and said . . .' A desiccated, aristocratic bleat. '"Keep reading in the papers about this Greek chap, Clitoris. Anybody know who he is?"' They all laughed, the younger lad with braying anguish; it was immediately clear his confusion at least equalled Lord Albemarle's.

Dundas came back with the tea and two very greasy doughnuts.

'Not for me, thank you,' Rivers said, patting his stomach. 'I have to be careful.'

Dundas nodded uncomprehendingly. Obviously duodenal ulcers and having to be careful were a million miles away from his experience. He ate both doughnuts with every sign of relish. Rivers sipped his tea and tried not to think that if Dundas's medical records were anything to go by (my God, they'd better be!) he could expect to see the doughnuts again before long.

They didn't talk much. Dundas was too tense, and Rivers respected his need for silence. When they'd finished, they walked across to the hangars together. Dundas disappeared inside the first hangar for a moment and came back carrying flying helmets, jackets and gauntlets. Rivers put a jacket on and followed Dundas across to the aeroplane.

'Here she is,' Dundas said, patting the fuselage. 'Terrible old bucket. Can't think why they've given us this one.'

Because it's the one they can best afford to lose, Rivers thought. He'd intended this reflection as a small private joke, but instead it brought him face to face with his own fear.

'Right,' Dundas said. 'If you'd like to hop in.'

Rivers climbed into the observer's seat and fastened the harness. Dundas bent over him to check the buckles. A faint smile acknowledged the reversal of the usual caring role. 'All right?' he said.

'Fine.'

'You've done a lot of flying, haven't you?'

'I don't know about a lot. Some.'

'But you've done spins and loops and things?'

'Yes.'

Dundas smiled. 'That's all right, then.'

Something about Dundas's smile held Rivers's attention. Suddenly, he felt certain Dundas was withholding something, even perhaps concealing it. Not malingering. In fact, rather the reverse. He thought Dundas might be minimizing his symptoms. It wasn't a good moment for that particular perception to strike.

Dundas pulled his helmet on, climbed in, exchanged a whole series of shouts and waves with the mechanics. The engine stuttered, began to roar, and then they were taxiing away from the hangar.

Rivers looked round him, at hedgerows thick with

64

blossom, a sky tumultuous with rising larks; then he snapped his goggles into place, and the splendour contracted to a muddy pond.

He was now definitely afraid. The situation might almost be regarded as a small experiment, with himself as the subject. The healthy reaction to fear in a normal human being is the undertaking of some manipulative activity designed to avoid or neutralize the danger. Provided such activity is available, the individual ought to be unaware of feeling fear. But no such activity was available. Like every other man who sits in the observer's seat, he was entirely dependent on his pilot. And what a pilot. He had long believed that the essential factor in the production of war neurosis among the two most vulnerable groups, observers and trench soldiers, was the peculiarly passive, dependent and immobile nature of their experience. It isn't often that a hypothesis conceived in the scientist's cortex is confirmed by his gut, but his gut certainly seemed to be doing its best to prove this one. He bit his lips to control the pain and concentrated hard on the back of Dundas's head, at the wisps of reddish-gold hair escaping from beneath the helmet, the pink neck, the edge of white scarf, the brown leather of his flying jacket, scuffed and scarred with wear.

'ALL RIGHT?' Dundas yelled.

They had reached their take-off position. The engine raced. Rivers felt himself pushed hard back against the vibrating seat. The plane lifted, bumped, lifted again, and then climbed steeply away from the huddle of buildings.

He looked over the side, shielding his mouth from the wind. The countryside stretched below them, grey striations of lanes and roads, the glitter of a pond, great golden swathes of laburnum, a line of hedgerow white with blossom, blue smoke from a bonfire drifting across a field of green wheat.

A movement from Dundas brought him back to the task in hand. Dundas was making a spinning movement with his hand. The comforting roar of the engine faltered, then became an infuriated mosquito whine as the plane started to spin. Dundas's eyes were fixed on his instruments. Rivers watched the sun revolve in a great spiral round the falling plane. Abruptly, the sun vanished, and the green fields rushed up to meet them. Dundas pulled on the stick, but something was wrong. The horizon was tilted. Rivers leant forward and tilted his hand to the left. Slowly the horizon straightened.

Dundas had lost his sense of the horizontal. Already.

'HOW WAS IT?' Rivers yelled.

Dundas waved his hand in an incomprehensible gesture, then put one hand on top of his head and pressed repeatedly, indicating he'd felt his head being squashed into his body. He made the spinning movement again. Rivers shook his head and made a looping movement. After a moment's hesitation, Dundas's thumb went up.

The plane banked steeply as Dundas turned and made for the city. He was not meant to do this, and Rivers guessed he was trying to make the flight last as long as possible. In a short time he saw beneath him the sulphurous haze of London. This was the view seen by the German pilots as they came in on moonlit bombing raids, following the silver thread of the Thames, counting bridges, watching for the bulge of the Isle of Dogs.

Rivers tapped Dundas on the shoulder. Dundas

turned round and nodded. So much of his face was hidden by the goggles it was impossible to read his expression. Rivers sat back and again concentrated on his own sensations. After the fifth loop he began to feel he was loose in his seat, a reaction he remembered from other flights and knew to be a frequent, though not universal, reaction of healthy fliers. They again came out with one wing down. Dundas leant over the side and retched, but didn't vomit. Rivers jerked his thumb at the ground, but Dundas ignored him.

With no idea at all now which manoeuvre to expect, Rivers sat back and tried to relax as the plane climbed. The vast blue haze of London fell away beneath the left wing-tip. Higher and colder. Wisps of cloud hid the sun; columns of shadows flitted rapidly across the city. Rivers felt calm, suddenly. There were worse ways to die, and he'd seen most of them.

Again the engine faltered, giving way to the mosquito whine as the plane began to fall. Dundas came out of the spin, white, giddy, confused and clearly finding it difficult to focus on his instruments. Rivers could see him peering at them. He yelled, 'DOWN!' and jerked his finger at the ground. Dundas leant out of the plane and was sick.

They had a bumpy landing, though not worse than many others Rivers had experienced. After the plane had taxied to a halt, Dundas stayed in his seat for a few moments before jumping down. He staggered slightly and held on to the wing. Rivers climbed down and immediately went up to him.

'I'm all right,' Dundas said, letting go of the wing.

Two mechanics were walking towards the plane. Dundas turned to them and made some comment on the flight. The three went into a huddle, and Rivers walked to one side. Dundas was smiling and talking cheerfully, but then Dundas was a very good actor.

When he came across to join Rivers, he said, 'Sorry about that.'

'Shall we go and sit down?'

Dundas looked towards the canteen, but shook his head. 'I think I'd just as soon get back, if you don't mind.'

Rivers's legs were trembling as they walked back to the car. He was angry with himself for getting into such a state—angry, ashamed and inclined to pretend he'd been less frightened than he knew he had been. He observed this reaction, thinking he was in the state of fatigue and illness that favours the development of an anxiety neurosis, and behaving in the way most likely to bring it about. He was doing exactly what he told his patients not to do: repressing the awareness of fear.

In the car going back to the hospital, Dundas examined his reactions minutely. During the first spin, in addition to the squashed head feeling, he'd felt sick. 'Not so much sick. More a sort of bulge in my throat. And then during the loop I felt really sick. And faint. The sky went dark.'

'And in the last spin?'

'That was terrible. I felt really confused.'

After leaving Dundas in the hospital entrance hall, Rivers went into his room and threw his cap and cane on to the chair. Henry Head came in a moment later. 'How was he?'

'Bad.'

'Sick?'

'And faint.'

'Are you all right?'

'No, I seem to be suffering from terminal stiff

upper lip. You know the way I go on about not repressing fear? What did I do?' He spread his hands.

'It's the Public School Factor, Will. We're all too well trained.'

'It's the Silly Old Fool Factor. Too many young men around.'

Head smiled. 'No, well, I know what you mean. One doesn't want to seem *totally* decrepit.'

'I had this sudden sense that Dundas was hiding something. And that didn't—'

'He is.'

Rivers looked surprised.

'He's got a bottle of Bumstead's Gleet Cure in his locker.'

'*Has he?*'

'Sister Mitchell noticed it. Syphilis wouldn't make him go faint, mind.'

'Lying awake worrying about it might.' Rivers sat in silence for a moment. 'Well. Redirects the investigation a bit, doesn't it?'

'Makes it a helluva lot simpler.' Head dropped into a sergeant-major's baritone. '"Show us yer knob, lad." Are you coming to dinner?'

'Yes, and then I must dash. I'm supposed to be seeing somebody at eight.'

*   *   *

Rivers had the top floor of a large house near Hampstead Heath. The house was within a hundred yards of the great gun, and there were times when its proximity showed in every line of his face.

Prior arrived exactly on time, and was about to ring the bell when he saw Rivers walking rapidly up the hill.

69

'Have you rung?' Rivers asked, getting out his key.

'No, I saw you coming.'

Rivers opened the door and stood aside to let Prior in. Mrs Irving, Rivers's landlady, was hovering in the hall, wanting to complain about the Belgian refugees on the second floor whose failure to understand the extent of the food shortages was making her life a misery. When that subject was exhausted, there were the raids to be discussed. Wasn't it scandalous they'd been kept awake all night and not a word about it in *The Times*? Then there was her daughter, who'd been summoned back from France, ostensibly because her mother was ill, in fact because she was incapable of sorting out her servant problems. Girls kept leaving her employ on the flimsy excuse that they could earn five times as much in the munition factories. There was no accounting for modern girls, she said. And Frances was so *moody*.

At last Mrs Irving was called away, by Frances presumably, at any rate by a young woman with braided hair who gave Rivers a cool, amused, sympathetic smile before she closed the door of the drawing-room.

'I hope she's letting you live rent free,' Prior said.

They walked up the stairs together. Rivers paused on the second floor to look down into the garden. The laburnum, he said, was particularly fine. Prior didn't believe in this sudden interest in horticulture. The pause was to give him time to get his breath back. His chest was tighter than it had been on his last visit, and Rivers would have noticed that. Damn Rivers, he thought, knowing the response was utterly unfair. Whenever he needed Rivers he became angry with him, often to the point where he couldn't talk about what was worrying him. He mustn't let that happen tonight.

Normally Prior took a long time to get started, but this evening he was no sooner settled in his chair than he launched into an account of his visit to Mrs Roper. What emerged most vividly was the eye in the door. He reverted to this again and again, how elaborately painted it had been, even to the veins in the iris, how the latrine bucket had been placed within sight of it, how it was never possible to tell whether a human eye was looking through the painted one or not. It was clear from Prior's expression, from his whole demeanour, that he was seeing the eye as he spoke. Rivers was always sensitive to the signs of intense visualization in other people, since this was a capacity in which he himself was markedly deficient, a state of affairs which had once seemed simple and now seemed very complicated indeed. He switched his attention firmly back to Prior, asked a few questions about his previous relationship with Mrs Roper, then listened intently to his account of the nightmare. 'Whose eye was it?' he asked, when Prior had finished.

Prior shrugged. '*I* don't know. How should I know?'

'It's your dream.'

Prior drew a deep breath, reluctant to delve into a memory that could still make his stomach heave. 'I suppose Towers is the obvious connection.'

'Had you been thinking about that?'

'I remembered it when I was in the cell with Beattie. I ... I actually saw it for a moment. Then later I remembered I used to go and buy gob-stoppers from Beattie's shop.' He paused. 'I don't know whether you remember, but when I picked up Towers's eye, I said, "What shall I do with this

71

gob-stopper?"'

'I remember.'

A long silence.

Rivers said slowly, 'When one eye reminded you of the other, was that just the obvious connection? I mean, because they were both eyes?'

Prior produced one of his elaborate shrugs. 'I suppose so.'

Silence.

'I don't know. It *was* in the prison, but later … I don't know. I knew I was going to have a bad night. You you you just get to know the the feeling. I felt sorry for Beattie. And then I started thinking about William—that's the son—and … you know, naked in his cell, stone floor, snow outside…' He shook his head. 'It was … quite powerful, and I … I *think* I resented that. I resented having my sympathies manipulated. Because it's nothing, is it?' A burst of anger. '*I lost three men with frost-bite*. And so I started thinking about that, about those men and … It was a way of saying, "All right, William, your bum's numb. Tough luck." Though that's irrelevant, of course.' He smiled wryly. 'It isn't a suffering competition.'

'And then you thought about Towers?'

'Yes. But not in the same way as … as as the other men, I mean, I wasn't focusing on the horror of it. It was … I don't know.' He held out his hand to Rivers, palm upwards. 'A sort of talisman. Do you know what I mean? If *that* happens to you…' The outstretched hand started to shake. 'There's no possible room for doubt where your loyalties are.'

Prior looked down at his shaking hand, and seemed to become aware of it for the first time. He swallowed. 'Sorry, will you excuse me a moment?'

72

He crashed out of the room. Doors opened and closed as he tried to locate the bathroom. Rivers got up to help, then heard retching, followed by a gush of water, followed by more retching. Prior wouldn't want to be seen in that condition. He sat down again.

It was obviously his day to cope with people being sick.

He rested his chin on his clasped hands, and waited. It had taken two months' hard work at Craiglockhart to get Prior to the point where he remembered picking up Towers's eye, and even then he'd had to resort to hypnosis, something he always did with great reluctance. Prior had arrived at the hospital mute, rebellious, possibly the least co-operative patient Rivers had ever encountered, and with a very marked tendency to probe. To insist on a two-way relationship. He had accused Rivers of being merely 'a strip of empathic wallpaper' and asked him what the hell use he thought that was. Later this had become something of a joke between them, but the probing went on, combined with a sort of jeering flirtatiousness that had been surprisingly difficult to handle.

Prior's nightmares had been dreadful. He'd always insisted he couldn't remember them, though this had been obviously untrue. Eventually, he'd told Rivers in a tone of icy self-disgust that his dreams of mutilation and slaughter were accompanied by seminal emissions.

Prior came back into the room. 'Sorry about that,' he said casually, settling back into his chair.

He hadn't reached the bathroom in time. The front of his tunic was wet where he'd had to sponge it down. He noticed Rivers noticing the stain, and his face tightened. *He's going to make me pay for seeing* that, Rivers thought. No point questioning the logic of it. That was Prior. 'Would you like a break?' Rivers asked, trying to relieve the tension.

Prior nodded.

'Let's go by the fire.'

They left the desk and settled themselves in armchairs. Rivers took off his glasses and swept a hand down across his eyes.

'Tired?'

'Slightly. As Mrs Irving was saying, we had our own personal air-raid last night. I suppose somebody panics and starts firing.'

A pause while they stared into the fire. Prior said, 'I bumped into a patient of yours the other night. Charles Manning.'

Rivers had started to clean his glasses. 'I umm—'

'Can't talk about another patient. No, of course you can't. *He* talked, though. You know, when he mentioned your name I thought "war neurosis"—well, he does tend to twitch a bit, doesn't he?—but no, apparently not. Met a handsome soldier. Nasty policeman's hand on shoulder. What do you know, suddenly he requires treatment. What was the ...? Henry Head, that was it. "Henry Head can cure sodomites." So off he goes to Head, who says, "Sorry, like to help. Snowed under." With sodomites, presumably. The mind does rather boggle doesn't it? "Why don't you try Rivers?"' Prior waited. When there was no response he went on, 'Manning was surprisingly open about his little tastes. Cameronians with sweaty feet, apparently. Touching, isn't it, how some people develop a real devotion to the Highland regiments? I wonder, Rivers...' Prior was making little smacking movements with his lips, a don worrying away at

74

some particularly recondite problem. 'How would you set about "curing" somebody of fancying Cameronians with sweaty feet?'

Rivers said coldly, 'I should apply carbolic soap to the feet.'

'Really? A leap ahead of Dr Freud there, I think.'

Rivers leant forward. '*Stop this*. Dr Head is "snowed under" by young men who've had large parts of their brains shot away. In a rational society, a man who spent his days like that wouldn't have to spend his evenings, his own time, remember, with men who could perfectly well be left to get on with their own lives in their own way. The fact that he's prepared to do it is a tribute to Head.'

'He's a friend of yours?'

'Yes.'

'I suppose he could refuse to take them?' Prior said.

'No, he can't do that. Two years' hard labour, remember?'

A short silence. 'I'm sorry.'

Rivers spread his hands.

But Prior wouldn't let go. 'All the same there must *be* times when one patient actually does *need* to talk about another. I mean, it must be obvious the conversation about the Cameronians could *only* have taken place in bed?'

'The thought had occurred.'

'Well, suppose I need to talk about it? Suppose I'm racked with guilt?'

'Are you?'

'The point is—' Abruptly, Prior gave up. 'No. I don't seem to feel sexual guilt, you know. At all, really. About anything.'

Not true, Rivers thought. Prior had felt enormous

75

guilt about the nocturnal emissions that accompanied his nightmares. Guilt about an involuntary action.

'I used to,' Prior said.

'When was that?'

'When I was twelve. Where we lived there was a young man who used to be wheeled around on a trolley. I don't know what was wrong with him, tuberculosis of the spine, something like that, something terrible. And the trolley creaked, so you could always hear it coming. And he was pointed out to us as an illustration of what happened if you indulged in self-abuse.'

'Who told you that?'

'Scoutmaster. Mr Hailes. He actually said what came out was spinal fluid. And of course you've only got a limited supply of that, and mine was going down pretty fast. I used to lie awake and try not to do it, and I'd get more and more frightened. Unfortunately, there was only one thing that took my mind off the fear. So I did it again. And all the time this creaking trolley was getting nearer and nearer. And we'd been told the first signs of collapse were pallor and shadows under the eyes. And I used to get out of bed in the morning and look in the mirror, and what do you know? Pallor. Shadows under the eyes.' He laughed. 'It's funny now, but at one time I actually thought about suicide.'

'What got you out of it?'

Prior smiled. 'Not what. Who. Paddy MacDowell.'

'The man who organized the Sheffield strike?'

The smile broadened. 'Yes, at a later stage. He was otherwise engaged at the time. "Bashing his bishop." That's what we used to call it. Mac's bishop got

76

bashed oftener than anybody else's. He used to more or less pull it out and do it in public—and he was taller and stronger than any of us. So that planted the first seed of doubt. And then Hailes said the way to purity was to keep a glass of cold water by your bed, and then when temptation struck, you could plunge "the Inflamed Organ"—he always called it that—into the water. Well, I relayed this to Mac. Mac was *common*, he didn't go to Scouts—and he said, "But if it's stiff how do you get it into the glass without spilling the water?" And I suddenly had this picture of poor bloody Hailes standing there with his limp "organ" in a glass of water and I just knew he was talking rubbish. Poor little sod, he must've forgotten what an erection looked like. Anyway, after that I gave up on guilt. I think I got through a lifetime's supply in six months.'

'Was it a close friendship? With MacDowell?'

'You mean, did we—'

'*No*, I—'

'Yes, it was close. We were that age, I suppose.'

Prior was looking much more relaxed. 'Do you want to go on?' Rivers asked.

A slight hesitation. 'No, but I think I'd better.' For a while he didn't speak, then, measuring the words with movements of his steepled fingertips, he said, 'Dreams are attempts to resolve conflict. Right? Well, I can't see any conflict in this one.'

'You stabbed somebody in the eye.'

'Rivers. It was a *door*.'

'The *eye* was alive.'

'Yes.'

'So why do you say there was no conflict?'

'Because I was so identified with William or Beattie or ... I don't know. William, probably, because I was

77

naked. And I was attacking what seemed to me the most awful feature of their situation, which is the eye. The constant surveillance. So I don't see that there's any conflict. I mean it might be very inconvenient in real life but in the dream there was no doubt whose side I was on. Theirs.'

Rivers waited. When it was clear Prior could offer nothing more he said, 'You say the worst feature of their situation is the eye?'

'Yes.'

'The constantly being spied on?'

'Yes.'

Rivers asked gently, 'In that meeting with Mrs Roper, who was the spy?'

'I—' Prior's mouth twisted. 'I was.'

Another pause. Rivers prompted. 'So?'

'*So,*' Prior said in a disgusted singsong, jabbing with his index finger, '"eye" was stabbing myself in the "I". And God knows one wouldn't want a reputation for puns like that!'

A pause. Rivers asked, 'What do you think about that? Does it seem...'

'It's possible, I suppose. I hate what I do. And I suppose I probably felt I was in a false position. Well, obviously I did, I'd have to be mad not to.'

'I want you to do something for me,' Rivers said. 'I want you to write down any dreams you have that are as ... as bad as this one. Just record them. Don't try to interpret. And send them to me. I'll be seeing you again on—'

'No, I'm sorry, I can't. It'll have to be the following week. If that's all right? I'm going to see Hettie Roper.'

'Back to Salford? Where will you be staying?'

'At home.' He pulled a face. 'Yes, I know. How can

I stay anywhere else?'

Rivers nodded. He was remembering a visit of Prior's parents to Craiglockhart. In one afternoon they'd undone every slight sign of progress and precipitated an asthmatic attack. 'Does your father know what you're doing? I mean, does he know what the job involves?'

'My God, I hope not.' Prior shifted restlessly. 'This is a dirty little war, Rivers. I can honestly say I'd rather be in France.'

'Yes. I'm sure you would.'

Prior gave him a sharp look. 'You're worried, aren't you? Why? Because I'm going home?'

'No, not particularly.'

'Oh, I *see*. Yes. It was a suicide dream.' His expression changed. 'You needn't worry. If anybody comes a cropper over this one, *it will not be me.*'

He looked quite different, suddenly: keen, alert, cold, observant, detached, manipulative, ruthless. Rivers realized he was seeing, probably for the first time, Prior's public face. At Craiglockhart he'd been aggressive and manipulative, but always from a position of comparative helplessness. At times he'd reminded Rivers of a toddler clinging to his father's sleeve in order to be able to deliver a harder kick on his shins. Now, briefly, he glimpsed the Prior other people saw: the Lodes, the Ropers, the Spragges, and it came as a shock. Prior was formidable.

CHAPTER SIX

Against a yellow backcloth a woman draped in brilliant green veils writhed and twisted. She looked like an exotic lizard or a poisonous snake. That, apparently, had been Wilde's intention. Robert Ross had been telling them about it before the performance, recalling a day in Paris, Wilde darting across the boulevards to look in shop windows, asking, 'What about that?' or 'Or perhaps she should be naked except for the jewels?' Yellow and green was *his* colour scheme, though Wilde could not have foreseen what, for Charles Manning, was its most disturbing feature: that the yellow was the exact shade of munition girls' skins. Others wouldn't notice that, of course. It only struck *him* because one of his duties at the Ministry was to serve as the military member on a committee set up to inspect the health and safety standards of munitions factories. One saw row after row of such girls, yellow-skinned, strands of ginger hair escaping from under their green caps, faces half hidden by respirators.

Ross had been quite interesting on Wilde's plans for *Salome*, rather more interesting than the performance so far. The most startling piece of information was that Wilde himself had once played Salome, which did rather boggle the imagination, since in photographs he looked far from sylph-like, even by the normal standards of prosperous middle-aged men. Manning directed his attention back to the stage. Since he'd made the effort to attend—and it had *been* an effort, he was feeling very far from well—he ought at least to give the play a chance, particularly since it had obviously meant a great deal to Wilde. Iokanaan's head had been brought in on a charger and Salome was kneeling, hands outstretched towards it. Manning felt an unexpected spasm of revulsion, not because the head was horrifying, but because it wasn't. Another thing Wilde couldn't have foreseen: people in the audience for whom severed heads were not necessarily made of papier mâché.

Salome began to fondle the head. '*Ah! thou wouldst not suffer me to kiss thy mouth, Iokanaan. Well! I will kiss it now. I will bite it with my teeth as one bites a ripe fruit. Yes, I will kiss thy mouth, Iokanaan. I said it: did I not say it? I said it. Ah! I will kiss it now.*'

Manning was bored. If he were honest all this meant nothing to him. He could see what Wilde was doing. He was attempting to convey the sense of a great passion constricted, poisoned, denied legitimate outlets, but none the less forced to the surface, expressed as destruction and cruelty because it could not be expressed as love. It was not that he thought the theme trivial or unworthy or out of date—certainly not that—but the language was impossible for him. France had made it impossible.

He'd only to think for a second of the stinking yellow mud of the Salient, that porridge in which the lumps were human bodies, or parts of them, for an impassable barrier to come between his mind and these words.

*   *   *

A line of men in gas masks clumps along the

duckboards. Ahead of the marching column what looks like a lump of mud sticks to the edge of the track. Closer, it turns out to be a hand. Clumping feet. His own breathing harsh inside the respirator, and then wriggling worm-like across the mud, a voice, sly, insinuating, confidential: 'Where's Scudder? Where's Scudder? Where's—'

*   *   *

On stage another question was being asked: '*But wherefore dost thou not look at me, Iokanaan? Thine eyes that were so terrible, so full of rage and scorn, are shut now. Wherefore are they shut?*'

*   *   *

He's dead, for Christ's sake, Manning thought. His knee had gone into spasm, and he was in acute pain. He glanced sideways at Ross, whose gaze was fixed on the stage, registering every nuance of the performance. He looked ill. Even in this golden reflected light, he looked ill. Oh, God, Manning thought, I wish this was over.

At last Herod cried, *Kill that woman!* and the soldiers rushed towards Salome, daughter of Herodias, and crushed her beneath their shields.

A moment's silence, then the applause burst out and Maud Allan, impersonal beneath the heavy make-up, was curtsying, blowing kisses, smiling, the severed head dangling from one small white hand.

Ross was surrounded as soon as the lights went up. Manning pushed through and shook hands with him, added his murmur to the general buzz of congratulation, then pointed to his knee, and to the back of the auditorium. Ross nodded. 'But you will come backstage?'

Pushing against the crowd to get to the top exit, Manning realized how painful his leg was. He opened the door marked FIRE EXIT and went through. A stone corridor, dimly lit, stretched ahead of him, with none of the gilt and plush of the rest of the theatre. The men's lavatory was at the end of the corridor, down a short flight of stairs. He peed, and then lingered over the business of washing his hands, wanting to postpone the moment when he would have to go backstage and swap the usual chit-chat. He would much rather have gone home. He was sleeping in his own house again, making the need to keep an eye on the builders his excuse, though he was glad of the chance to get away from the club. That silly incident, the newspaper clipping sent to his house, had disturbed him, simply because it could have been sent by *anybody*. He no longer felt he could trust people, members of his club, people he worked with. Even tonight his unwillingness to attend had not been primarily from fear of being seen with Ross—though that *was* a factor—so much as from simple reluctance to mix. Perhaps he was becoming too much of a recluse. Rivers certainly seemed to think he was.

He looked into the mirror. The overhead light cast deep shadows across his face.

*   *   *

Clumping feet. His own breathing harsh inside the respirator, and then wriggling worm-like across the mud, a voice, sly, insinuating, confidential:

*   *   *

83

'What did you think of it?'

A man had come out of one of the cubicles and was staring at him in the mirror. His sudden silent appearance startled Manning. 'Not for me, I'm afraid,' Manning said, starting to dry his hands. 'What did you think?'

The man, who had not moved, said abruptly, 'I thought it was the mutterings of a child with a grotesquely enlarged and diseased clitoris.'

'Did you? I just thought it had dated rather badly.'

'No,' the man said, as if his opinion were the only one that could carry weight. 'It isn't dated. In fact, in terms of what they're trying to do, it's an extremely clever choice.'

Manning looked into the mirror, determined not to be thrown by this ludicrous and yet curiously menacing figure. 'You think enlarged clitorises are a modern problem, do you?'

'All the discontents of modern women can be cured by clitoridectomy.'

'It's a bit more complicated than that, surely.'

It was as if he hadn't spoken. The man came closer until his face was beside Manning's in the glass. 'There are women in this city whose clitorises are so grotesquely enlarged, so horribly inflamed, they can be satisfied ONLY BY BULL ELEPHANTS.'

Silence. Manning couldn't think of anything to say.

'Didn't I see you in the box with Robert Ross?'

Manning turned to face him. Looking him straight in the eye and loading every word with significance, he said, 'I am from the Ministry of Munitions.' He touched the side of his nose, raised a cautionary finger and departed.

Walking along the corridor, he was surprised to

find himself trembling. The man was a complete lunatic. One didn't have to be Rivers to diagnose that, and yet he had been, in a rather horrible way, impressive.

In the crush of Maud Allan's dressing-room, he accepted a glass of wine and edged his way towards Ross. 'I've just met the most extraordinary man in the downstairs lavatory.'

'Hmm.'

'No, not "hmm." Mad. He went on and on about diseased clitorises.'

'It'll be Captain Spencer. Grein said he'd seen him.'

'Who is he?' Manning asked.

'The source of all the trouble, my dear. He's the man who saw the Black Book. Who *knows the names.*'

'But he's mad.'

'That won't stop them believing him. The fact is...' Ross looked around cautiously. 'She shouldn't have sued. I know I'm the *last* person to say that, but—'

'What else could she have done?'

Ross shook his head. 'Once they're in court they can name *anybody.*'

'Are they leaving you alone?'

'No. I have a police officer more or less permanently stationed in the drawing-room. I'd offer the poor man a bed if I didn't think it would be misinterpreted.'

When they left, twenty minutes later, Manning noticed Captain Spencer standing under a street lamp on the other side of the road, watching. Manning reached out to touch Ross's sleeve, then thought better of it, and let his hand drop.

CHAPTER SEVEN

On the train to Manchester, Prior read the Roper correspondence.

Dear Winnie,
Don't worry about me pet I am orlrite Hettie come home for Xmas and we had a good time even little Tommy purked up a bit and you no what he's like you notice this new year there wasnt the same nonsense talked as there was last I think last year knocked the stuffing out of a lot of people except that bloody buggering Welsh windbag he dont change his tune much the poor lads

Hettie made me go to the sales with her cos she new I wanted a blowse there was a nice black one *no trimings* but Hettie says aw Mam your making yourself an old woman anyway you no Hettie I come away with a navy blue with a little yellow rose on it I think it looks orlrite cant take it back if it dont with it being in the sale we bumped into Mrs Warner you no her from the suffragettes and of corse she asked after you but she was only standoffish you could see her wanting to get away she says she thort to much was made of Xmas and turcy was a very dry meat I says well Ive never tasted it so I wouldnt no You no what Ronnie Carker used to say dont you theyre only mecking use of you, Beattie when *they* go home at night they dont even have to pick their nickers up mind you if Ronnie was there they wouldnt need to take them of either

As regards your late visitor you want to remember youve had a lot of worry with Alfs Mam being bad and then thier Ivy being so funny but whatever you do dont let it go past the fortnite YOU COME HOME otherwise youll end up with some bloody mucky cow with a neck you can plant taties in women like that do *no end of damidge* Ive seen bits of young lasses dragging themselves round years after

Did Alf get the letter I sent it on thursday but the post is very slow isnt it I spose its the backlog from Xmas if he did get it ask him to send me the stuff as soon as poss if he didn't tell him not to worry Ill rite again I want it for a man who stopped here just before Xmas he needs it to do somethink a bit risky *but only for him* he doesnt no anythink about you and Alf so theres no danger of you getting dragged in Anyway wil close now hoping this finds you as it leaves me

Buckets of love
Mam

Dear Mam,
School again, dunno who's more fed up, me or the kids. The hall roof sprang a leak during the holidays. No hope of getting it mended, of course, and it was blowing a gale today. Absolutely streaming down the panes and no lights on and Weddell rabbiting on about the Empire and how we must all tighten our belts and brace ourselves, though you don't see *him* bracing himself much, and he couldn't tighten his belt not with that belly on him. I just kept praying one of the drops from the ceiling was going to land on his bald pate, but

no luck. And all the kids coughing like mad. One starts off and then they all start. So we got 'Our glorious Empire . . .' *cough cough*. 'We must fight to the last man.' *cough cough* 'Our valiant lads . . .' *cough cough*. Oh, and he's worked out how many old boys are in the trenches. Quite a lot, which surprised me, I'd've thought they all had rickets. There's rickets in my class. You know that very domed forehead they get? Once you know to look out for that you realize how much of it there is. And then we have to listen to all this puke about what we're fighting for. Still, it's better than it was before Christmas. I really did think I was going to throw up then. Peace on earth to men of goodwill, and how we were all showing goodwill by blowing up the Jerries and saving gallant little Belgium. I tried to tell Standard Six what gallant little Belgium got up to in the Congo, but he soon put a stop to that. I told him I was only doing it to compare a *bad* colonial regime with the splendid record of our glorious Empire, but I don't think he believed me. He doesn't trust me further than he could throw me and that wouldn't be far. He's put me on teaching the little ones this term and I don't think that's a coincidence either.

8's been in touch. You know I've been worried sick about him ever since he got nabbed, but he says it's not too bad. One of the lads had a beard and they shaved him with a cut-throat razor. He ended up pretty cut about, but it's surprising what they can find to laugh at. He says he hasn't seen our William but of course he wouldn't with him being in solitary. It might be the last we hear, though, Mam, because he says the guard who smuggles the letters out is being moved.

One thing I have found out—from 10, you won't know him—is the state of things in Étaples. That's the big camp where they all get sent to train and he says he's never seen anything like it. He says they treat the conscripts like shit. Men tied to posts for the least little thing with their arms above their heads. Doesn't *sound* much, does it, but he says it's agony. He says as sure as anything there's going to be a blow up there. I hope so, I *do* hope so. A few officers shot by their own men, that's all it'll take, just the one little spark, and it'll spread like wildfire. I *know* it will.

Haven't heard anything from Mac. I try to keep busy, I'm running round like scalded cat half the time because I daren't let myself think. The little ones are nice, though. Nobody's got to them yet. I thought of a new nursery rhyme the other day.

> Georgie Georgie, pudding and pie
> Perhaps the girls'll make him cry

Let's keep our fingers crossed, eh?

You want to stock up on food, Mam. I know it's difficult when you've got Tommy to feed, but if you get the chance put a few tins by. If it ever comes to coupons, conchies' families'll be at the back of the queue, *if they get any at all*.

Don't worry about me, I'm all right. You think about yourself for a change,

Lots of love,
Hettie

P.S. If that bloody Mac doesn't write soon I'll bash his bloody head in.

Dear Ma,
Find the stuff you asked for enclosed. Tell your friend to follow the directions *exactly*. You will think me a softie I expect but I feel sorry for the dogs. If you get close enough to the poor brutes, I pity them. Dead in twenty seconds. Anyway, good luck. Reckon we'll have peace by *next* Christmas? Here's hoping,

Alf

P.S. Winnie says to say she came all right.

My darling Hettie,
You'll be wondering why you haven't heard sooner. Well, there's been all hell let loose. Do you remember that lad with the hump on his back? Would insist on going in front of the tribunal instead of getting out of it on health grounds, which he certainly would have done. I've been trying to get him a passage to Ireland and eventually succeeded, but he was picked up just as he was getting on to the boat. The hump gave him away. We'd tried everything to hide it. Charlie suggested putting a dress on him and trying to make him look like a pregnant woman walking backwards, but I don't know how you do that. Anyway, he's back in Wandsworth, where they're doing their best to flatten it for him no doubt. But it's a nuisance because it means *we* have to lie low and that means everybody else has had their trips to the Emerald Isle postponed. It clogs the entire system up, and I lose patience, I'm afraid. I *know* individuals matter, but getting six or seven men across to Ireland isn't going to stop the war. There's only one way do that, and we both know what it is.

90

I'm staying with Charlie Greaves's mother. DON'T WRITE. I know you know the address, but the trouble is you're not the only one who knows it. *All incoming post is opened.* I don't want you in this any deeper than you are already. And I'm *not* treating you like 'the little woman'. There's got to be people they *don't* know about, otherwise there's no safe houses, and no network to pass people on. Speaking of which, I sent a lad to your Mam just before Christmas. Did you happen to bump into him? I wondered afterwards if I'd done the right thing. Not that I've any doubts about him, he's a good lad, keen as mustard, but he does get carried away. I don't suppose it matters, but if you write to your Mam you might mention it, though I suppose he'll have moved on by now. How is she, by the way? I wish we could get Tommy out of there. He's not doing her any good at all.

I'm writing this in bed, which is a big brass one, masses of room, and bouncy. It's tippling down outside and the wind's blowing, and I'd give anything to have you in here with me. *Soon.*

All my love,
Mac

It seemed strange to Prior to be reading his friends' private letters, though these had all—with the exception of Alf's letter and its inconvenient mention of dogs—been read aloud at the Old Bailey. Even Hettie's little nursery rhyme had boomed around No. 1 Court, as the Attorney-General argued it implied her involvement in the conspiracy. No, there was no privacy left in these letters; he was not violating anything that mattered. And yet, as the train thundered into a tunnel and the carriage filled with the acrid smell of smoke, Prior turned to face his doubled reflection in the window and thought he didn't like himself very much. It was the last letter he minded: the gentleness of Mac's love for Hettie exposed, first in open court and now again to him.

They'd found that letter in the pocket of Hettie's skirt when they went to the school to arrest her.

CHAPTER EIGHT

Harry Prior was getting ready to go out. A clean shirt had been put to air on the clothes-horse in front of the fire, darkening and chilling the room. Billy Prior and his mother sat at the table, she with her apron on, he in shirt and braces, unable either to continue their interrupted conversation or to talk to Harry. He bent over the sink, lathering his face, blathering and spluttering, sticking his index fingers into his ears and waggling them. Then, after rinsing the soap off, he placed one forefinger over each nostril in turn and slung great gobs of green snot into the sink.

Prior, his elbow touching his mother's side, felt her quiver fastidiously. He laced his fingers round the hot cup of tea and raised it to his lips, dipping his short nose delicately as he drank. How many times as a child had he watched this tense, unnecessary scene, sharing his mother's disgust as he would have shared her fear of lightning. Now, as a man, in this over-familiar room—the tiles worn down by his footsteps, the table polished by his elbows—he thought he could see the conflict more even-handedly than he had seen it then. It takes a great deal of aggression to quiver fastidiously for twenty-eight years.

He thought, now, he could recognize his mother's contribution to the shared tragedy. He saw how the wincing sensitivity of her response was actually feeding this brutal performance. He recalled her gentle, genteel, whining, reproachful voice going on and on, long after his father's stumbling footsteps had jerked him into wakefulness; how he had sat on the stairs and strained to hear, until his muscles ached with the tension, waiting for her to say the one thing *he* would not be able to bear. And then the scuffle of running steps, a stifled cry, and he would be half way downstairs, listening to see if it was just a single slap, the back of his father's hand sending his mother staggering against the wall, or whether it was one of the bad times. She never had the sense to *shut up*.

But then, he thought, his face shielded by the rim of his cup, one might equally say she had never been coward enough to refrain from speaking her mind for fear of the consequences. It would be very easy, under the pretext of 'even-handedness', to slip too far the other way and blame the violence in the home not on his brutality, but on her failure to manage it.

As a child, Prior remembered beating his clenched fist against the palm of the other hand, over and over again, saying, with every smack of flesh on flesh, PIG PIG PIG PIG. Obviously, his present attempt to understand his parents' marriage was more mature, more adult, more perceptive, more sensitive, more insightful, more almost anything you cared to mention, than PIG PIG PIG PIG, but it didn't content him, because it was also a lie: a way of claiming to be 'above the battle'. And he was not above it: he was its product. *He* and *she*—elemental forces, almost devoid of personal characteristics— clawed each other in every cell of his body, and would do so until he died. 'They fight and fight and never rest on the Marches of my breast,' he thought, and I'm fucking fed up with it.

His father had got his jacket and cap on now, and stood ready to go out, looking at them with a hard, dry, stretched-elastic smile, the two of them together, as they had always been, waiting for him to go. 'I'll see you, then,' he said.

There was no question, as in the majority of households there would have been, of father and son going for a drink together.

'When will you be back?' his mother asked, as she had always done.

'Elevenish. Don't wait up.'

She always waited up. Oh, she would have said there was the fire to damp down, tomorrow's bait to be got ready, the table to be laid, the kettle to be filled, but all these tasks could have been done earlier. Prior, once more lowering his eyes to the cup, tried not to ask himself how many violent scenes might have been avoided if his mother had simply taken his father at his word and gone to bed. Hundreds? Or none? The man who spoke so softly and considerately now might well have dragged her out of bed to wait on him, when he staggered in from the pub with ten or eleven pints on board.

Leave it, he told himself. *Leave it.*

*　　　*　　　*

After his father had gone, Prior and his mother went on sitting at the table while they finished drinking their tea. She never mentioned France or Craiglockhart. She seemed to want to ignore everything that had happened to him since he left home. This was both an irritation and a relief. He asked after boys he'd known at school. This one was dead, that one wounded, Eddie Wilson had deserted. He remembered Eddie, didn't he? There were deserters in the paper every week, she said. The policeman who found Eddie Wilson hiding in his

95

mother's coal-hole had been awarded a prize of five shillings.

'There was a letter in the paper the other week,' she said. 'From Father Mackenzie. You remember him, don't you?'

She found last week's paper and handed it to him. He read the letter, first silently and then aloud, in a wickedly accurate imitation of Father Mackenzie's liturgical flutings. '"There may be some among you, who, by reason of your wilful and culpable neglect of the Laws of Physical development, are not fit to serve your country, but—" Oh, for Christ's sake!' He threw the paper down. '*Some among them* carry their wilful and culpable neglect to the point of getting rickets. If he's physically well developed it's because his mother could afford to shove good food in his gob four times a day.' And goodness wasn't he well developed, Prior thought, remembering Father Mackenzie in his socks.

'He just thinks a lot of people are shirking, Billy. You've got to admit he's got a point.'

'Do you know the height requirement for the Bantam regiments? *Five feet*. And do you know how many men from round here *fail that*?'

'Billy, sometimes you sound exactly like your father.'

He picked up the paper and pretended to read.

'There's a lot of talk about a strike at the munition works. Your father's all for it. Well, *he* would be, wouldn't he?'

'What's it about?'

'I don't know.' She groped for an unfamiliar word. 'Dilution?'

'Sounds right.'

'Well, you can imagine your dad. "Bits of lasses

earning more than I do." "You mark my words," he says, "after the war they'll bring in unskilled labour. The missus'll be going to work, and the man'll be sat at home minding the bairn. It's the end of craftsmanship. This war's the Trojan horse, only they're all too so-and-soing daft to see it.'"

Typical, Prior thought. However determined his father might be to raise the status of the working class as a whole, he was still more determined to maintain distinctions within it.

'Oh, and he doesn't like false teeth. That's another thing,' his mother went on. 'Mrs Thorpe's got them, you know. "Mutton dressed up as lamb," he says. The way he goes on about her teeth you'd think she'd bit him. And then there's Mrs Riley's dustbin. *Lobster* tins, would you believe. "They were glad of a bit of bread and scrape before the war."'

'He's got a funny idea of socialism.'

She shrugged. 'I wouldn't know. Things like women's rights, he was never in favour of that.'

'*No.*'

'I remember him going on at Beattie Roper about that.'

A pause. 'I went to see Beattie.'

She looked stunned. 'In prison?'

'Yes.'

'You've no call to go getting yourself mixed up in that.'

Faced with this sudden blaze of anger, he said, 'I have to. It's my job.'

'Oh.' She nodded, only half believing him.

'How's Hettie?'

His mother froze. 'I wouldn't know. I never see her.'

There had been a time, when he was seventeen,

97

when he and Hettie Roper had been 'walking out', and, for once, the 'quaint expression' had been painfully accurate. 'Walking' was exactly what they did. And talking too, of course: passionate, heated talk, about socialism and women's rights, spiritualism, Edward Carpenter's ideas on male comradeship, whether there could be such a thing as free love. He remembered one day on the beach at Formby, sitting in the dunes as the sky darkened, and the sun hung low over the sea. All day he had been wanting to touch her, and had not dared do it. The sun lingered, tense and swollen, then spilled itself on to the water. 'Come on,' he said, picking up his jacket. 'We'd better be getting back.'

That night, as on so many other nights, his mother had been waiting up for him. A book was open on her knee, but she hadn't bothered to light the gas. And then the questions started. He realized then that she hated Hettie Roper. He didn't know why.

'Does she still run the shop?' he asked.

'No point. Nobody'd buy anything off her if she did.'

'Does she work?'

'Not that I know of.'

'So how does she live?'

A shrug. 'She's still got the allotment.'

'I thought I'd pop round and see her.'

Silence.

Reminding himself he was no longer seventeen, Prior stood up and put his cup on the draining-board. 'I won't be long.'

*   *   *

Before the war, women used to sit on their steps in the

warm evenings until after dark, postponing the moment when the raging bedbug must be faced, and taking pleasure in the only social contact they could enjoy without fear of condemnation. A woman seen chatting to her neighbours during the day quickly felt the weight of public disapproval. 'Eeh, look at that Mrs Thorpe. Eleven kids. You'd think she could find herself summat to do, wouldn't you?' Now, looking up and down the street, Prior saw deserted doorsteps. Women were out and about, but walking purposefully, as if they had somewhere to go.

He supposed it was Mrs Thorpe's name that came particularly to mind because she'd been one of the worst offenders, with her lard-white breasts the size of footballs, and Georgie or Alfie or Bobby worrying away at them, breaking off now and then for a drag on a tab end. Or perhaps, subconsciously, he'd already identified her, for there she was, coming towards him, divested of the clogs and shawl he'd always seen her in and wearing not merely a coat and hat but flesh-coloured stockings *and shoes*. It was scarcely possible the attractive woman with her should be Mrs Riley, but he didn't know who else it could be.

They greeted him with cries of delight, hugging, kissing, standing back, flashing their incredible smiles. There was a saying round here: for every child born a tooth lost, and certainly, before the war, Mrs Thorpe and Mrs Riley had advertised their fecundity every time they opened their mouths. Now, in place of gaps and blackened stumps was this even, flashing whiteness. 'What white teeth you have, Grandma,' he said.

'All the better to eat you with,' said Mrs Riley. 'And who are *you* calling Grandma?'

Mrs Thorpe asked, 'How long have you got, love?' And then, before he had time to answer, 'Eeh, aren't we awful, always asking that?'

'Two days.'

'Well, make the most of it. Don't do anything we wouldn't do, mind.'

He smiled. 'How much scope does that give me?'

'Fair bit, these days,' said Mrs Riley.

He remembered, suddenly, that he'd sucked the breasts of both these women. His mother had been very ill for two months after his birth, and he'd been fed on tins of condensed milk from the corner shop, the same milk adults used in their tea. Babies in these streets were regularly fed on it. Babies fed on it regularly died. Then Mrs Thorpe and Mrs Riley had appeared, at that time, he supposed, lively young girls each with her own first baby at her breast. They had taken it in turns to feed him and, in so doing, had probably saved his life. He had known this a long time, but somehow, when Mrs Thorpe and Mrs Riley had been shapeless bundles in shawls, it had not *registered*. Now, though not easily discomforted, he felt himself start to blush.

'Look at that,' said Mrs Riley. 'He's courting, I can always tell.'

'*Are* you courting?' Mrs Thorpe asked.

'Yes. Her name's Sarah. Sarah Lumb.'

'Good strong name that,' said Mrs Riley.

'She's a good strong lass.'

'Mebbe has need to be,' said Mrs Riley, looking him up and down, speculatively. 'Do y' fancy a drink?'

'No, I'd like to, but I've got to see somebody.'

'Well, if you change your mind we'll be in the Rose and Crown.'

100

And off they went, cackling delightedly, two married women going out for a drink together. Unheard of. And in his father's pub too. No wonder the old bugger thought Armageddon had arrived.

Prior walked on, noticing everywhere the signs of a new prosperity. Meat might be scarce, bread might be grey, but the area was booming for all that. Part of him was pleased, delighted even. 'Bits of lasses earning more than I do'? *Good.* Lobster tins in Mrs Riley's dustbin? *Good.* He would have given anything to have been simply, unequivocally, unambiguously pleased. But he passed too many houses with black-edged cards in the window, and to every name on the cards he could put a face. It seemed to him the streets were full of ghosts, grey, famished, unappeasable ghosts, jostling on the pavements, waiting outside homes that had prospered in their absence. He imagined a fire blazing up, a window shaking its frame, a door gliding open, and then somebody saying, 'Wind's getting up. Do you feel the draught?' and shutting the door fast.

The glow he'd felt in talking to Mrs Thorpe and Mrs Riley faded. He slipped down the back alley between Marsh Street and Gladstone Terrace, making for Tite Street and Beattie Roper's shop, a journey he must have taken thousands of times as a child, a boy, a young man, but now he moved silently across the cobbles, feeling almost invisible. He was no more part of the life around him than one of those returning ghosts.

He came out at the top of Hope Street and started to walk down it. Hope Street ran parallel with the canal and was known, predictably, as No-Hope Street, because of the alacrity with which its inhabitants transferred themselves from one to the

101

other. At least before the war they did. Suicides were rare now. The war had cheered everybody up.

Half way down, on the corner of Hope Street and Tite Street, was Beattie's shop, its windows boarded up. He knocked loudly on the door.

'You'll not get an answer there, love,' a woman said, passing by. He waited until she'd turned the corner, then knelt and peered through the letter-box. The counters were cleared, the floor swept clean. He called, 'Hettie. It's me, Billy.' The door into the living-room stood open. He felt her listening. 'Hettie, it's me.'

She came at last, kneeling on her side of the door to check he was alone. There was a great rattling of bolts and chains, and she stood there, a thin, dark, intense woman, older than he remembered. No longer pretty.

'Billy.'

'I've been to see your mother.'

'Yes. She wrote.'

A long hesitation, which told him immediately what he wanted to know. He took off his cap and stepped forward. Almost simultaneously, she stood aside and said, 'Come in.'

The living-room was empty. Both doors, one to the scullery, the other to the stairs, were closed. He looked round the room, taking his time. A fire blazed in the grate. The kettle stood on the hob beside it. The table, with its green cloth, still took up most of the space, six empty chairs ranged neatly round it. Hettie followed his gaze, and he could see how changes she'd become accustomed to—the empty chairs— became strange again, and unbearable as she saw them through his eyes. 'Oh, Billy,' she said, and then she was in his arms and crying.

He cuddled her, lifting her off her feet, rocking her from side to side. Only when the sobs subsided did he loosen his grip, and let her slide to the ground. Her spread fingers encountered belt, buckles, buttons, tabs, stars: the whole hated paraphernalia. He said quickly, 'I see you've still got Tibbs.'

A fat tabby cat lay coiled on the rug, the pale underside of his chin exposed. Ghost smells of cat pee and creosote drifted in from the shop.

'Yes,' she said, laughing and sniffing. 'Pees on everything now.'

Her laughter acknowledged the fund of shared memories. Thank God, Prior thought, pulling out a chair and sitting down.

She fetched the tea-pot and started making tea. 'How's me mam? She *says* she's all right.'

'Thin. But she's eating. She's come off the strike.'

'Hmm. How long for? I tell her she shouldn't do it, but she says, "How else can I convince them?"'

'Have you been to see her?'

'I'm going next week. I gather we've got you to thank for that?'

'I put in a word.'

She poured the tea. 'How come you're in a position to put in a word?'

'Got a job in the Ministry, that's all. They're not sending me back 'cause of the asthma.'

'But what do you do?'

He laughed. 'Exactly what I did before the war. Push pieces of paper across a desk. But I managed to get me hands on your mam's file—via a young lady in the filing department—and then I thought I'd go and see her.'

'And you just *bluffed* your way in?'

'Well, not exactly, I had Ministry of Munitions

103

headed notepaper. That gets you anywhere.'

'Huh! I wish *we* had some.'

She believed him. Just as once her mother had believed Spragge. She was sitting at the head of the table, in her mother's chair, no doubt because that made her mother's absence seem less glaring, and he was sitting, almost certainly, where Spragge had sat. He looked across to the dresser, and there sure enough was the photograph of William.

Hettie saw him looking at it, and reached behind her. 'I don't think you've seen this one, have you?' she said, and handed it across.

William was leaning against a stone wall, his arms loosely folded, and he was smiling, though the smile had become strained as the photographer fiddled with his camera. He was wearing bicycle clips. A pencilled date on the back said 'May 1913'. Prior thought he knew the place, they'd gone there together, the three of them. Behind the wall, not visible in the photograph, a steep bank shelved away, covered with brambles and bracken, full of rabbits whose shiny round droppings lay everywhere.

'Why does it look so long ago?' he said, holding the photograph out in front of him. Without conscious duplicity (though not without awareness), he was groping for the tone of their pre-war friendship.

She laughed, a harsh yelp that didn't sound like Hettie.

'No, but it does, doesn't it?' he persisted. 'I mean, it *looks* longer than it is. You know, I was thinking about that on the way over. About...' He took a deep breath. 'You know if you were writing about something like ... oh, I don't know, enclosures, or the coming of the railways, you wouldn't have people standing round saying...' He put a theatrical hand to

104

his brow. '"Oh, dear me, we *are* living through a period of terribly rapid social change, aren't we?" Because nobody'd believe people would be so ... *aware*. But here we are, living through just such a period, and everybody's bloody well aware of it. I've heard nothing else since I came home. Not the words, of course, but the *awareness*. And I just wondered whether there aren't periods when people *do* become aware of what's happening, and they look back on their previous unconscious selves and it seems like decades ago. Another life.'

'Yes, I think you're right.' She thought for a moment. 'I went to London a couple of months ago, to see one of the few suffragette friends who still wants to know me. And we were sitting in her house, and there was a raid, and we actually heard shrapnel falling on the trees, and do you know it sounded exactly like rain. And she was ... *full of herself*. Short hair, breeches, driving an ambulance, all things she'd never've been allowed to do in a million years. And suddenly she grabbed hold of me and she said, "Hettie, for women, this is the first day in the history of the world."'

'And the last for a lot of men.'

Her face darkened. 'Don't beat *me* over the head with that, Billy. *I*'m the pacifist, remember.'

'At least you've got the vote.'

'No, I haven't. I'm not thirty. Mam hasn't, she's in prison. Winnie hasn't, same reason. William hasn't, he's had his vote taken away 'cause he's a conchie. So as far as votes go this family's one *down* on before the war.'

'Where is William?' Prior said, looking at the photograph again.

'Dartmoor. He took the Home Office scheme. He's

105

doing "useful work unconnected with the war".' She snorted. 'Breaking stones.'

'I'm surprised he took it.'

'You wouldn't be if you saw him. He's that thin, you wouldn't know him.'

'I had Mike Riordan in my platoon. You remember Mike? I didn't know *him* either. Only in his case it was the face that was missing.'

'It isn't a competition, Billy.'

'No. You're right.'

She touched his sleeve. 'I wish we were on the same side.'

'Well, as far as your mam's concerned we are. You surely don't think I'm on Spragge's side?'

Her expression changed. 'Oh, that man. Do you know, I met him once, just for a couple minutes, and I *knew* there was something wrong with him.'

'You didn't know about the poison?'

'No, she kept all that from me. I wish she hadn't, I'd've told her she was daft to trust him. And that smirking bastard at the Old Bailey. It was awful, Billy. You're stood in that dock and you *feel* guilty, even though you know you haven't done it. For months afterwards I felt people could look straight through me.' She stopped. 'Here, drink your tea. It'll get cold.'

'How are you managing?'

'I survive. Your dad brings me a bit of meat now and then. Don't look so surprised, Billy.' A pause. 'I tell you who's been good. Mrs Riley. Every time she bakes she brings something round. You know mebbe just half a dozen rock buns, but every bit helps. I've nothing to thank the others for, except a few bricks through the window. What gets me you know is the way they used to cut me mam dead in the street, they'd just look through her. But let them be in trouble, or their daughters be in trouble, and there they were, banging on the back door. I says, "You're a fool, Mam. Why should you risk prison for them?" But it was, "Oh, well, she had to have instruments last time," or "Poor bairn, she's only seventeen." And she'd do it for them. And it all came out at the trial. You know, killing a baby when its mother's two months gone, that's a terrible crime. But wait twenty years and blow the same kid's head off, that's all right.'

Prior winced, thinking how strange it was that such words should come so easily from her mouth, that she should have so little conception of what memories they conjured up for him.

'What about Mac? Do you ever see him?'

Her face became guarded. 'No.'

'Never?'

'You know bloody well, Billy, he wouldn't dare come here.'

Prior sat back in his chair. 'I know he couldn't stay away.' He waited. 'I thought I heard somebody just now.'

Her eyes went to the scullery door.

'Walking up and down.'

'It's a restless house. You've got to remember me mam held seances here. In this room.'

'You don't believe in that.'

'I know me mam wasn't a fraud. *Something* happened. Whether it was just the force of people's need or not, I don't know, but there used to be nights when this table was shaking. It changes a place. I sit here on me own some nights and I hear footsteps going round and round the table.'

He had a dreadfully clear perception of what her
107

life must be like, alone in this house, with the empty chairs and the boarded-up windows. It didn't surprise him that she heard footsteps going round the table.

'Talking of Mac,' he said, and felt her stiffen. 'I thought I'd go round and see his mam. I don't suppose he still sees her, does he?'

'That's a good idea, Billy. I'd willingly go, but I doubt if she'd thank me for it. In fact, I doubt if she'd invite me in.'

'No, she's a great patriot, Lizzie.' He was smiling to himself. 'You know the last time I was home I bumped into her. Well.' He laughed. 'Fell over her. You know the alley behind the Rose and Crown? "Just resting," she says. I got her on her feet and she took one look at the uniform and she says, "Thank God for an honest man." And out it all came. Apparently on the day war broke out she did seven men for free because they'd just come back from the recruiting office. *They said.* "And do you know," she says. "Five of them were still walking round in civvies a year after." She says she had a go at Wally Smith about it. And he says, "Well they wouldn't let me in because of me teeth." And Lizzie says, "What the fuck do they want you to do? *Bite the buggers?*"'

Hettie was looking very uncomfortable. Since she was far from prudish he could only suppose the story of Lizzie and her August 4th burst of generosity was likely to be painful to the person on the other side of the scullery door. He thought of saying, 'Oh, come on, Mac, stop arsing about,' but he didn't dare risk it. Better make his plea first, then leave them alone to talk about it.

'I'd like to see Mac, Hettie.'

'So would I,' she flashed. 'Fat chance.'

'No, I mean I really do need to see him. If I'm going to do anything for your mam, I've got to talk to him first. He—'

'He didn't know anything about it.'

'No, but he knew Spragge. Spragge was with him the night before he came here. He gave Spragge the address.'

'Do you think he doesn't know that? Spragge took in an awful lot of people, Billy. He had *letters*.'

'I know. I'm not ... I'm not *blaming* Mac. I just want to talk to him. He might remember something that would help. You see, if we could prove Spragge acted as an *agent provocateur* with somebody else—or even tried to—that would help to discredit his evidence in your mam's case.'

She glanced at the scullery door. 'I know somebody who bumps into Mac now and then. I'll see if I can get a message through.'

'That's all I ask.' He stood up. 'And now I'd better be off.'

She didn't try to detain him. At the door he paused and said loudly, 'I thought I'd go for a walk by the cattle pens. I thought I'd go there now.'

She looked up at him. 'Goodnight, Billy.'

CHAPTER NINE

It was not quite dusk when Prior reached the cattle pens, empty at this time of the week and therefore unguarded. Mac, if he came at all, would wait till dark, so there was time to kill. He lit a cigarette and strolled up and down, remembering the taste of his first cigarette—given to him by Mac—and the valiant efforts he'd made not to be sick.

He stood for a while, his hands gripping the cold metal of one of the pens. He was recalling a time when he'd been ill—one of the many—and he'd gone out and wandered the streets, not well enough yet to go back to school but bored with being in the house. It had been a hot day, and he was muffled up, a prickly scarf round his neck, a poultice bound to his chest. The heat beat up into his face from the pavements as he dragged himself along, stick-thin, white, bed-bound legs moving in front of him, the smell of Wintergreen rising into his nostrils. The name made him think of pine trees, snow-covered hills and the way the sheets felt when you thrust your hot legs into a cool part, away from the sticky damp.

He heard their hoofs before he saw them and, like everybody else, stopped to watch as the main street filled with cattle being driven to the slaughterhouse. A smell of hot shit. Dust rising all round, getting into his lungs, making him cough and bring up sticky green phlegm. He backed away from the noise and commotion, ran up a back alley between the high dark walls, then realized that, as in a nightmare, a

110

cow was following him, with slithering feet and staring eyes, and men chasing after her. More men came running from the other end of the alley. They cornered her, closing in from both sides, and the terrified animal slipped in her own green shit and fell, and they threw heavy black nets around her and dragged her back to the herd, while all along the alley housewives whose clean washing had been swept aside erupted from their backyards, shouting and waving their arms.

At the moment the nets landed Prior had looked across the heaving backs and seen a boy, about his own age, standing pressed back against the wall, his white, still face half hidden by a mass of cottery black hair. Mac.

The sight of the cow in the net stayed with him. Many a night he dreamt about her and woke to lie staring into the swirling darkness. Sometimes when he woke it was already light, and then, afraid to go back to sleep, he would creep downstairs, open the door quietly and slip out into the empty, dawn-smelling streets. The only other person about at that hour was the knocker-up, an old woman with bent back and wisps of white hair escaping from a black woollen shawl, who went from house to house, tapping on the upper windows with her long pole, waiting for the drowsy or bad-tempered answer, and moving on. Drifting along behind her, he'd found his way to the cattle pens, and to the deepest friendship of his childhood.

He left the pens now and walked into the high shed, which was as vast as a cathedral, and echoing. He walked up and down, dwarfed by the height, imagining the place as it used to be and presumably still was, if you came at the right time of week. He

111

remembered the rattle of rain on the corrugated iron roof, imagined it pouring down as it had on the night he first stayed here with Mac. He looked round, and the empty stalls filled with terrified cattle, huge shadows of tossing horns leapt across the ceiling as the guards moved up and down with lanterns, checking that the overcrowded animals were not suffocating to death. If they suffocated before they could be slaughtered, their meat was unfit for human consumption, though it found its way on to the market as 'braxy', in shops patronized only by the very poor. There was no profit to be had from braxy, so if an animal was distressed and appeared to be near death the guards would rouse the slaughterman to come and dispatch it. These guards were supposed to be on duty all night, but since they'd been away for long stretches on the drovers' road they naturally wanted to sleep with their wives or girlfriends, and that was where Mac came in. The job was subcontracted to him at a penny a night, and he was good at it. He could calm a cow, even a cow who'd already scented blood, to the point where she would yield milk into a lemonade bottle. Prior could almost see him now, wedged into a wall of sweating flesh, slithering on the green shit that always had about it the smell of terror, coaxing, whispering, stroking, burrowing his head into the cow's side, and then coming back in triumph with the warm milk. They'd swigged it from the bottle, sitting side by side on the bales of straw that stood in one corner of the shed, and then, slowly and luxuriously, like businessmen savouring particularly fine cigars, they smoked the tab ends Mac had picked up from the streets.

Prior wandered across to the bales of straw and sat down, his cigarette a small planet shining in the darkness, for the night was closing in fast. He could just see the nail in the wall which had always been their target in peeing competitions, and from the nail he moved in imagination to the school playground. He had a lot of playground memories of Mac, and classroom memories too, though few of these were happy. Mac was dirty and his hair was lousy. He wore men's shoes, and a jacket whose sleeves came to the tips of his fingers, and he was always being beaten. As children do, Prior supposed, he'd started by assuming that Mac was beaten more often than anybody else because he was naughtier than anybody else. He was inclined to believe now that the *only* valuable part of his education at that abysmal school had been learning that this was not true. Lizzie's profession was well known. On the one occasion she'd come to school, her speech had been slurred and she'd raised her voice in the corridor; they'd all watched her through the classroom windows, every varied pitch of her indignation expressed in the jiggling of the feather on her hat. No doubt she'd come down to protest because they'd beaten Mac too hard. If so, the visit did no good: he was beaten again as soon as she left. Prior remembered those beatings. He remembered the painful pressure of emotions he'd felt: fear, pity, anger, excitement, pleasure. He wondered now whether the pleasure could possibly have been as sexual as he remembered it. Probably not.

After one such occasion Prior had sat with his back to the railings that divided the boys' playground from the girls', munching a sandwich and watching Mac. Mac was running up and down the playground with Joe Smailes on his back, staggering beneath the weight, his grubby hands with their scabbed knuckles

113

clasping Joe Smailes's podgy pink thighs. Mac was a bread horse: he gave other boys rides on his back in exchange for the crust from their bread or the core of their apple. Lizzie had not been poor, as the neighbourhood understood poverty, but she was too disorganized by drink to provide regular meals. What disturbed Prior this time, what ensured that his eyes never left Mac's face as he staggered up and down, was the knowledge that he'd deserved a beating every bit as much as Mac, but because *he* was clean, tidy, well turned out, likely to win a scholarship and bring desperately needed credit to the school, he'd been spared. He bit into his second sandwich, thought, munched, choked. Suddenly he ran across the playground, thrust what was left of the sandwich into Mac's hands, burst into tears, and ran away.

Who needed Marx when they had Tite Street Board School, Prior thought, stubbing out his cigarette carefully between strips of golden straw. Still absorbed in memories of the past, he got to his feet and started to walk up and down. The moon had risen; its light was bright enough to cast his shadow across the floor. His first awareness of Mac was of a shadow growing beside his own, then the touch of a hand on his shoulder, and a light amused voice asking, 'Am I to understand you've been up my mother?'

Prior turned. 'What makes you say that?'

'All that stuff about "Thank God for an honest man", I don't know what else it could mean.'

'Now would *I* do that?'

'I don't know. Before the war you'd've fucked a cow in a field if you could've found one to stand still for you.'

114

And the bull. 'Mac, I swear—'

'Aw, forget it. If I was sensitive about that I'd've croaked years ago.' Mac was smiling. This was almost, but not quite, a joke.

Prior said, 'Shall we sit down?'

They sat on bales of straw a few feet apart, united and divided by the rush of memory. They could see clearly enough, by moonlight and the intermittent glow of cigarettes, to be able to judge each other's expression.

'It *was* you in the kitchen, then,' Prior said. 'I thought it was.'

'Why, who'd you think it might be?'

Prior hesitated. 'I was afraid it might be some poor frightened little sod of a deserter, I was afraid he'd—'

'What would you have done?'

'Turned him in.'

Mac looked at him curiously. 'Even though he's "a poor frightened little sod"?'

'*Yes*. What about the poor frightened little sods who *don't* desert?'

'Well, at least we know where we stand.'

'I don't want to start by telling you a pack of lies.'

Mac laughed. 'You told Hettie a few. That girl in the filing department, the one who got you the files, my God, Billy, you must be ringing *her* bell.'

'Say it, Mac.'

'All right, I'll say it. It strikes me you'd be a bloody good recruit, *for them*. You with your commission and your posh accent, and your...' With a kind of mock delicacy, Mac touched his own chest. '*Low* friends. Officers' mess one night, back streets of Salford the next. Equally at home or...' He smiled, relishing the intimacy of his capacity to wound. 'Equally *not* at home, in both.'

115

'Whereas *you* of course are firmly embedded in the bosom of a loving proletariat? Well, let me tell you, Mac, the part of the proletariat I've been fighting with—the vast majority—they'd string *you* up from the nearest fucking lamp-post and not think twice about it. And as for your striking munition workers...' Prior swept the shed with a burst of machine-gun fire.

There was a moment's shocked silence, as if the childish gesture had indeed produced carnage.

'And don't think they wouldn't do it, they would. *I know them.*'

Mac said, 'I'm surprised you feel *quite* so much pleasure at the idea of the workers shooting each other.'

'No pleasure, Mac. Just facing reality.' Prior produced a flask from his tunic pocket and handed it over. 'Here, wash it down.'

Mac unscrewed the cap, drank, blinked as his eyes watered, then passed the flask back, its neck unwiped. After a moment's hesitation Prior drank, thinking, as he did so, that the sacramental gesture was hollow. Milk in unwiped lemonade bottles was a lifetime away.

'You still haven't explained,' Mac said.

'About the files? I work in the Intelligence Unit.'

Mac made a slight, involuntary movement.

'They'd've been here by now.'

Mac smiled. 'Must be quite nice, really. A foot on each side of the fence. Long as you don't mind what it's doing to your balls.'

'They're all right, Mac. Worry about your own.'

'Oh, I *see*. I wondered when that was coming. *Men* fight, is that it?'

'No. I can see it takes courage to be a pacifist. At

116

least, I suppose it does. You see, my trouble is I don't know what courage means. The only time I've ever done anything even slightly brave, I couldn't remember a bloody thing about it. Bit like those men who bash the wife's head in with a poker. "Everything went black, m'lud."'

Mac nodded. 'Well, since you're being honest, I think a load of fucking rubbish's talked about how much courage it takes to be a pacifist. When I was deported from the Clyde, they came for me in the middle of the night. One minute I was dreaming about a blonde with lovely big tits and the next minute I was looking up at six policemen with lovely big truncheons. Anyway, they got me off to the station and they started pushing me around, one to the other, you know, flat-of-the-hand stuff, and they were all grinning, sort of *nervous* grins, and I knew what was coming, I knew they were working themselves up. It's surprising how much working up the average man needs before he'll do anything *really* violent. Well, you'd know all about that.'

'Yes,' Prior said expressionlessly.

'I was shitting meself. And then I thought, well. They're not going to blind you. They're not going to shove dirty great pieces of hot metal in your spine, they're not going to blow the top of your head off, they're not going to amputate your arms and legs without an anaesthetic, so what the fuck are you worried about? If you were in France you'd be facing all that. And of course there's always the unanswered question. *Could* you face it? Could you *pass the test*? But where I think we differ, Billy, is that *you* think that's a Very Important Question, and I think it's fucking trivial.'

Prior glanced sideways at him. 'No, you don't.'

117

'All right, I don't.'

'You could always say you're showing *moral courage*.'

'No such thing. It's a bit like medieval trial-by-combat, you know. In the end moral and political truths have to be proved *on the body*, because this mass of nerve and muscle and blood is what we are.'

'That's a very dangerous idea. It comes quite close to saying that the willingness to suffer proves the rightness of the belief. But it *doesn't*. The most it can ever prove is the believer's sincerity. And not always that. Some people just like suffering.'

Mac was looking round the shed. He said, 'I don't think I do,' but he seemed to have tired of the argument, or perhaps the whisky had begun to soften his mood. 'I often think about those days.'

Prior waited. 'You *can* trust me, you know.'

'I trusted Spragge.'

'You didn't have pissing competitions with Spragge.'

'Oh, that's it, is it? *Piss* brothers?'

Prior laughed. 'Something like that.'

A long silence. 'What do you want?'

'I want you to tell me about Spragge.'

Mac gave a choking laugh. 'He's your fucking employee.'

'Not any more. The trial blew his cover.'

'Good.'

'He was with you, wasn't he, the night before?'

'I sent him there.'

Mac must find that almost intolerable, Prior thought. His debt to the Ropers was total. Without Beattie, he'd've been a scabby, lousy, neglected kid, barely able to read and write, fit only for the drovers' road and the slaughterhouse. Beattie had taken him

118

in. By the age of thirteen he'd been living more with her than with his own mother. As soon as the older boys in the street gang stopped speculating about sex and started climbing Lizzie's stairs in search of more concrete information, Mac had found his own home unbearable. He'd disappeared altogether for a time, going up the drovers' road one summer, returning, older, harder, the first traces of cynicism and deadness round his mouth and eyes. Then Beattie took charge. 'What the hell's the matter with you?' she asked. 'You can read, can't you? Just 'cos the teachers think you're stupid, doesn't mean you are. Some of *them* aren't too bright. Here, read this. No, go on, *read it*. I want to know what you think.'

'He was after *you*, wasn't he?' Prior asked.

'Yes.'

'Do *you* think she meant to kill Lloyd George?'

'Nah. You know Beattie. She finds a spider in the sink, she gets a bit of newspaper and puts it in the yard.'

'Hmm. I just wonder what she'd do if she found Lloyd George in the sink.'

'Run the fucking taps.'

They looked at each other and burst out laughing.

'Look, if there *was* anything, the idea came from Spragge. And I think helping people escape from a detention centre sounds about right. And Spragge had tried it on before.'

'Who with?'

'Charlie Greaves, Joe Haswell. He offered them explosives to blow up a munitions factory. Said he knew where he could get some. Well, for God's sake. They're not exactly lying around, are they? As soon as they said no, he started backing off. Pretended he hadn't meant it.'

119

'And you still sent him to Beattie?'

'This is *hindsight*, man. It sticks in my mind *now* because of what happened. At the time I just thought, oh God, another mad bugger.'

'Could you get them to write it down? With dates, if possible.'

'I don't even know where they are.'

'It's for Beattie, Mac.'

Mac let out a sharp breath. 'What do you want it for?'

'To discredit Spragge, of course.'

'They won't reopen the case.'

'Not publicly. But they might let her out. Quietly. She's going to die in there, Mac. She won't last anywhere near ten years.'

A dragging silence.

'I'm not asking them to incriminate themselves. All they have to do is say "He offered us explosives and we refused."'

'And you think they're going to be believed?'

'I think there's a better chance than you might think. There's a lot of questions being asked about the way spies are used in munition factories. Some of them are better at starting strikes than you are, Mac.'

'All right.' Mac stood up. 'It'll take a few weeks.'

'As long as that?'

'I've told you. I don't know where they are.'

'Where can I contact you?'

Mac laughed. 'You fucking can't. Here, give me your address.'

Prior took the notepad and pencil, and scribbled. 'All right?'

'*Don't* write to Hettie. The post's opened. And one more thing.' Mac came very close, resting his hands heavily on Prior's shoulders. 'If this is a trap, Billy, you're dead. I'm not a fucking Quaker, remember.'

For a moment the pressure on his shoulders increased, then Mac turned and strode away.

*   *   *

Prior decided to take the short-cut home across the brick fields. This patch of waste land always reminded him of France. Sump holes reflected a dull gleam at the sky, tall grasses bent to the wind, pieces of scrap metal rusted, rubbish stank, a rusting iron bedstead upreared itself, a jagged black shape that, outlined against the horizon, would have served as a landmark on patrol.

One of the ways in which he felt different from his brother officers, one of the many, was that *their* England was a pastoral place: fields, streams, wooded valleys, medieval churches surrounded by ancient elms. They couldn't grasp that for him, and for the vast majority of the men, the Front, with its mechanization, its reduction of the individual to a cog in a machine, its blasted landscape, was not a contrast with the life they'd known at home, in Birmingham or Manchester or Glasgow or the Welsh pit villages, but a nightmarish culmination. 'Equally not at home in either,' Mac had said. He was right.

Prior lingered a while, listening to the night noises, remembering the evenings in his childhood when he'd sat on the stairs, unable to sleep, until his father had come in and gone to bed, and he knew his mother was safe. Engines rumbled, coughed, whistled, hissed. Trucks shunted along, bumpers clanged together. A few streets away a drunk started singing: 'There's an old mill by the stream, Nelly Dean.'

He ought to be getting back. He'd already been

away much longer than he'd meant. He began walking rapidly across the brick fields. One moment he was striding confidently along and the next he was falling, sliding rather, down a steep slope into pitch-black. He lay on his back at the muddy bottom of the hole and saw the tall weeds wave against the sky. He wasn't hurt, but the breath had been knocked out of him. Gradually, his heart stopped thumping. The stars looked brighter down here, just as they did in a trench. He reached out for something to hold on to, and his groping fingers encountered a sort of ledge. He patted along it and then froze. It was a firestep. It couldn't be, but it was. Disorientated and afraid, he felt further and encountered a hole, and then another beside it, and another: funk holes, scooped out of the clay. *He was in a trench.* Even as his mind staggered, he was groping for an explanation. Boys played here. Street gangs. They must have been digging for months to get as deep as this. But then probably the trench was years old, as old as the real trenches, perhaps. He clambered out, over what he suspected was No Man's Land, and there, sure enough, were the enemy lines.

Smiling to himself, unwilling to admit how deeply the bizarre incident had shocked him, he walked on, more cautiously now, and reached the railings at the far side. He was trembling. He had to hold on to the railings to steady himself.

The shock made him rebellious. He decided he wouldn't go straight home after all. Witnessing these nasty little rows between his parents did them no good, and him a great deal of harm. The time had come to call a halt. He would go to the pub. Which pub? His way home took him past the Rose and Crown, whose brass door flashed to and fro, letting out great belches of warm beery air. He would go there. He would do what other men do who come home on leave. Get drunk and forget.

He was greeted by a fug of human warmth, so hot he felt the skin on his nose tingle as the pores opened. He stood looking round at the flushed and noisy faces, and in the far corner spotted Mrs Thorpe and Mrs Riley with a great gaggle of other women. He decided he ought to stand them a drink. After all, they'd stood him many a drink in their day. A cry of recognition greeted him as he approached, and the whole boozy crowd of them opened up and took him in.

Two hours later Harry Prior was stumbling home, gazing in bleary appreciation at the full moon, riding high and magnificent in the clear sky. He paused on the bridge that spanned the canal to take a quick leak and admire the view. The moon was reflected in the water. He looked down at it, as a jet of hot piss hit the wall and trickled satisfyingly between the cobbles, and wondered why it should be bobbling up and down. He checked to see the real moon was behaving itself, then peered more closely at its reflection.

It wasn't the bloody moon at all, it was an arse. My God, the lad was going at it. Harry had half a mind to cheer him on, but then he thought, no, better not. A person might very easily be mistaken for a peeping Tom. He leant further over, pressing himself against the rough granite, wishing he could see more. All he could see of the woman was knees. Who the bloody hell wants to watch a male arse bobbing up and down? Bloody golf-balls. Still, it didn't half give you ideas. Bugger all doing at home, knees glued together. He rubbed himself against the wall for comfort, then wandered disconsolately on.

'There's somebody on the bridge.'

Prior turned, but he couldn't see anything. He listened to the fading footsteps. 'They're going.'

She'd gone tense and braced herself against him. He'd have to start from the beginning. He kissed her mouth, her nose, her hair, and then, lowering his head in pure delight, feeling every taboo in the whole fucking country crash round his ears, he sucked Mrs Riley's breasts.

PART TWO

CHAPTER TEN

Prior returned to London to find the city sweltering in sticky, humid, thundery heat. Major Lode was more difficult than ever, and not merely because of the weather. An attempt was under way to centralize the intelligence services under the control of the War Office, and Lode was fighting for the survival of the unit. The change was being pushed through at an exalted level and very little filtered down to Prior, but he observed Lode daily becoming fiercer, the blue eyes more vulnerable, the moustache in ever greater need of protective dabbings and strokings, as his empire collapsed around him. The files, 'the brain cells of the unit' Lode proclaimed (God help it, thought Prior), were to be transferred to the War Office. The task of 'tidying them up' before they were transferred was allotted to Prior. At first he took this to be merely a routine clerical task, perhaps designed to keep him out of trouble, but it quickly became clear that Lode wanted 'sensitive material' referred to him. In other words, evidence for the worst of the unit's cock-ups was to be removed. The job, though huge—the files numbered more than eight hundred—suited Prior very well, since it solved what had hitherto been his main problem: how to get enough access to past files to compile a dossier on Spragge.

He was busy and, within reason, happy, though he did not feel particularly well. Then, four days after his return, something disturbing happened.

He'd gone out to lunch in a nearby pub, bought himself a pint of beer and opened *The Times*, as he always did, at the casualty lists. The name leapt out at him.

Hore, Captain James Frederick. Killed in action on the 5th April, dearly beloved younger son...

Jimmy Hore. They'd met on a riding course, trotting round a ring with their stirrups crossed in front of them, their hands clasped behind their heads. Acquiring the correct seat. The seat of gentlemen. Prior, who'd already experienced the realities of trench warfare, had been angry and amused, though he kept both reactions to himself, since he was convinced nobody else could appreciate the idiocy of the situation as he did. Certainly not this blank-faced moron trotting towards him, but then, as they trotted past each other, he caught Jimmy's eye and realized his face wasn't blank at all, but rigid with suppressed laughter. That glance of shared amusement had been too much for Jimmy, who burst out laughing and fell off his horse.

Prior looked round the pub. Prosperous-looking men in pin-striped suits jostled at the bar, chinking coins, bestowing well-oiled smiles on the pretty, chestnut-haired barmaid. And Jimmy was dead. All the poor little bugger had ever wanted to do was get married to ... whatever her name was. And work in a bank. Prior would have liked nothing better, at that moment, than for a tank to come crashing through the doors and crush everybody, the way they sometimes crushed the wounded who couldn't get off the track in time. The violence of his imaginings—he saw severed limbs, heard screams—terrified him.

He couldn't eat. He would just drink up and go. But when he lifted his glass, his attention was caught

128

by the amber lights winking in the beer. Sunlight, shining through the glass, cast a ring of shimmering gold on the surface of the table that danced when his hand moved. He started to play with it, moving his hand to and fro.

He was back at his desk. No interval. One second he was in the pub, the next sitting behind his desk. He looked across at the closed door. Blinked. Thought, I must've gone to sleep. He felt relaxed, but without the clogged feeling that follows midday sleep. He'd been reading *The Times . . . Jimmy Hore was dead*. He couldn't remember leaving the pub. He must have walked all the way back in a complete dream. He looked at his watch, and his brain struggled to make sense of the position of the hands. Ten past four.

Three hours had passed since he broke for lunch, and of that he could account for perhaps twenty to twenty-five minutes. The rest was blank.

*   *   *

He made himself work until six. After all, in France he'd done paperwork on a table that kept jumping several feet into the air. He could surely manage to ignore a little disturbance like this. Though, as file after file passed across his desk, he was aware, somewhere on the fringes of his consciousness, that it was not 'a little disturbance'. Something catastrophic had happened.

Shortly after six he thought he recognized voices, and went out of his room and a little way along the corridor. Major Lode and Lionel Spragge were deep in conversation by the lifts. It was not possible to hear what they were saying, but he noticed that Lode shook Spragge's hand warmly as the lift arrived.

Prior slipped back into his room, but left the door open.

He was ready to produce some small query that would bring Lode into his room, but in the event he didn't need to. Lode stood in the doorway, grinning. 'Just seen Spragge,' he said in his clipped, staccato voice. 'What have you been doing to him?'

'Me? Nothing.'

'Says you offered him a job.'

'I didn't offer him anything. Wishful thinking, I'm afraid.'

'Well, he certainly seems to *think* you did. I had to tell him there was nothing doing. Nap*poo*.' Lode looked at him for a moment, then said in a menacing, nannyish singsong, 'He's got it *in* for *you*.'

Bastard, Prior thought, as Lode closed the door behind him. It's not my fault your frigging unit's being closed down.

Towards six it began to thunder, a desultory grumble on the horizon, though the sun still shone. Prior worked for a further half hour, then gave up. He'd been having bad headaches ever since he got back to London and blamed them on the weather, though in fact he knew they'd started after his fall into the children's trench. He would go somewhere fairly reasonable to eat. Cosset himself.

A sudden downpour began just as he reached the main steps. He looked up, trying to judge how long it would last. A white sun shone through a thin layer of cloud, but there were darker clouds massing over Nelson's Column. He went back upstairs to fetch his greatcoat. As he passed Lode's room, he heard an unfamiliar voice say, 'Do you think he believed it?'

Lode replied, 'Oh, I think so. I don't see why he shouldn't.'

130

Prior went along to his own room, shrugged himself into the heavy greatcoat, and walked back to the lift. For once it arrived immediately in a great clanking of cables and gates. He told himself there was no reason to connect the overheard conversation with himself, but he found it difficult not to. The atmosphere in the unit was rather like that. Plots and counterplots, many of them seemingly pointless. So far he'd managed to hold himself aloof.

The underground was crowded. Currents of hot, dead air moved across his face as he waited on the edge of the platform. He couldn't carry his greatcoat—that was forbidden—and the sweat streamed down his sides. He found himself wondering whether this reaction was not excessive, whether he was not really ill. A subterranean rumbling, and the train erupted from the tunnel. He found himself a seat near the door and glanced at the girl beside him. Her hair was limp, her neck had a creased, swollen whiteness, and yet she was attractive in her rumpled skirt and white blouse. He glanced at her neckline, at the shadow between her breasts, then forced himself to look away. He found that rumpled look in women amazingly attractive.

He ate at a small café not far from Marble Arch. It wasn't as pleasant as it had looked from the outside: the walls had faded to a sallow beige, the windows streamed with condensation, blasts of steamy air belched from the swing doors into the kitchen as waitresses banged in and out. After his meal he lit a cigarette, drank two cups of hot, sweet, orange-coloured tea and persuaded himself he felt better.

A twisting flight of stairs led down to his basement flat. The dustbins from all the apartments in the house were kept in the small forecourt outside his

131

living-room window. The smell of rotting cabbage lingered. At night there were rustlings that he tried to convince himself were cats. He put his key in the lock and walked in. The hall was dark, but not cool. He threw his briefcase and coat down on to a chair, then, pulling his tie off, went along the corridor to the bathroom, ran a cold bath and nerved himself to get in. His skin under the water looked bloated, and there were lines of silver bubbles trapped in his pubic hair. He ran his fingers through, releasing them, then clasped the edges of the bath and lowered his head beneath the water.

He got out, wrapped himself in a towel, opened the french windows into the small yard and lay down on the bed. Despite the open windows there was no decrease in stuffiness. The only way you could get a movement of air through the place was to have the french windows *and* the front door open. But then you let the smell of cabbage in as well.

His head was aching. He turned and looked at the photograph of Sarah by his bed. She was sitting on the bottom step of some kind of monument, younger, plump, though not fat, with her hair dressed low so that it almost covered her forehead. She was pretty, but he thought she looked more ordinary than she did now, when her cheekbones had become more prominent, and she wore her hair back from the high rounded forehead. Her smile was different too. In the photograph it looked friendly, confiding, almost puppyish. Now, though still warm, it always kept something back. She was coming to see him sometime in the next few weeks, or at least it seemed *almost* certain that she was. He was afraid to count on it. He was afraid to picture her in the flat, because he knew that if he did the emptiness when her

132

imagined presence failed him would be intolerable.

What he needed was to get out. These days he tried to circumvent the nightmares by going for a long walk early in the evening and then having three very large whiskies before bed. He'd reluctantly come to the conclusion that Rivers was right: sleeping draughts stopped working after the first few weeks, and when they stopped the nightmares returned with redoubled force. At least with the walk and the whisky he could count on a few good hours before they started.

Walking the city streets on a hot evening, he seemed to feel the pavements and the blank, white terraces breathe the day's stored heat into his face. His favourite walks were in Hyde Park. He liked the dusty gloom beneath the trees, the glint of the Serpentine in the distance. Close to, by the water's edge, there was even the whisper of a breeze. He stopped and watched some children paddling, three little girls with their dresses tucked into their drawers, then switched his attention to two much bigger girls, who came strolling along, arm in arm, but they read the hunger in his eyes too clearly and hurried past, giggling.

He felt restless, and, for once, the restlessness had nothing to do with sex. He had a definite and very strange sensation of wanting to *be* somewhere, a specific place, and of not knowing what that place was. He began to stroll towards the Achilles Monument. This was a frequent objective on his evening walks, for no particular reason except that its heroic grandeur both attracted and repelled him. It seemed to embody the same unreflecting admiration of courage that he found in 'The Charge of the Light Brigade', a poem that had meant a great deal to him as a boy, and still did, though what it meant had become considerably more complex. He stared up at the stupendous lunging figure, with its raised sword and shield, and thought, not for the first time, that he was looking at the representation of an ideal that no longer had validity.

Feeling dissatisfied, as if he'd expected the walk to end in something more than this routine encounter with Achilles, he turned to go, and noticed a man staring at him from under the shadow of the trees. We-ell. Young men who linger in the park at dusk can expect to be stared at. Deliberately, he quickened his pace, but then the back of his neck began to prickle, and a second later he heard his name called.

Lionel Spragge came lumbering up to him, out of breath and plaintive. 'Where are you going?' he demanded.

'Home.'

At that moment a gang of young people, five or six abreast, came charging along the path, arms linked, broke round Spragge like a river round a stone, and swept on. Two more boys, running to catch up, elbowed him out of the way. Under cover of this disturbance, Prior walked away.

'Hey, hang on,' Spragge came puffing up behind him. 'You can't just go walking off like that.'

'Why not?'

Spragge tapped his watch. 'Achilles. Nine o'clock.'

'Well?'

Spragge looked genuinely bewildered. 'Why make the appointment if you don't want to talk?'

Prior was beginning to feel frightened. 'I came out for a walk.'

'You came to see me.'

'Did I? I don't think so.'

'You *know* you did.' He stared at Prior. 'Well, if this doesn't take the biscuit. You said, "I can't talk now. Statue of Achilles, nine o'clock." What's the point of denying it? I mean what *is* the *point?*'

Spragge stank. His shirt was dirty, there was three days' growth of stubble on his chin, he'd been drinking, his eyes were bloodshot, *but the bewilderment was genuine.*

Prior said, 'Well, I'm here now anyway. What do you want?'

'If you hadn't turned up I'd've come to your house.'

'You don't know where I live.'

'I do. I followed you home.'

Prior laughed. A bark of astonishment.

'I was behind you on the platform. I sat three seats away from you on the train.' Spragge waggled his finger at his temple. 'You want to watch that. First step to the loony bin.'

'Piss off.'

Spragge caught his arm. 'Don't you want to know what I've got to say?'

'Not particularly.'

'Yes, you do,' Spragge said confidingly, leaning close, breathing into his face. 'Come on. Sit down.'

They found a place. At the other end of the bench an elderly woman sat, feeding a squirrel on nuts. Prior watched the animal's tiny black hands turning the nut delicately from side to side. 'Make it quick, will you?'

'I've remembered where I saw you.'

'Have you?'

'Meeting in Liverpool. You were speaking for the war, your father was speaking against.'

'Get to the point.'

135

'Oh, I know a lot about you. It's amazing what you can find out when you try, and finding out things was my job, wasn't it? When I had a job.'

'You didn't find things out,' Prior said crisply. 'You made them up.'

'You and the Ropers. You were like this.' Spragge jabbed his crossed fingers into Prior's face. 'Thick as thieves. *And* MacDowell.'

'That's why I got the job.'

'Oh, yeh, chuck me out and push you in.'

'I came a year after you left.'

'You told me I'd got a job.'

'No, I didn't.'

'Yes, you did. I went straight back home and told the wife. And then when I didn't hear anything I went to see Lode, and he threw me out. Bloody laughed at me.' Spragge turned his downwards-slanting turquoise eyes on Prior. 'You were just pumping me. Trying to make out I put the old cunt up to it.'

Prior got up. 'Wash your mouth out.'

'I thought that'd get you. You and her, you were—'

Prior crossed his fingers. 'Like this?'

Spragge stared at him, a vein standing out at his temple, like a worm under the clammy skin. 'People don't change.'

'No, I agree, they don't. I was a socialist then, I'm a socialist now. As far as the war goes, I don't have to prove my patriotism to *you*. I didn't offer you a job. I'm sorry if you told your wife I did, but that's your responsibility, not mine. Now bugger off and leave me alone.'

Prior walked away. He was aware of Spragge shouting, but was too angry to hear what he said. He thought Spragge might follow him, and that if he did there would be a fight. Spragge was taller, but older and flabbier. And he didn't care anyway. He wanted a fight. Spragge's face floated in front of him: the slightly bulbous nose, the sheen of sweat, the enlarged pores around the nostrils, the tufts of grey hair protruding from them. He'd never experienced such intense awareness of another person's body before, except in sex. What he felt was not simple dislike, but an intimate, obsessive, deeply *physical* hatred.

Back in the flat he rinsed his face in cold water and, trembling slightly, lay down on the bed. He plumped the pillows up behind him and groped in the pocket of his tunic for a cigarette. Weren't any. Then he remembered he'd been wearing his greatcoat. He got up, checked the pockets and found a packet of cigars. He didn't smoke cigars. But he must have bought them, and either smoked or offered them to somebody else, because there were two missing from the pack. Just as he must have arranged to meet Spragge. Spragge wouldn't have lied about that. It was too blatant, too easily discounted. No, he'd made the appointment all right. God knows when, or why.

He got up from the bed, feeling the palms of his hands sticky. He went to the front door and locked it, then stood with his back to it, looking down the dark corridor to the half-open door of his bedroom, feeling a momentary relief at being locked in, though he quickly realized this was nonsense. Whatever it was he needed to be afraid of, it was on this side of the door.

CHAPTER ELEVEN

After a pause, Rivers asked, 'Have there been any further episodes since then?'

'Yes, but I don't think any of them involved other people. I don't *think* they did.' Prior's mouth twisted. 'How would I know?'

'Nobody's said anything?'

'No.'

'How many?'

'Seven.'

'As many as *that*?'

Prior looked away.

'How long do they last?'

'Longest, three hours. Shortest ... I don't know. Twenty minutes? The long ones are frightening because you don't know what you've done...' He attempted a laugh. 'You just know you've had plenty of time to do it.'

'I don't think you should assume you've done anything wrong.'

'Don't you? Well, if it's so bloody good, why do I need to forget it?'

Rivers waited a while. 'What do you think you might have done?'

'I don't know, do I? Nipped across to Whitechapel and ripped up a few prostitutes.'

Silence.

'*Look*,' Prior said, with the air of one attempting to engage the village idiot in rational discourse, 'you know as well as I do that that ...' He flung himself

138

back in his chair. 'I'm not going to do this, I just refuse.'

Rivers waited.

Still not looking at him, Prior said, or rather chanted, 'I have certain impulses which I do not give way to except in strict moderation and at *the other person's* request. At least, in *this* state I don't. I'm simply pointing out that in the the the the *other* state I might not be so *fucking* scrupulous. And don't look at me like that.'

'I'm sorry.'

'You think this is a load of self-dramatizing rubbish, don't you?'

Rivers said carefully, 'I think you've been alone with the problem too long.'

'There's nothing ridiculous in anything I've said.'

Rivers looked at the pale, proud, wintry face and caught a sigh. 'I certainly wouldn't call it ridiculous.'

'The fact is I don't know and neither do you, so you're in no position to pontificate.'

Silence. Rivers said, 'How are the nightmares?'

'Bad. Oh, I had one you'll like. I was was walking along a path in a kind of desert and straight ahead of me was an eyeball. Not this size.' Prior's cheeks twitched like boiling porridge. 'Huge. And alive. And it was directly in front of me and I knew this time it was going to get me.' He smiled. 'Do whatever it is eyeballs do. Fortunately, there was a river running along beside the path, so I leapt into the river and I was all right.' He gazed straight at Rivers. 'But then I suppose all your patients jump into fucking rivers sooner or later, don't they?'

The antagonism was startling. They might have been back at Craiglockhart, at the beginning of Prior's treatment. 'How did you feel about being in the river?'

'Fine. It sang to me, a sort of lullaby, it kept telling me I was going to be all right and I *was* all right—as long as I stayed in the river.'

'You didn't feel you wanted to get out?'

'In the dream? No. Now, YES.'

Rivers spread his hands. 'Your coming here is entirely voluntary.'

'With *that* degree of dependency? Of course it's not fucking voluntary.' He started to say something else and bit it back. 'I'm sorry.'

'Don't be, there's no need.' Suddenly Rivers leant across the desk. 'I'm not here to be liked.'

'I *am* sorry,' Prior said, his face and voice hardening. 'I thought I was supposed to be accepting my emotions? Well, my emotion is that I'm sorry.'

'In that case I accept your apology.'

A pause. 'Do you know what I do when I come round from one of these spells? I look at my hands because I half expect to see them covered in hair.'

Rivers made no comment.

'You've read Jekyll and Hyde?'

'Yes.' Rivers had been waiting for the reference. Patients who suffered from fugue states invariably referred to the dissociated state—jocularly, but not without fear—as 'Hyde'. 'In real life, you know, the fugue state is—well, I was going to say "never", but, in fact, there is one case—is almost never the darker side of the personality. Usually it's no more than a difference in mood.'

'But we don't *know*. You see, the conversation I'm trying not to have is the one where I point out that you could find out in five minutes flat and you say, "Yes, I know, but I won't do it."'

Silence.

140

'*Well?*'

'I'm sorry, I thought you said you didn't want that conversation.'

'You know, for somebody who isn't here to be liked you have the most wonderful manner. You used hypnosis at Craiglockhart.'

'Yes, but in that case we could check the memory. You see, one of the things people who believe in ... the extensive use of hypnosis claim—well, they don't even claim it, they assume it—is that memories recovered in that way are genuine memories. But they're very often not. They can be fantasies, or they can be responses to suggestions from the therapist. Because one's constantly making suggestions, and the ones you're not aware of making—not conscious of—are by far the most powerful. And that's dangerous because most therapists are interested in dissociated states and so they—unconsciously of course—encourage the patient further down that path. And one can't avoid doing it. Even if one excludes everything else, there's still the enlargement of the pupils of the eyes.'

Prior leant forward and peered. 'Yours are enlarged.'

Rivers took a deep breath. 'You can get your memory back by the same methods we used at Craiglockhart. You were very good at it.'

'Is that why you do this?' Prior swept his hand down across his eyes.

Rivers smiled. 'No, of course not, it's just a habit. Eyestrain. Now can we—'

'No, that's not true. If it was eyestrain, you'd do it at random and you don't. You do it when ... when something touches a nerve. Or or ... It *is* a way of hiding your feelings. You've just said it yourself, the

141

eyes are the one part you can't turn into wallpaper—
and so you cover them up.'

Rivers found this disconcerting. He tried to go on
with what he'd been going to say, and realized he'd
lost the train of thought. After so many hours of
probing, manipulating, speculating, provoking,
teasing, Prior had finally—and almost casually—
succeeded. He couldn't ignore this; it had to be dealt
with. 'I think ... if as you say it *isn't* random—and I
don't *know* because it's not something I'm aware
of—it's probably something to do with not wanting
to see the patient. For me the patient's expressions
and gestures aren't much use, because I have no
visual memory, so I think perhaps I stop myself
seeing him as a way of concentrating on what he's
saying. All right? Now perhaps we can—'

'No visual memory at all?'

'None at all.'

'I don't see how you think.'

'Well, I suspect you're a very visual person. Could
we—'

'Have you always been like this?'

Rivers thought, *all right*. He stood up and
indicated to Prior that they should exchange seats.
Prior looked surprised and even uneasy, but quickly
recovered and sat down in Rivers's chair with
considerable aplomb. Rivers saw him look round the
study, taking in his changed perspective on the room.
'Isn't this against the rules?' he asked.

'I can't think of a single rule we're not breaking.'

'Can't you?' Prior said, smiling his delicate smile. 'I
can.'

'I'm going to show you how boring this job is.
When I was five...'

Prior shifted his position, leant forward, rested his

142

chin on his clasped hands, and said, in meltingly empathic tones, 'Yes? Go on.'

Rivers was not in fact breaking the rules. He intended to do no more than offer Prior an illustration from his own experience that he'd already used several times in public lectures, but he hadn't reckoned on doing it while confronted by a caricature of himself. 'One of the expressions of having no visual memory is that I can't remember the interior of any building I've ever been in. I can't remember this house when I'm not in it. I can't remember Craiglockhart, though I lived there for over a year. I can't remember St John's, though I've lived there twenty years, but there is one interior I *do* remember and that's a house in Brighton I lived in till I was five. I can remember *part* of that. The basement kitchen, the drawing-room, the dining-room, my father's study, but I can't remember anything at all about upstairs. And I've come to believe—I won't go into the reasons—that something happened to me on the top floor that was so terrible that I simply had to forget it. And in order to ensure that I forgot I suppressed not just the *one* memory, but the capacity to remember things visually at all.' Rivers paused, and waited for a response.

'You were raped,' Prior said. 'Or beaten.'

Rivers's face went stiff with shock. 'I really don't think I was.'

'No, well, you wouldn't, would you? The whole point is it's too terrible to contemplate.'

Rivers said something he knew he'd regret, but he had to say it. 'This was my father's vicarage.'

'I was raped in a vicarage once.'

It was on the tip of Rivers's tongue to say that no doubt Prior had been 'raped' in any number of

143

places, but he managed to restrain himself. 'When I said terrible I meant to a child of that age. I was five remember. Things happen to children which are an enormous shock to the child, but which wouldn't seem terrible or or or even particularly important to an adult.'

'And equally things happen to children which are genuinely terrible. And would be recognized as terrible by *anybody* at *any* age.'

'Yes, of course. How old were you?'

'Eleven. I wasn't meaning myself.'

'You don't classify that as "terrible"?'

'*No*. I was receiving extra tuition.' He gave a yelping laugh. 'God, was I receiving extra tuition. From the parish priest, Father Mackenzie. My mother offered him a shilling a week—more than she could afford—but he said, "Don't worry, my good woman, I have seldom seen a more promising boy."' He added irritably, 'Don't look so shocked, Rivers.'

'I am shocked.'

'Then you shouldn't be. He got paid in kind, that's all.' Suddenly Prior leant forward and grasped Rivers's knee, digging his fingers in round the kneecap. 'Everything has to be paid for, doesn't it?' He grasped the knee harder. '*Doesn't it?*'

'No.'

Prior let go. 'This terrible-in-big-black-inverted commas thing that happened to you, what do *you* think it was?'

'I don't know. Dressing-gown on the back of a door?'

'As bad as *that*? Oh, my God.'

Rivers pressed on in defiance of Prior's smile. 'I had a patient once who became claustrophobic as the result of being accidentally locked in a corridor with

144

a fierce dog. Or it seemed fierce to him. In that—'

'Oh, I see. Even the bloody dog wasn't *really* fierce.'

'In that case his parents didn't even know it had happened.'

'You say you were five when this ... non-event didn't happen?'

'Yes.'

'How old were you when you started to stammer?'

'Fi-ive.'

Prior leant back in Rivers's chair and smiled. '*Big dog.*'

'I didn't mean to imply there was—'

'For God's *sake*. Whatever it was, you *blinded* yourself so you wouldn't have to go on seeing it.'

'I wouldn't put it as dramatically as that.'

'You destroyed your visual memory. You put your mind's eye *out*. Is that what happened, or isn't it?'

Rivers struggled with himself. Then said simply, 'Yes.'

'Do you ever think you're on the verge of remembering?'

'Sometimes.'

'And what do you feel?'

'Fear.' He smiled. 'Because the child's emotions are still attached to the memory.'

'We're back to the dressing-gown.'

'Yes. Yes. I'm afraid we are, because I do sincerely believe it may be as simple as that.'

'Then one can only applaud,' Prior said, and did. Three loud claps.

'You know ...' Rivers hesitated and started again. 'You must be wary of filling the gaps in your memory with ... with monsters. I think we all tend to do it. As soon as we're left with a blank, we start projecting our worst fears on to it. It's a bit like the guide for medieval map-makers, isn't it? *Where unknown, there place monsters.* But I do think you should try not to do it, because what you're really doing is subjecting yourself to a constant stream of suggestion of of a very negative kind.'

'All right. I'll try not to. I'll substitute the Rivers guide to map-making: *Where unknown, there place dressing-gowns.* Or just possibly, *dogs.* Here, have your chair back.' Prior settled himself back into the patient's chair, murmuring, 'Do you know, Rivers, you're as neurotic as I am? And that's saying quite a lot.'

Rivers rested his chin on his hands. 'How do you feel about that?'

'Oh, my God, we *are* back to normal. You mean, "Do I feel a nasty, mean-spirited sense of triumph?" No. I'm mean-spirited enough, I'm just not stupid enough.' Prior brooded a moment. 'There's one thing wrong with the Rivers guide to map-making. Suppose there really are monsters?'

'I think if there are, we'll meet them soon enough.'

Prior looked straight at Rivers. 'I'm frightened.'

'I know.'

*　　　*　　　*

When Prior finally left—it had been a long, exhausting session—Rivers switched off the desk lamp, went to sit in his armchair by the fire, and indulged in some concentrated, unobserved eye-rubbing. *Did* he do it 'when something touched a nerve'? It was possible, he supposed. If there was a pattern, Prior would certainly have spotted it. On the other hand, Prior was equally capable of making the whole thing up.

He didn't regret the decision to give Prior what he'd always claimed he wanted—to change places—because in the process he'd discovered an aspect of Prior that mightn't have been uncovered in any other way. Not so much the 'extra tuition'—though that was interesting, particularly in view of Prior's habit of aggressive flirtation—as the assumption that Rivers's loss of visual memory must have some totally traumatic explanation. That had revealed more about Prior than he was aware of.

Though Prior had been a formidable interrogator. *Whatever it was, you blinded yourself so you wouldn't have to go on seeing it ... You put your mind's eye out.* Simply by being rougher than any professional colleague would ever have been, Prior had brought him face to face with the full extent of his loss. People tended to assume he didn't know what he'd lost, but that wasn't true. He did know, or glimpsed at least. Once, in the Torres Straits, he'd attended a court held by the British official in collaboration with the native chiefs, and an old woman had given evidence about a dispute in which she was involved. As she spoke, she'd glanced from side to side, clearly reliving every detail of the events she was describing, and very obviously *seeing* people who were not present in court. And he had looked at her, this scrawny, half-naked, elderly, illiterate woman, and he had envied her. No doubt he'd encountered Europeans who had visual memories of equal power, but his own deficiency had never before been brought home to him with such force.

It *was* a loss, and he had long been aware of it, though he had been slow to connect it with the Brighton house experience. Slower still to recognize

147

that the impact of the experience had gone beyond the loss of visual memory and had occasioned a deep split between the rational, analytical cast of his mind and his emotions. It was easy to overstate this: he had, after all, been subject to a form of education which is designed to inculcate precisely such a split, but he thought the division went deeper in him than it did in most men. It was almost as if the experience—whatever it was—had triggered an attempt at dissociation of personality, though, mercifully, not a successful one. Still, he had been, throughout most of his life, a deeply divided man, and though he would once have said that this division exercised little, if any, influence on his thinking, he had come to believe it had determined the direction of his research.

Many years after that initial unremembered experience, he and Henry Head had conducted an experiment together. The nerve supplying Head's left forearm had been severed and sutured, and then over a period of five years they had traced the progress of regeneration. This had taken place in two phases. The first was characterized by a high threshold of sensation, though when the sensation was finally evoked it was, to use Head's own word, 'extreme'. In addition to this all-or-nothing quality, the sensation was difficult to localize. Sitting blindfold at the table, Head had been unable to locate the stimulus that was causing him such severe pain. This primitive form of innervation they called the protopathic. The second phase of regeneration—which they called the epicritic—followed some months later, and was characterized by the ability to make graduated responses and to locate the source of a stimulus precisely. As the epicritic level of innervation was restored, the lower, or protopathic, level was partially integrated with it and partially suppressed, so that the epicritic system carried out two functions: one, to help the organism adapt to its environment by supplying it with accurate information; the other, to suppress the protopathic, to keep the animal within leashed. Inevitably, as time went on, both words had acquired broader meanings, so that 'epicritic' came to stand for everything rational, ordered, cerebral, objective, while 'protopathic' referred to the emotional, the sensual, the chaotic, the primitive. In this way the experiment both reflected Rivers's internal divisions and supplied him with a vocabulary in which to express them. He might almost have said with Henry Jekyll, *It was on the moral side, and in my own person, that I learned to recognize the thorough and primitive duality of man; I saw that, of the two natures that contended in the field of my consciousness, even if I could rightly be said to be either, it was only because I was radically both ...*

It was odd how the term 'Jekyll and Hyde' had passed into the language, so that even people who had never read Stevenson's story used the names as a shorthand for internal divisions. Prior spoke of looking at his hands to make sure they had not been transformed into the hairy hands of Hyde, and he was not alone in that. Every patient Rivers had ever had who suffered from a fugue state sooner or later referred to that state as 'Hyde', and generally this was a plea for reassurance. In a hospital setting, where the fugue state could be observed, such reassurance was easily given, but it was less easy to reassure Prior. Partly because the fugue state *couldn't* be observed, but also because Prior's sense of the darker side of his personality was unusually strong. He might talk about being incapable of sexual guilt, but, Rivers

149

thought, he was deeply ashamed of his sadistic impulses, even frightened of them. He believed there were monsters on his map, and who was to say he was wrong?

There was one genuinely disturbing feature of the case: that odd business of making an appointment in the fugue state and keeping it in the normal state. It suggested the fugue state was capable of influencing Prior's behaviour even when it was not present, in other words, that it was functioning as a co-consciousness. Not that a dual personality need develop even from that. He intended to make sure it didn't. There would be no hypnosis, no artificial creation of dissociated states for experimental purposes, no encouraging Prior to think of the fugue state as an alternative self. Even so. It had to be remembered Prior was no mere bundle of symptoms, but an extremely complex personality with his own views on his condition. And his imagination was already at work, doing everything it could to transform the fugue state into a malignant double. He believed in the monsters—and whatever Rivers might decide to do, or refrain from doing—Prior's belief in them would inevitably give them power.

CHAPTER TWELVE

'Now I want you to draw me an elephant,' Head said.

His voice distorted, as if he were blowing bubbles in soapy water. Lucas replied, 'Yeth ah seen dom. Up. Uvver end.'

He took the notepad and pencil, and began to draw. Rivers was sitting beside Head, but neither of them spoke since Lucas's concentration must not be disturbed. They had been doing the tests for half an hour and Lucas was already tired. His tongue protruded between his teeth, giving him the look of a small boy learning to read, except that, in Lucas's case, the protrusion was permanent.

Rivers noticed Head looking at the shrapnel wound on Lucas's shaved scalp, and knew he was thinking about the technical problems of duplicating this on the skull of the cadaver he'd been working on that morning. It was an interesting technique, Rivers thought. Head measured the dimensions of the wound on the living patient, then traced the outline on to the skull of a cadaver, drilled holes at regular intervals around the outline, and introduced a blue dye into the holes. The entire skull cap could then be lifted off and the brain structures underlying the dyed area dissected and identified. In this way the area of brain death could be correlated precisely with the nature of the patient's language defects.

A laborious business, made more so by the need to duplicate the wounds of *two* patients on every cadaver. One of the more surprising consequences of the war was a shortage of suitable male corpses.

Rivers lifted his hands to his chin, smelling the medical school smell of human fat and formaldehyde, only partially masked by carbolic soap. He watched Head's expression as he looked at Lucas's shaved scalp, and realized it differed hardly at all from his expression that morning as he'd bent over the cadaver. For the moment, Lucas had become simply a technical problem. Then Lucas looked up from his task, and instantly Head's face flashed open in his transforming smile. A murmur of encouragement, and Lucas returned to his drawing. Head's face, looking at the ridged purple scar on the shaved head, again became remote, withdrawn. His empathy, his strong sense of the humanity he shared with his patients, was again suspended. A necessary suspension, without which the practice of medical research, and indeed of medicine itself, would hardly be possible, but none the less identifiably the same suspension the soldier must achieve in order to kill. The end was different, but the psychological mechanism employed to achieve it was essentially the same. What Head was doing, Rivers thought, was in some ways a benign, epicritic form of the morbid dissociation that had begun to afflict Prior. Head's dissociation was healthy because the researcher and the physician each had instant access to the experience of the other, and both had access to Head's experience in all other areas of his life. Prior's was pathological because areas of his conscious experience had become inaccessible to memory. What was interesting was why Head's dissociation didn't lead to the kind of split that had taken place in Prior. Rivers shifted his position, and sighed. One began by finding mental illness mystifying, and ended

152

by being still more mystified by health.

Lucas had finished. Head leant across the desk and took the drawing from him. 'Hmm,' he said, looking at the remarkably cow-like creature in front of him. A long pause. 'What's an elephant got in front?'

Again the blurting voice, always on the verge of becoming a wail. 'He got a big'—Lucas's good hand waved up and down—'straight about a yard long.'

'Do you know what it's called?'

'Same what you. Drive. Water with.'

'Has he got a *trunk*?'

Lucas wriggled in his wheelchair and laughed. 'He lost it.'

He reached for his drawing, wanting to correct it, but Head slipped it quickly into the file. 'Sums now.'

They went quickly through a range of simple sums. Lucas, whose ability to understand numbers was unimpaired, got them predictably right. It was Head's custom to alternate tasks the patient found difficult or impossible with others that he could perform successfully. The next task—designed to discover whether Lucas's understanding of 'right' and 'left' was impaired—involved his attempting to imitate movements of Head's arms, first in a mirror and then facing him across the desk.

Rivers watched Head raise his left hand— 'professional in shape and size; ... large, firm, white and comely'—and thought he probably knew that hand better than any part of his own body. He'd experimented on it for five years, after all, and even now could have traced on to the skin the outline of the remaining area of protopathic innervation—for the process of regeneration is never complete. A triangle of skin between the thumb and forefinger retained the primitive, all-or-nothing responses and

153

remained abnormally sensitive to changes in temperature. Sometimes, on a cold day, he would notice Head shielding this triangle of skin beneath his other hand.

For a while, after the tests were complete, Head chatted to Lucas about the results. It was Head's particular gift to be able to involve his patients in the study of their own condition. Lucas's face, as Head outlined the extent of his impairments, was alight with what one could only call clinical interest. When, finally, an orderly appeared and wheeled him out of the room, he was smiling.

'He has ... improved,' Head said. 'Slightly.' He brushed his thinning hair back from his forehead and for a moment looked utterly bleak. 'Tea?'

'I wouldn't mind a glass of milk.'

'*Milk?*'

Rivers patted his midriff. 'Keeps the ulcers quiet.'

'Why, are they protesting?'

'God, how I hate psychologists.'

Head laughed. 'I'll get you the milk.'

Rivers glanced at *The Times* while he waited. In the Pemberton Billing trial they'd reached the medical evidence—such as it was. As Head came back into the room, Rivers read aloud: '"Asked what should be done with such people. Dr Serrel Cooke replied, 'They are monsters. They should be locked up.'" The voice of psychological medicine.'

Head handed him a cup. 'Put it down, Rivers.'

Rivers folded the paper. 'I keep trying to tell myself it's funny.'

'Well, it is, a lot of it. It was hilarious when that woman told the Judge his name was in the Black Book.' He waited for a reply. 'Anyway, when do you want to see Lucas? Tomorrow?'

154

'Oh, I think we give the poor little blighter a rest, don't we? Monday?'

They talked for a while about Lucas, then drifted into a rambling conversation about the use of pacifist orderlies. The hospital contained a great many paralysed patients in a building not designed to accommodate them. There were only two lifts. The nurses and the existing orderlies—men who were either disabled or above military age—did their best, but the lives of patients were inevitably more restricted than they need have been. What was desperately required was young male muscle, and this the pacifist orderlies—recruited under the Home Office scheme—supplied. But they also aroused hostility in the staff obliged to work with them. It had now reached a point where it was doubtful whether the hospital could go on using them. The irrationality of getting rid of much needed labour exasperated Rivers, and he had spoken out against it at the last meeting of the hospital management committee, rather too forcefully, perhaps, or at least Head seemed to think so. 'I'm not g-going b-back on it,' he said. 'I've spent m-most of my l-life t-t-toning down what I w-wanted to s-say. I'm not d-doing it any more.'

Head looked at him. 'What happened to the gently flowing Rivers we all used to know and love?'

'Went AWOL in Scotland. Never been seen since.'

'Yes.'

'Yes what?'

'Yes, that was my impression.'

*　　　*　　　*

The lift door was about to close. Rivers broke into a

run, and Wantage, one of the non-pacifist orderlies, clanged the gate open again. 'There you are, sir,' he said, stepping back. 'Room for a thin one.'

He was returning a man in a wheelchair to the ward. Rivers squeezed in beside the wheelchair and pressed the button for the top floor.

Wantage was the most popular of the orderlies, partly because his built-up boot supplied an instant explanation for why he wasn't in France. He was a fat, jolly man with a limitless capacity for hate. He hated skivers, he hated shirkers, he hated conchies, he hated the Huns, he hated the Kaiser. He loved the war. He had the gentlest hands in the hospital. He would have given anything to be able to go and fight. Whenever Rivers saw him lurching along behind a wheelchair, he was reminded of the crippled boy in the Pied Piper story, left behind when the other children went into the mountain.

At the second floor the lift stopped and a young nurse got in. Viggors, the patient in the wheelchair, spoke to her, blushing slightly—she was evidently a great favourite—and then sat, slumped to one side, his eyes level with her waist, gazing covertly at her breasts. Wantage chattered on. On the third floor the lift stopped again and Wantage pushed the wheelchair out.

Rivers was left wishing he hadn't seen that look. Every day in this hospital one was brutally reminded that the worst tragedies of the war were not marked by little white crosses.

For safety reasons—*his* patients were mobile and could use the fire escapes—both his wards were on the top floor. The hospital had been built as a children's hospital; the top floor had been the nursery and the walls were decorated with Baa-baa Black

156

Sheep, Little Bo Peep, Red Riding Hood, Humpty-Dumpty. The windows were barred. On his arrival Rivers had asked for these bars to be removed, but the War Office refused to pay for any alterations beyond the absolute minimum: the provision of adult-size baths and lavatories. *Not* washbasins. Lawrence was there now, shaving in a basin that barely reached his knees. The eye, deprived of normal perspective, saw him as a giant. No amount of experience seemed to correct the initial impression.

Rivers collected his overnight key from sister and walked along the corridor to his own room. The room was vast, with a huge bay window overlooking Vincent Square. He went through into the adjoining room and asked his secretary to send Captain Manning in.

Manning had been admitted because the anxiety attacks he'd suffered ever since his return from France had become more severe, partly as a result of his obsession with the Pemberton Billing affair. Rivers would have liked to tell him to ignore the trial for the farrago of muck-raking nonsense it was, but that was not possible. Manning had been sent a newspaper cutting about Maud Allan and the 'cult of the clitoris'. More recently he'd received a copy of the 47,000 article. Manning was being targeted, presumably by someone who knew he was a homosexual, and he could hardly be expected to ignore that.

'Have you been waiting long?' Rivers asked.

'Couple of minutes.'

Manning looked tired. No doubt last night had been spent dreading coming into hospital. 'How are you settling in?'

'All right. I've been given a room to myself. I didn't

157

expect that.'

'Have you brought the article with you?' Rivers asked.

Manning handed it over. It was not, as Rivers had been assuming, a newspaper cutting, but a specially produced copy, printed on to thick card. At the top—typewritten—was the message: *In the hope that this will awaken your conscience.*

'Did you read it at the time?' Manning asked. 'When it first came out?'

'No.' Rivers smiled faintly. 'A pleasure postponed.'

AS I SEE IT—THE FIRST 47,000

Harlots on the Wall
There have been given many reasons why England is prevented from putting her full strength into the War. On several occasions in the columns of the *Imperialist* I have suggested that Germany is making use of subtle but successful means to nullify our effort. Hope of profit cannot be the only reason for our betrayal. All nations have their Harlots on the Wall, but these are discovered in the first assault and the necessary action is taken. It is in the citadel that the true danger lies. Corruption and blackmail being the work of menials is cheaper than bribery. Moreover, fear of exposure entraps and makes slaves of men whom money could never buy. There is all the more reason, as I see it, to suppose that the Germans, with their usual efficiency, are making use of the most productive and cheapest methods.

Often in this column I have hinted at the possession of knowledge which tends to substantiate this view. Within the past few days the most extraordinary facts have been placed before me which co-ordinate with my past information.

Spreading Debauchery
There exists in the *cabinet noir* of a certain German Prince a book compiled by the Secret Service from the reports of German agents who have infested this country for the past twenty years, agents so vile and spreading debauchery of such a lasciviousness as only German minds could conceive and only German bodies execute.

Sodom and Lesbia
The officer who discovered this book while on special service briefly outlined for me its stupefying contents. In the beginning of the book is a precis of general instructions regarding the propagation of evils which all decent men thought had perished in Sodom and Lesbia. The blasphemous compilers even speak of the Groves and High Places mentioned in the Bible. The most insidious arguments are outlined for the use of the German agent in his revolting work. Then more than a thousand pages are filled with the names mentioned by German agents in their reports. There are the names of 47,000 English men and women.

It is a most catholic miscellany. The names of privy councillors, youths of the chorus, wives of Cabinet Ministers, dancing girls, even Cabinet Ministers themselves, while diplomats, poets, bankers, editors, newspaper proprietors and members of His Majesty's household follow each other with no order of precedence.

159

As an example of the thoroughness with which the German agent works, lists of public houses and bars were given which had been successfully demoralized. These could then be depended upon to spread vice with the help of only one fixed agent. To secure those whose social standing would suffer from frequenting public places, comfortable flats were taken and furnished in an erotic manner. Paphian photographs were distributed, while equivocal pamphlets were printed as the anonymous work of well-known writers.

The Navy in Danger

No one in the social scale was exempted from contamination by this perfect system. Agents were specially enlisted in the navy, particularly in the engine-rooms. These had their special instructions. Incestuous bars were established in Portsmouth and Chatham. In these meeting places the stamina of British sailors was undermined. More dangerous still, German agents, under the guise of indecent liaison, could obtain information as to the disposition of the fleet.

Even the loiterer in the streets was not immune. Meretricious agents of the Kaiser were stationed at such points as Marble Arch and Hyde Park Corner. In this black book of sin details were given of the unnatural defloration of children who were drawn to the parks by the summer evening concerts.

The World of High Politics

Impure as were all these things, the great danger was seen in the reports of those agents who had obtained *entrée* to the world of high politics. Wives

160

of men in supreme position were entangled. In Lesbian ecstasy the most sacred secrets of State were betrayed. The sexual peculiarities of members of the peerage were used as a leverage to open fruitful fields for espionage.

In the glossary of this book is a list of expressions supposed to be used among themselves by the soul-sick victims of this nauseating disease so skilfully spread by Potsdam.

Lives are in Jeopardy

In his official reports the German agent is not an idle boaster. The thought that 47,000 English men and women are held in enemy bondage through fear calls all clean spirits to mortal combat. There are three million men in France whose lives are in jeopardy, and whose bravery is of no avail because of the lack of moral courage in 47,000 of their countrymen, and numbering among their ranks, as they do, men and women in whose hands the destiny of this Empire rests.

As I see it, a carefully cultivated introduction of practices which hint at the extermination of the race is to be the means by which the German is to prevent us avenging those mounds of lime and mud which once were Britons.

The Fall of Rome

When in time I grasped the perfection of this demoniacal plan, it seemed to me that all the horrors of shells and gas and pestilence introduced by the Germans in their open warfare would have but a fraction of the effect in exterminating the manhood of Britain as the plan by which they have already destroyed the first 47,000.

As I have already said in these columns, it is a terrible thought to contemplate that the British Empire should fall as fell the great Empire of Rome, and the victor now, as then, should be the Hun.

The story of the contents of this book has opened my eyes, and the matter must not rest.

Rivers threw the page down. 'If only *German* minds can conceive of this lasciviousness and only *German* bodies execute it, how on earth do the 47,000 manage to do it?' He took off his glasses and swept his hand down across his eyes. 'Sorry, I'm being donnish.' He looked at Manning, noting the lines of strain around his eyes, the coarse tremor as he raised the cigarette to his mouth. For somebody like Manning, profoundly committed to living a double life, the revelation that both sides of his life were visible to unknown eyes must be like having the door to the innermost part of one's identity smashed open. 'Has anybody else been sent this?'

'Ross. One or two others.'

'Friends of Ross?'

'Yes.'

'Ross is a ... quite a dangerous man to know.'

'What can I do, Rivers? It's not a recent friendship.'

Rivers sighed. 'I don't think you can do anything.'

Manning sat brooding. 'I think it would help if I felt I could understand it. I mean, I can see the war's going pretty badly and there are always going to be people who want scapegoats instead of *reasons*, but ... Why this? I can *see* why people with German names get beaten up ... or or interned. And conchies. I don't approve, but I can understand it. I don't understand this.'

'I'm not sure I do. I *think* it's the result of certain impulses rising to the surface in wartime, and having to be very formally disowned. Homosexuality, for instance. In war there's this enormous glorification of love between men, and yet at the same time it arouses anxiety. Is it the right kind of love? Well, one way to make sure it's the right kind is to make public disapproval of the other thing crystal clear. And then there's pleasure in killing—'

Manning looked shocked. 'I don't know that—'

'No, I meant civilians. Vicarious, but real nevertheless. And in the process sadistic impulses are aroused that would normally be repressed, and that also causes anxiety. So to put on a play by a *known* homosexual in which a woman kisses a man's severed head...'

'I talked about the trial to Jane. I said I thought the real target was Ross, and one or two others, and she said of course I did. Seeing—what was it? "Seeing his own sex as peripheral to the point at issue was a feat of mental agility of which no man is capable."'

'I look forward to meeting Mrs Manning one day.'

'She says the the ... *sentimentality* about the role women are playing—doing their bit and all that—really masks a kind of deep-rooted fear that they're getting out of line. She thinks pillorying Maud Allan is actually a way of teaching them a lesson. Not just lesbians. *All* women. Just as Salome is presented as a strong woman by Wilde, and yet at the same time she has to be killed. I mean it is quite striking at the end when all the men fall on her and kill her.'

'What do you think about that?'

'I think it's a bit naïve. I think it ignores Wilde's identification with Salome. He isn't saying women

163

like this have to be destroyed. He's saying people like me have to be destroyed. And how right he was. *Is*.'

This was all very well, Rivers thought, but Manning was ill, and it was not literary discussion that was going to cure him.

'Do you think Spencer's mad?' Manning asked abruptly.

'On the basis of his evidence, yes. Though whether he'll be recognized as mad...'

'It's an odd contrast with Sassoon, isn't it?'

Rivers looked surprised.

'Spencer being fêted like this. Sassoon says something perfectly sensible about the war, and he's packed off to a mental hospital.'

Of course, Rivers thought, all the members of Robert Ross's circle would know the story of Sassoon's protest against the war, and the part he'd played in persuading Sassoon to go back.

Manning said, 'I suppose I shouldn't mention him?'

'Why not?'

'Because he's a patient.'

'He's somebody we both know.'

'Only he's been on my mind lately. I was wondering if they'd have the nerve to send this to *him*. Or to anybody out there.'

'I think the sort of mind that produces this can't conceive of the possibility that any of "the 47,000" might be in France.'

So far Manning had found it impossible to talk about the war. Manning himself would have denied this. He would have said they talked about it all the time: strategy, tactics, war aims, the curiously inadequate response of civilian writers, the poems of Sassoon and Graves. Suddenly, Rivers thought he

164

saw a way of beginning, very gently, to force the issue. 'Are you familiar with the strict Freudian view of war neurosis?' he asked. Manning, he knew, had read a certain amount of Freud.

'I didn't know there was one.'

'Oh, yes. Basically, they believe the experience of an all-male environment, with a high level of emotional intensity, together with the experience of battle, arouses homosexual and sadistic impulses that are normally repressed. In vulnerable men—obviously those in whom the repressed desires are particularly strong—this leads to breakdown.'

'Is that what *you* believe?'

Rivers shook his head. 'I want to know what *you* think.'

'I don't know what makes other people break down. I don't think sex had much to do with *my* breakdown.' A slight smile. 'But then I'm not a repressed homosexual.'

Rivers smiled back. 'But you must have a ... an instinctive reaction, that it's *possible*, or it's obvious nonsense, or—'

'I'm just trying to think. Do you know Sassoon's poem "The Kiss"?'

'The one about the bayonet. Yes.'

'I think that's the strongest poem he's ever written. You know, I've never served with him so I don't know this from personal experience, but I've talked a lot to Robert Graves and he says the extent to which Sassoon contrives to be two totally different people at the Front is absolutely amazing. You know he's a tremendously successful and *bloodthirsty* platoon commander, and yet at the same time, back in billets, out comes the notebook. Another anti-war poem. And the poem uses the experience of the platoon

165

commander, but it never uses any of his attitudes. And yet for once, in that *one* poem, he gets both versions of himself in.'

Yes, Rivers thought. 'Yes,' he said. 'I see that.'

'And of course it's crawling with sexual ambiguities. But then I think it's too easy to see that as a matter of personal ... I don't know what. The fact is the *army*'s attitude to the bayonet is pretty bloody ambiguous. You read the training manuals and they're all going on about importance of close combat. Fair enough, but you get the impression there's a value in it which is independent of whether it gains the objective or not. It's proper war. *Manly* war. Not all this nonsense about machine-guns and shrapnel. And it's reflected in the training. I mean, it's one long stream of sexual innuendo. *Stick him in the gooleys. No more little fritzes.* If Sassoon had used language like that, he'd never have been published.' Manning stopped abruptly. 'You know I think I've lost the thread. No, that's it, I was trying ... I was trying to be honest and think whether I hated bayonet practice more because ... because the body that the sack represents is one that I ... come on, Rivers. Nice psychological term?'

'Love.'

'I don't know what the answer is. I don't *think* so. We *all* hate it. I've no way of knowing whether I hate it more, because we don't talk about it. It's just a bloody awful job, and we get on and do it. I mean, you split enormous parts of yourself off, anyway.'

'Is that what you did?'

'I suppose so.' For a moment it seemed he was about to go on, then he shook his head.

When he was sure there'd be no more, Rivers said, 'You know we are going to have to talk about the

166

war, Charles.'

'I do talk about it.'

Silence.

'I just don't see what good it would do to churn everything up. I know what the theory is.' He looked down at his hands. 'My son Robert, when he was little ... he used to enjoy being bathed. And then quite suddenly he turned against it. He used to go stiff and scream blue murder every time his nurse tried to put him in. And it turned out he'd been watching the water go down the plug-hole and he obviously thought he might go down with it. Everybody told him not to be stupid.' Manning smiled. 'I must say it struck me as an *eminently* reasonable fear.'

Rivers smiled. 'I won't let you go down the plug-hole.'

*   *   *

At dinner the talk was all of the Pemberton Billing trial. Everybody was depressed by the medical evidence, since this was the first time psychologists had been invited to pronounce in court on such a subject. 'What do we get?' somebody asked. 'Serrel Cooke rambling on about monsters and hereditary degeneracy. The man's a joke.'

If he is, I've lost my sense of humour, Rivers thought.

After dinner he was glad to escape from the hospital and go for a stroll round the square. London had become a depressing place. Every placard, every newsboy's cry, every headline focused on the trial. Lord Alfred Douglas was in the witness-box now, apparently blaming England's poor showing in the war on the plays of Oscar Wilde. Any serious consideration of the terrible state of affairs in France was pushed into second place by the orgy of irrational prejudice that was taking place at the Old Bailey. Manning was quite right of course, people didn't want reasons, they wanted scapegoats. You saw it in the hospital too, where hostility to the pacifist orderlies mounted as the news from France grew worse, but there was some element of logic in that. Men were being whipped back into line. Into *the* Line. Unless he were suffering from the complaint Jane Manning had diagnosed, of being incapable of seeing his own sex as peripheral to anything. But no, he thought Manning was right. Maud Allan was in the firing line almost by accident. The real targets were men who couldn't or wouldn't conform.

Rivers's thoughts turned to Sassoon. Manning's experience clearly showed that every member of Robert Ross's circle was at risk, liable to the same treatment as Ross himself. It didn't help that Ross was opposed to the war, though he had not approved of Sassoon's protest, arguing—quite rightly in River's opinion—that it would destroy Sassoon without having any impact on the course of events. Ross's own method of opposition, according to Manning, was to show photographs of mutilated corpses to any civilian who might benefit from the shock. Rivers was glad Sassoon was well away from Ross, and the trial.

Once, at Craiglockhart, he'd tried to warn Sassoon of the danger. As long ago as last November he'd told him about the *cabinet noir*, the Black Book, the 47,000 names of eminent men and women whose double lives left them open to German blackmail.

—*Relax, Rivers. I'm not eminent.*

—*No, but you're a friend of Robert Ross, and you've*

publicly advocated a negotiated peace. That's enough! You're vulnerable, Siegfried. There's no point pretending you're not.

—And what am I supposed to do about it? Toe the line, tailor my opinions ... But what you're really saying is, if I can't conform in one area of life, then I have to conform in the others. Not just the surface things, everything. Even against my conscience. Well, I can't live like that. Nobody should live like that.

It had been pleasant talking to Manning about Siegfried. Apart from Robert Graves, whom Rivers saw occasionally, Manning was the only acquaintance they had in common.

The square was deserted. On nights of the full moon people hurried back to the safety of their cellars. Rivers's footsteps seemed to follow him, echoing along the empty pavement. The moon had drifted clear from the last gauzy wrack of cloud, and his shadow stretched ahead of him, the edges almost as sharp as they would have been by day.

So calm, so clear a night. We're in for it, he thought. That was one thing he'd never had to cope with at Craiglockhart: bombs falling within earshot of patients who jumped out of their skins if a teaspoon rattled in a saucer. He turned and began to walk rapidly towards the dark and shuttered building.

CHAPTER THIRTEEN

Head is the one awake inside the sleeping hospital. Masked and gowned, a single light burning above his head, he stands beside a dissecting table on which a man lies, face upwards, naked, reeking of formaldehyde. The genitals are shrivelled, the skin the dingy gold of old paper. Head finishes drawing an outline on the shaven head, says, 'Right then,' and extends his gloved hand for the drill. But something's wrong. Even as the drill whirs, the golden-skinned man stirs. Rivers tries to say, 'Don't, he's alive,' but Head can't, or won't, hear him. A squeak of bone, a mouth stretched wide, and then a hand grasps Head's hand at the wrist, and the cadaver in all its naked, half-flayed horror rises from the table and pushes him back.

The corridor outside Rivers's room is empty, elongated, the floor polished and gleaming. Then the doors at the end flap open with a noise like the beating of wings and the cadaver bounds through, pads from door to door, sniffs, tries to locate him more by smell than sight. At last it finds the right door, advances on the bed, bends over him, thrusts its anatomical drawing of a face into his, as he struggles to wake up and remember where he is.

Christ. He lay back, aware of sweat on his chest and in his groin. He was in a hospital bed, too high, too narrow, the mattress covered with rubber that creaked as he moved. He could see that ruin of a face bending over him. In these moments between sleep

170

and waking, he was able to do—briefly—what other people take for granted: see things that were not there.

Quickly, before the moment passed, he began to dissect the images of which the dream was composed. The dissecting-room in the dream had not been the room at the Anatomical Institute where he'd watched Head at work that morning, but the anatomy theatre at Bart's, where he had trained.

The whole emotional impression left by the dream was one of ... He lay, eyes closed in the darkness, sifting impressions. Contamination. To imagine Head, the gentlest of men, drilling the skull of a conscious human being was a sort of betrayal. The link with Head's carrying out the tests on Lucas was obvious. Rivers had thought, as he watched Head looking at Lucas, that the same suspension of empathy that was so necessary a part of the physician's task was also, in other contexts, the root of all monstrosity. Not merely the soldier, but the torturer also, practises the same suspension.

The dream was about dissociation. Like most of his dreams these days, a dream about work. He never seemed to dream about sex any more, though before the war sexual conflicts had been a frequent subject of dreams. A cynic might have said he was too exhausted. He thought it was probably more complicated, and more interesting, than that, but he had little time for introspection. Certainly no time for it now. He sat up and flapped his pyjama jacket to make the sweat evaporate, then lay back and tried to compose himself for sleep. He never slept well on the nights he stayed at the hospital, partly because of the uncomfortable bed, partly because the expectation of being woken kept his sleep light.

171

He was just beginning to drift off when the whistles blew.

By the time the orderly knocked on his door, he was out of bed and fastening his dressing-gown. He followed the man along the corridor to the main ward where Sister Walters greeted him. She was a thin, long-nosed Geordie with a sallow skin and a vein of class-hatred that reminded him of Prior. Oddly enough, it seemed to be directed entirely at her own sex. She hated the VADs, most of whom were girls of good family 'doing their bit' with—it had to be admitted—varying degrees of seriousness. She loved her officer patients—my boys, she called them—but the VADs, girls from a similar social background after all, she hated. One night last December, as the guns thudded and the ground shook beneath the direct hit on Vauxhall Bridge, they'd sat drinking cocoa together, and the barriers of rank had come down, enough at least for her to say bitterly, 'They make me sick, the way they go on. "Oooh! Look at me! I'm dusting!" "I'm sweeping a floor." Do you know, when I was training we got eight quid *a year*. That was for a seventy-hour week, and you got your breakages stopped off that.'

Cocoa was being made now and carried round on trays. Rivers went from bed to bed of the main ward. Most of the men were reasonably calm, though jerks and twitches were worse than normal. In the single rooms, where the more seriously disturbed patients were, the signs of distress were pitiful. These were men who had joked their way through bombardments that rattled the tea-cups in Kent, now totally unmanned. Weston had wet himself. He stood in the middle of his room, sobbing, while a nurse knelt in front of him and coaxed him to step out of the

172

circle of sodden cloth. Rivers took over from her, got Weston into clean pyjamas and back into bed. He stayed with him till he was calm, then handed over to an orderly and went in search of Sister Walters.

She handed him his cocoa. 'Captain Manning's smoking. Do you think you could—'

'Yes, of course.'

At Craiglockhart the corridors had reeked of cigarettes, and there the staff had contrived not to notice. Here, with two wards full of paralysed patients, the no-smoking rule had to be enforced. Rivers tapped once and walked in.

Manning was sitting up in bed. 'Hello,' he said, sounding surprised.

'I'm afraid I've got to ask you to put that out. Two lifts. Twenty wheelchairs.'

'Yes, certainly.' Manning stubbed his cigarette out. 'Stupid of me. I didn't know you did nights.'

'Only at full moons.'

'I thought that theory of mental illness had been exploded.'

Rivers smiled. 'You know what I mean.'

'Sister Walters says they got Vauxhall Bridge twice. Is that right?'

'Yes. Though we don't need to worry when they hit it. Only when they miss.'

'Reminds me of last Christmas. Do you remember that raid? I was staying with Ross, Sassoon was there as well, and it was very funny because it was the first raid I'd experienced, and I was all set to be the cool, collected veteran, calming down the poor nervous civilians. I was a complete bloody wreck. Ross's housekeeper was better than me. Sassoon was the same. In fact I remember him saying, "All that fuss about whether I should go back or not. I won't be any

173

bloody good when I do.'''

A ragged sound of singing. 'Listen,' Manning said. He began to sing with them, almost under his breath.

Bombed last night
And bombed the night before
Gunna get bombed tonight
If we never get bombed any more.
When we're bombed we're scared as we can be...

'First time I've heard that outside France.' A pause. 'You know, I've been thinking about what you said ... about remembering and trying to talk about it.'

Rivers propped his chin on his hands and said, 'Go on.' Even as he spoke, he recalled Prior's wickedly accurate imitation of this position. *Damn* Prior.

'You know these attacks I have? Well, they tend to start with a sort of waking dream. It's nothing very much actually, it's not horrifying, it's just a line of men marching along duckboards wearing gas masks and capes. Everything's a sort of greenish-yellow, the colour it is when you look through the visor. The usual ... porridge.' He swallowed. 'If a man slips off the duckboard it's not always possible to get him out and sometimes he just sinks. The packs are so heavy, you see, and the mud's fifteen feet deep. It's not like ordinary mud. It's like a bog, it ... sucks. They're supposed to hold on to the pack of the man in front.'

'And you say this ... dream triggers the attack?'

'I don't know. I suppose so.'

'What in particular?'

Manning tried to answer and then shook his head.

'If you had to pick out the worst thing, what would it be?'

174

'There's a hand coming out of the mud. It's holding the duckboard and ... nothing else. Everything else is underneath.'

A short silence.

'Oh, and there's a voice.' Manning reached for his cigarettes and then remembered he couldn't smoke. 'It's not coming *from* anybody. It's just ... there.'

Rivers waited. 'What does it say?'

'"Where's Scudder?"' Manning smiled. 'It's a rather nasty, *knowing* little voice. "Where's Scudder? Where's Scudder?"'

'Do you answer?'

Manning shook his head. 'No point. It knows the answer.'

Silence, except for the sound of singing, fading now, and then, in the distance, the thudding of the guns.

Rivers said, 'You know, if we went down to my room you could smoke.'

Manning looked surprised. '*Now?*'

'Why not? Unless you think you can get back to sleep?'

Manning didn't answer that. There was no need.

*　　　*　　　*

'There,' Rivers said, putting an ashtray at Manning's elbow. The lamp created a circle of light around the desk, a world.

'You don't, do you?' Manning said, lighting up.

'A cigar now and then.'

Manning inhaled deeply, his eyes closed. 'One of the reasons I don't talk about it,' he said, smiling, 'apart from cowardice, is that it seems so futile.'

'Because it's impossible to make people

175

understand?'

'Yes. Even a comparatively small thing. The feeling you get when you go into the Salient, especially if you've been there before and you know what you're facing. You really do say goodbye to everything. You just put one foot in front of another, one step, then the next, then the next.'

Rivers waited.

'It's . . . ungraspable,' Manning said at last. 'I don't mean *you* can't grasp it because you haven't been there. I mean, *I* can't grasp it and I *have* been there. I can't get my mind round it.'

'You were going to tell me about Scudder.'

'Was I?'

Their eyes met.

Manning smiled. 'Yes, I suppose I was. He was a man in my company. You know, the whole thing's based on the idea that if you've got the right number of arms and legs and you're not actually mentally defective you can be turned into a soldier. Well, Scudder was the walking proof that it isn't true. He was hopeless. He knew he was. The night before we were due to move up, he got drunk. Well, a lot of them got drunk, but he was . . . legless. He didn't turn up for parade, and so he was court-martialled. I went to see him the night before. He was being held in a barn, and we sat on a bale of straw and talked. It turned out he'd been treated for shell shock the previous year. With electric shocks. I didn't know they did that.'

'Oh, yes,' Rivers said. 'They do.'

'He was at Messines when the mines went up. Apparently he used to dream about mines and blood. And he used to jerk his head and make stupid noises. That's what the doctor called them. *Stupid noises*.

Anyway it worked, after a fashion. The electric shocks. The night after he had the treatment he didn't dream about mines. He dreamt he was back in the trenches having electric shock treatment. I stayed with him a couple of hours, I suppose.' Manning smiled faintly. 'He was a most unfortunate-looking youth. I mention that in case there's a doctrinaire Freudian lurking under your desk.'

Rivers pretended to look. 'No-o. There isn't one behind it either.'

Manning laughed. 'The thing was he was extremely bright. And I don't know whether it was snobbery or . . . or what it was, but I'd been assuming he wasn't. Actually I don't think it was snobbery, it was just he was so bloody *bad* at everything. You couldn't believe there was an intelligent mind behind all those . . . cock-ups. But there was.' His expression became momentarily remote. 'After that, I noticed him more. I thought—'

'What did he get?'

'At the court martial? Two hours' field punishment a day. When everybody else was resting—uh!—he'd be cleaning limbers, that sort of thing. I used to stop and have a word with him. I don't think it helped because it took him away from the other men, and in the end it's the other men who keep you going.'

'Go on. You say you thought—'

'I thought he was clumsy. And then after this talk I watched him, I watched him at bayonet practice, running in and lunging and . . . *missing*. You know, the thing's this big, and he was missing it. And suddenly I realized it was nothing to do with clumsiness. He couldn't switch off. He couldn't . . . turn off the part of himself that minded. I'm quite certain when he finally got the bayonet in, he saw it

177

bleed. And that's the opposite of what should be happening. You know I saw men once ... in close combat, as the manuals say, and one man was reciting the instructions. *Lunge*, one, two: *twist*, one, two, *out*, one, two ... Literally, killing by numbers. And that's the way it has to be. If a man's properly trained he'll function on the day almost like an automaton. And Scudder was the opposite of that. Somehow the whole thing had gone into reverse. I think probably because of the breakdown, because I can see the same sort of thing happening to me. Like red—the colour red—whatever it is, even if it's a flower or a book—it's always blood.'

Rivers had gone very still. He waited.

'When I was out there, I could be in blood up to the elbows, it didn't bother me. It's almost as if instead of normal feelings being cut off, there aren't any divisions left at all. Everything washes into everything else. I don't know if that makes sense.'

'Very much so.'

A pause. 'Anyway, we moved forward. It was raining. I don't know why I bother to say that. It was always raining. The heavens had opened. And we were told to report to *the graveyard*.' Manning laughed, a genuine full-blooded laugh. 'I thought, my God somebody's developed a sense of humour. But it was absolutely true. We were *billeted* in the graveyard. And it was extraordinary. All the tombs had been damaged by shells and you could see through into the vaults, and this was in an area where there were corpses everywhere. The whole business of collecting and burying the dead had broken down. Wherever you looked there were bodies or parts of bodies, and yet some of the younger ones—Scudder was one—were fascinated by these vaults. You'd

178

come across them lying on their stomachs trying to see through the holes, because the vaults were flooded, and the coffins were floating around. It was almost as if these people were *really* dead, and the corpses by the road weren't. Any more than we were really alive.

'We were shelled that night. Three men wounded. I was organizing stretcher-bearers—not easy, as you can imagine—and I'd just finished when Hines walked up and said, "Scudder's gone." He'd just got up and walked away. The other men thought he'd gone to the latrine, but then he didn't come back. We got together a search-party. I thought he might have fallen into one of the vaults, and we crawled round calling his name, and all the time I knew he hadn't. I decided to go after him. I know, not what a company commander ought to have done, but I had a very good second in command and I knew he couldn't have got far. You see, everything was coming forward for the attack, and the road was absolutely choked. I hoped I could get to him before the military police picked him up. He'd have been shot. We were far enough forward for it to count as desertion in the face of the enemy. I was struggling and floundering along, and it really was almost impossible, and then I saw him. He hadn't got very far. When I caught up with him, he didn't even look at me. Just went on walking. And I walked beside him and tried to talk to him, and he obviously wasn't listening. So I just pushed him off the road, and we slithered down and stopped on the rim of a crater. There's always gas lingering on the water. When you get close your eyes sting. He was blue. And I tried to talk to him. He said, "This is mad." And I said, "Yes, I know, but we've all got to do it." In the end I simply named people. Men in his platoon. And I said, *"They*'ve got to do it. You'll only make it harder for them." In the end he just got up and followed me, like a little lamb.'

Manning stirred and reached for another cigarette. 'We went forward almost as soon as we got back. The orders were full of words like "trenches" and "attacking positions". There weren't any trenches. The attacking position was a line of sticks tied with bits of white ribbon. We were late arriving, and it was getting light. If we hadn't been late, we'd've crawled straight past them in the dark. The "line" was a row of shell-craters, filled with this terrible sucking mud. And you just crouched beneath the rim, and ... waited. We advanced. No close work, but machine-guns directly ahead up the slope. A *lot* of casualties. *A lot*, and no hope of getting them back. It was taking the stretcher-bearers a couple of hours to go a hundred yards. So there we were, crouched in another row of shell-holes exactly like the first. And all hell was let loose. As soon as it died down a bit, I tried to crawl from one hole to another. It took me an hour to crawl between two holes. And in the other hole I found four men, none of them wounded, and I thought, thank God, and then suddenly one of them said, "Where's Scudder?" Well, there was nothing I could do about it. I couldn't move, the shelling was so heavy. And then there was a lull, and we heard a cry. It seemed to be coming from a crater slightly further back, not far, and we crawled along and found him.

'He'd either slipped or been blown down the slope. Blown, I suspect, because he'd got quite a way in. He was already up to his chest. We tried to get him out, but even forming a line and holding out a rifle we couldn't reach him. He could just get the tips of his fingers on the butt, but his hands were slippery with

180

mud and they kept sliding off. I could see if we went on trying somebody else was going to slip in. And Scudder was panicking and . . . *pleading* with us to do something. I have never seen anything like his face. And it went *on* and *on*. He was slipping away all the time, but *slowly*. I knew what I had to do. I got the men lined up and told him we were going to try again, and while he was looking at the others I crawled round the other side, and fired.' Manning closed his eyes. 'I missed. And that was terrible, because then he knew what was happening. I fired again, and this time I didn't miss.

'We spent the rest of the night there, in that hole. It was very odd. You know, I don't think any of the men would have said, "You did the wrong thing. You should have let him die slowly." And yet nobody wanted to talk to me. They kept their distance.'

A long silence. 'His mother wrote to me in hospital. To thank me. Apparently Scudder had written to her and told her I'd been kind to him.'

Rivers said firmly, 'You were.'

Manning looked at him and then quickly away. 'We were relieved the following night. I reported back to Battalion HQ and they expressed extreme displeasure. Apparently we'd been a bulge in the line. We'd been sitting in the wrong shell-holes. They were having dinner, veal and ham pie and red wine, and suddenly I realized they weren't even going to offer us a fucking drink. I had Hines with me, he was dead on his feet. So I leant across the table, took two glasses, gave one to Hines and said, "Gentlemen, the King." And of course they all had to struggle to their feet.' He laughed. 'And then we got the hell out of it before they could work out how to put an officer on a charge for proposing the loyal toast. We staggered down

181

that road giggling like a pair of schoolboys. We were still laughing when the shell got us. I got this. Poor old Hines ... I crawled across to him. And he looked straight at me and said, "I'm all right, Mum." And died.'

Rivers stirred. He was about to speak when he heard bugles in the streets. 'Let's have the curtains open, shall we?' he said.

He pulled the heavy curtains back, and grey dawn light flooded into the room. Manning flinched. He got up and joined Rivers by the window, and was just in time to see a taxi drive along the other side of the square. Rivers opened the windows, and the sound of birdsong filled the room.

'You know,' Manning said, 'when Ross told me they sounded the all-clear by driving boy scouts with bugles round the streets in taxis, I didn't believe him.'

They watched the taxi leave the square. Manning said, 'I used to find a certain kind of *Englishness* engaging. I don't any more.'

CHAPTER FOURTEEN

Sarah was coming. The thought buoyed Prior up as he walked along the Bayswater Road to the underground station. Only when he was on the train, staring sightlessly at his reflection in the black glass, did his thoughts turn to Spragge. He hadn't seen him face to face since that evening in the park, but he'd suspected more than once that Spragge was following him. Possibly it was just nerves. His nerves *were* bad, and the intolerable sticky heat didn't help. The gaps in his memory were increasing both in length and frequency, and they terrified him.

Like the undiscovered territory on medieval maps, Rivers said. *Where unknown, there place monsters.* But a better analogy, because closer to his own experience, was No Man's Land. He remembered looking down a lane in France. The lane had a bend in it, and what was beyond the bend was hidden by a tall hedge. Beyond that was No Man's Land. Beyond that again, the German lines. Full of men like himself. Men who ate, slept, shat, blew on their fingers to ease the pain of cold, moved the candle closer, strained their eyes to read again letters they already had by heart. He knew that, they all knew it. Only it was impossible to believe, because the lane led to a country where you couldn't go, and this prohibition alone meant that everything beyond that point was threatening. Uncanny.

Something about the lifeless air of the underground encouraged morbid thoughts. Above ground, in the relatively cool, coke-smelling air of King's Cross, he felt more cheerful. Please God, he thought, no gaps while Sarah's here.

He waited by the barrier, sick with excitement. The train slid to a halt, grunted, wheezed, belched, subsided into a series of disgruntled mutters, and then all along its length doors swung open, and people started to get out. The sheer excitement of knowing he was going to see her stopped him seeing her, and for one terrifying moment all the women on the platform were Sarah. Then his mind cleared, and there was only one woman, walking straight towards him.

He caught her in his arms and swung her off her feet. When, finally, he set her down they stared at each other. He noticed the yellow skin, the dark shadows round her eyes, the fringe of ginger hair which was not her own colour, but some effect of the chemicals she worked with.

'Well?' she said.

'You look beautiful. But then you always do.'

He took her bag and steered her towards the taxi rank.

'Can't we go on the underground?' she said, pulling back.

He looked surprised.

'I've never been on it.'

Her face lit up as she stepped out on to the descending staircase. She was too excited to talk until they were on the train, and had stopped at several stations, and the first novelty of hurtling in a lighted capsule through dark tunnels had worn off. Then she turned to him and said, 'You look a bit tired. Are you all right?'

'It's the heat,' he said. 'I haven't been sleeping

well.'

'You will tonight.'

He smiled. 'I was hoping not to sleep at all tonight.'
But that was too direct. She smiled but looked
away.

'How's your mother?'

'The same. The shop's not doing too well. No
demand for second-hand stuff these days.'

'What about Dr Lawson's Cure for Female
Blockages and Obstructions? I bet she's doing a
roaring trade in that.'

'Geraway, man. It's all sixpenny ticklers these
days.'

'*Is it?*' Prior asked innocently.

She smiled and eventually laughed.

'How was your trip home?' she asked after a while.

'Not bad. I met a few old friends.'

'Did you tell your mam about me?'

He hesitated.

'You didn't,' she said.

'I prepared the ground.'

'*Billy.* You think she won't like me, don't you?'

He knew she wouldn't. He had a very clear idea of
the sort of girl his mother wanted him to marry. One
of those green-skinned, titless girls who wore white
lawn blouses and remembered their handkerchiefs.
The Ministry was full of them. The extraordinary
thing was he *did* find them attractive, though not in a
way he liked. They woke his demons up, just as surely
as making love to Sarah put them to sleep. 'It's not
that,' he said.

'Isn't it?' She smiled, and he realized she simply
didn't care. 'What about your dad?'

'I don't tell him anything.'

'Do you think *he*'d like me?'

185

He'd never thought about it. As soon as he considered it, he knew his father *would* like her, and she'd like him. She wouldn't *approve* of the old sod, but she'd get on all right with him. Instantly the idea of taking her home became even less attractive. 'There's plenty of time,' he said.

* * *

Leading her down the steps to the basement he was ashamed of the overflowing bins and the smell, but he needn't have worried. Sarah was delighted with the flat. He realized, as he took her from room to room, that it could have been twice as dark, twice as stuffy, and she would still have been pleased with it. For two days and nights this would be their home, and that was all that mattered.

She ended the tour sitting on the single bed in his room, unselfconsciously bouncing up and down to test the mattress. Then she looked up and found him watching her, and her face was suffused with a blush that banished the yellow from her skin. His breath caught in his throat, and he swallowed hard. 'If you'd like to get washed or or bathed, it's next door.'

'Yes, I—'

'I'll get a towel.'

Prior wished sometimes he didn't *know* what it was like to be groped, to be pounced on before you're ready. As he pulled a towel out of the airing cupboard, he heard the bathroom door open and then felt her arms come round him and clasp his chest. She pressed her face between his shoulders, her mouth against his spine. 'Can you feel this?' she asked. And she began to groan, deep noises, making his spine and the hollows of his chest vibrate with her breath. He pushed her gently away. 'You must be tired,' he said.

She giggled, and he felt her laughter in his bones. 'Not *too* tired.'

* * *

They did have a bath, eventually. Afterwards, lying on the bed, she traced his ribs with the tips of her fingers, propped up on one elbow, her hair screening them both. 'You know the part of men I like best?' she said, moving her finger down.

'Men?' Cupping his hands around his mouth, he called into the passage, 'Ge-orge? Albert? Are you there?'

She smiled, but persisted. 'This part.' Her finger slid into the hollow beneath his ribs and down across his belly.

'There?'

'Yes.'

'Uh? Uh?' he said, thrusting his hips upward. 'Oh, *that.*'

'*"That"*!' He struggled to sit up, only to subside as she slid down the bed and took his flaccid penis into her mouth.

She looked up and smiled. 'He's nice too.'

'He's a bloody disgrace at the moment. Look at him.'

'You can't expect miracles.'

He closed his eyes. 'Go on doing that you might just get one.'

* * *

Hanging over her, watching the stretched mouth, the
187

slit eyes, the head thrown back until it seemed her spine must crack, he remembered other faces. The dying looked like that.

*   *   *

'What shall we do?' he asked. 'Are you hungry?'
'Not really.'
'We could go to Oxford Street. Look round the shops.'
'Don't sound so enthusiastic.'
'Or Kew.'
'What do *you* want to do?'
'Kew, I think. The weather can't last and we can do indoor things tomorrow.'
'More? You'll wear me out.'
'*Other* things.'
'Oh.'

*   *   *

Once in the gardens they wandered aimlessly, more interested in each other than in the plants. As the afternoon wore on, the heat thickened until there was a brassy glare in the sky, as if a furnace door had opened. Still they walked, each adjusting to the other's stride, hardly aware when their linked shadow faded from the grass.

Drops of rain striking their faces startled them out of their absorption. They looked around, dazed. The rain began to beat down, lashing their heads and shoulders. In less time than seemed possible, Sarah's hair was hanging in dark, reddish-brown strands and the sleeves of her blouse had become transparent. Prior looked for shelter, but could see only some
188

trees. They made for those and stood under them, but there was little protection. Rain streaked the trunks and splashed through the leaves on to the backs of their necks.

Sarah was beginning to shiver with cold. Prior didn't know where they were. He could see a little mock Grecian temple on a grassy mound, but that was open to the wind. From his previous visits he remembered the Palm House, which was certainly warm. That would be the best place if he could manage to locate it. He worked out where the main gate was, and thought he could remember that you turned left. 'I think we should make a run for it,' he said. 'This isn't going to go over.'

They ran, heads bent, Prior with his arm round Sarah, splashing through puddles. Rivulets of mud, washed out of flowerbeds, ran down the paths. Sarah refused the offer of his tunic and strode through it all, drenched, skirt caught between her legs, blouse transparent, hair stringy, skin glowing, with a stride that would have covered mountains. She had decided to *enjoy* it, she said.

The lake was a confusion of exploding circles and bubbles, too turbulent to reflect the inky sky. They ran the last few yards and entered the Palm House. Prior felt a rippling effect on his face and neck and then, immediately, an uncomfortable wave of damp heat. He began to cough. Sarah turned to him. 'Isn't this bad for your chest?'

'No,' he said, straightening up. 'In fact it's ideal.'

The aisles were crowded, so much so it was difficult to move. Thick green foliage surrounded them, and towered to the dazzling glass roof above their heads. Smells of wet earth, of leaves dripping moisture, a constant trickle of water, and somewhere a trapped

189

blackbird singing. But as they moved deeper into the crush, it was the smell of people that took over: damp cloth, wet hair, steamy skin.

Prior took Sarah's arm and pointed to the gangway above. 'Come on, it'll be less crowded.'

He had a dim feeling there might also be more air up there, for in spite of what he'd said to Sarah he was finding the atmosphere oppressive. Sarah followed slowly, wanting to look at the plants. She tugged at his arm and pointed to a flower that had the most incredibly pink penile-looking stamens. 'Isn't he beautiful?'

'I thought you were a rib-cage girl?'

'Not ribs. The—'

He laughed and pulled her to him. They were standing at the bottom of the spiral staircase. She slid her hand between his legs and rubbed. 'I could be converted.'

He pressed her more closely against him, his mouth buried in her wet hair, looking over her head, focusing on nothing. Suddenly his eye registered a familiar shape. The green blur cleared, and he found himself gazing, through the branches of some tall plant with holes in its leaves, into the face of Lionel Spragge. There could be no mistake. They stared at each other through the foliage, no more than four or five feet apart. Then Spragge turned and pushed into the crowd, which swallowed him.

Sarah looked up. 'What's the matter?'

'Let's go upstairs.'

He took her hand and pulled her towards the staircase. At every turn he looked down through the green leaves of the canopy at the heads and shoulders below, until eventually they ceased to look like individual people. As they climbed higher, the sound

190

of rain on the glass roof grew louder. The windows were misted up, and a steamy, diffuse, white light spread over everything. He looked down on to the gleaming canopy of leaves. And then at the aisles, searching for Spragge's broad shoulders and square head. He thought he saw him several times as he and Sarah walked round the gangway, but could never be sure. At first Sarah exclaimed over the different shapes and patterns of the leaves, which were indeed beautiful, as he acknowledged after a cursory glance. Then, gradually, sensing his withdrawal, she fell silent.

I should have spoken to him, Prior thought, though he couldn't imagine what he would have said. But somehow the not speaking seemed in retrospect to give the encounter a hallucinatory quality. He looked down again, and now he would have been relieved to see Spragge's square head moving below.

He felt Sarah watching him and made an effort to behave more normally, rubbing condensation from the glass, trying to see out. 'You know, I think we might just as well make a dash for it.'

He had begun to feel exposed, here above the leaves, with the white light flooding over everything. Down there in the crowd, Spragge had only to look up through a gap in the foliage and there he was, floodlit under the white light of the dome.

'Yes, all right,' Sarah said.

She sounded puzzled, but ready to go along with whatever he suggested. But she was no fool, his Sarah. He was going to have to tell her something.

Others had also decided to make a dash for it. A group of women with heavy drenched skirts were running stiff-legged towards the main gate.

'Can you run?' he asked.

191

A glint of amusement. 'Can *you*?'

Good question. By the time they reached the underground station, he was more out of breath than her. He remembered, as he pressed his hand to his side, Spragge saying, 'I was behind you on the platform.' Suddenly he didn't want the underground. He didn't want to be shut in. 'Look, I've got a better idea,' he said. 'Why don't we go on the river? If we get off at Westminster Bridge we could see the Abbey.'

The boat was already moored when they reached the landing stage, and beginning to be crowded. At the last moment, as the engine began to throb, a crowd of people swept on board, including what looked like a girls' school party. Prior stood up and gave one of the teachers his seat. 'I'll get you a cup of tea,' he whispered to Sarah and went to the bar.

As he stood waiting his turn, the roar increased, the river churned, and they began moving out into midstream. He got the tea, took it back to Sarah, and tried to drink his own, but found it too difficult to keep his feet on the tilting deck, so he moved away from her and went to stand in the doorway that connected the covered deck with the open benches in the stern. Even these were full, and in fact the rain had almost stopped. A white sun could be glimpsed now and then through a hazy veil of cloud.

On the front bench a group of elderly cockney men were making the best of a bad job, laughing and joking at everything. A little way behind, on the end of the third bench, sat a man with unusually broad shoulders. He looked like Spragge, but it was difficult to tell because he was wearing a hat and facing away from Prior. Prior craned to see the side of his face. It *was* Spragge. Had to be. And yet he wasn't sure. There was something odd about the way the man

192

didn't turn, didn't move. Edging along the railing towards him, Prior became aware of a slowness in his movements, as if he were wading through glue. He saw himself, in his mind's eye, go up to the man, tap him on the shoulder, wait for him to turn, and the face that turned towards him ... was his own. He sat down, his eyes level with the railings from which a row of glittering raindrops hung. He reached out his hand and, with the tip of his forefinger, destroyed them one by one. The wet, running uncomfortably under his shirt cuff, brought him back to himself. He looked again. It might or might not be Spragge, but it certainly looked nothing like *him*. The whole powerful, brutal bulk of the head and shoulders was as different from his own slight build as any two physiques could be, and yet again, as he got up and began to move forward, he felt he was looking at the back of his own head. He breathed deeply, gazing through the rails at the brown, swollen, sinuous river, making himself follow individual twigs and leaves as they were borne along, noticing how the different currents of water, as they met and parted, rippled like muscles under skin. They were approaching another bridge. He steadied himself, walked up to the man and tapped him on the shoulder.

Spragge's face was a relief. So much so that it took several seconds for the anger to surface. 'What the hell are you doing here?'

'Going back to London. What are *you* doing?'

He sounded genuinely surprised, but Prior had caught the hiccup of laughter in his voice. Spragge had spoken more loudly than he needed, playing to the small audience of cockneys, and to the larger audience on the benches behind.

Prior lowered his voice. 'Are you following me?'

'*Following* you?' Again very loud. 'Now why should I do that?'

He sounded like a bottom-of-the-bill music-hall actor conveying injured innocence. The impression was not of somebody who'd decided to act as one possible response to a situation, but of somebody who couldn't *not* act. You had the feeling he would act in front of the bathroom mirror. That if ever you succeeded in ripping the mask off there would be no face behind it. Prior felt a wave of revulsion. 'If you're following me,' he said, 'I'll—'

'Yes, what will you do?' Spragge waited, as if the question genuinely interested him. 'Call the police? Have me arrested? It's not against the law to go to Kew.' He smiled. 'Nice girl,' he said, nodding towards the prow. And then he cupped his hands against his chest.

'If you go anywhere near her, I'll break your fucking neck.'

Spragge laughed, jowls shaking. He put his hand on Prior's chest and slapped it, genially. 'That's all right,' he said. Then he sat down again and looked out over the river, with no more than a sideways glance at the cockneys, and a faint smile.

*   *   *

In something not moving, something too steady for a boat. Hands, mottled purple and green, moved along polished wood. Then he was back, staring up at a window made of chips of purple and green light. He looked for Sarah and couldn't see her. In a panic he leapt up and began searching the Abbey, thrusting tourists aside, trailing hostile stares.

He found her at last, standing by the effigy of an

194

eighteenth-century bishop, running her hand over the smooth marble. A shaft of sunlight had found the auburn lights in her hair.

She looked up as he arrived, breathless. 'You back now?'

The question was so apposite it silenced him. For a moment he thought, *she knows*. And immediately rejected the idea. Of course she didn't know.

They went home by taxi. Prior thought about Spragge, because he was afraid of thinking about anything else. What angered him was the thought that Spragge might have seen that little act of intimacy in the Palm House when Sarah had moved closer and rubbed his cock through the hard cloth of his breeches. A *good* moment. In all that press of wet, sweating, steamy-skinned people, they'd been alone, and then Spragge's face peering through the leaves. *Had* he seen? He must have. Prior was aware of feeling an almost excessive sense of exposure, of violation even, as if he'd been seen, arse upwards, in the act itself.

The taxi jolted and swayed. A memory started to surface that seemed to have nothing to do with the afternoon's events. He was ill with asthma, walking with his father's hand. Where could they have been going? His father had never taken him anywhere, he'd been too ashamed of the little runt that had mysteriously sprung from his loins. Perhaps his mother had been ill. Yes, that was it.

They'd sat on a bench somewhere, and a woman brought him lemonade. *Real* lemonade, his father had said proudly—but why proudly?—not that gassy bottled stuff. There had been lime jelly too, with jelly babies suspended in it. While he was picking at it, his father and the woman went upstairs. He could hear

195

voices from the open window above his head. *The boy, Harry*. Then his father's voice, thick and hurried. *He's all right. Wraps himself round that lot he won't have much to grumble about.*

'Wrapping himself round that lot' had not been easy. He loved jelly, but hated jelly babies, mainly because of the way people ate them, nibbling at their feet, then at their faces, then boldly biting off the head and turning the headless body round to display the shiny open wound. He contemplated eating his way round them, freeing them from their quivering prison, but he knew he couldn't do that. The jelly had been specially made—it wasn't grown-up food—and his father would be angry. So, one by one, he had forced them down, swallowing them whole, his eyes fixed on the trees so he wouldn't have to think about what he was doing. Even so, he'd gagged once or twice, his eyes had watered, while upstairs the thick whispers came and went and the bed springs creaked.

On the way home his father had said, casually, 'Better not tell your mam.' And then he'd sat him astride his shoulders and carried him all the whole way home, all the way up the street with everybody looking, his meaty hands clasped round his son's thin white thighs. For once he'd ridden home in triumph. And he hadn't told his mam, though he'd stood by her sick bed and listened to his father describe a visit to the park. He'd been invited to join the great conspiracy and even at the age of five he knew the value of it. He wasn't going to jeopardize future outings by telling her anything.

That night he'd woken up, hot and sticky, knowing he was going to be sick. He started to cry and after a long time his father came in, blundering round and stubbing his toes before he found the light. He looked

196

up at him, the huge man, looming over the bed. Then, slowly, erupting from his mouth, the jelly babies returned—intact, or very nearly so—while his father stood and gaped.

It must have been quite a sight, Prior thought, helping Sarah out of the cab and turning to pay the driver. Like watching a sea-horse give birth.

*   *   *

Once inside the flat he lit the gas fire and made two mugs of strong sweet tea, while Sarah went to take off her wet clothes. She came back wearing his dressing-gown, shivering from the cold. He sat her down between his knees and towelled her hair.

'You know you were saying about the bit you liked best? For me it's your hair,' he said, feeling his tongue thick and unwieldy, getting in the way of his teeth. 'It was the first thing I noticed. The different colours.'

'You told me,' she said, twisting round. 'And you needn't make it sound so romantic. You were wondering which colour was down there. Weren't you?'

He smiled. 'Yes.'

They sat sipping their tea. She said, 'Well, are you going to tell me?'

'Yes.' He picked up two handfuls of hair and tugged on them. 'But it's worse than you think. I need *you* to tell *me* what happened.'

'When?'

'On the boat.'

Her eyes widened, but she didn't argue. 'You gave your seat to that woman and got a cup of tea and then you went and stood over by the bar. I didn't see what happened then, I was looking at the bank. Then the

197

sun came out and some of the girls went out on deck and this woman thought she ought to go and keep an eye on them. So next time you came back there was a seat next to me. I asked you which bridge we were going under and you didn't answer. I could see you were in one of your moods. So I left you to it. Then when we got out, that man in the Palm House was waiting at the top of the steps. He said something about me—I honestly didn't hear what it was—and you hit him. He came back at you, and you lifted your cane and you were obviously going to brain him, so he backed off. He went across the bridge, and you got hold of me and dragged me into the Abbey. I kept saying, "What's the matter?" I couldn't get an answer, so I thought, sod it. And I went off and looked at things on me own.' She waited. 'Are you telling me you don't remember all that?'

'I remember the first bit.'

'You don't remember hitting him?'

'No.'

'Who is he?'

'Doesn't matter.'

'It does bloody matter.'

'It's got nothing to do with you.'

Her face froze.

As she pulled away, he said, 'No, look, I didn't mean it like that.' He buried his head in his hands. 'I'll tell you all about him if you like, but that's not the bit that matters. What matters is that I can't remember.'

'It's happened before?'

'It's been happening for oh ... two months.'

He could see her mind busily at work, trying to minimize the significance. 'But you lost your memory once before, didn't you? I mean, when you came back from France you said you couldn't remember

198

anything.' She switched to a tone of condemnation. 'You've let yourself get run down, that's what you've done.'

'Look, I need you to tell me about it.' He tried to sound light-hearted. 'You're the first person who's met him.'

'Don't you mean "me"? Well, it *is* you, isn't it?'

Prior shook his head. 'You don't understand.' He leapt up and took a piece of paper out of the top drawer of the sideboard. 'Look.'

Sarah looked down and read: *Why don't you leave my fucking cigars alone?*

'I found some cigars in my pocket. I threw them away.'

'But it's your writing.'

'YES. How can I say "I" about that?'

Sarah was thinking. 'When I said it was you, I didn't just mean ... the obvious. I meant I ... I meant I recognized you in that mood. Do you remember the first time we went out together? That day on the beach.'

'Yes, of—'

'Well, you were like that then. Hating everybody. You were all right on the train, but once we were on the beach, I don't know what happened, you just went right away from me and I couldn't reach you. I could feel the hatred coming off you. It was like anybody who hadn't been to France was *rubbish*. Well, you were like that on the boat. And there's no talking to you when you're in that mood. You just despise everybody.' She hesitated. 'Including me.'

'It's not a mood, Sarah. People remember moods.'

*   *   *

In bed that night, coiled round her, he kissed all along her spine, gently, so as not to wake her, his lips moving from one vertebra to the next.

Stepping stones to sanity.

But the day after tomorrow, she would be gone.

CHAPTER FIFTEEN

Sarah left early on the Monday morning. They clung together by the barrier at King's Cross, breathing in coke fumes, and did not say goodbye.

*   *   *

He worked late, putting off the moment when he'd have to face the empty flat. On his way home he kept telling himself it wouldn't be too bad, or at least it wouldn't be as bad as he expected.

It was worse.

He wandered from room to room, searching for traces of her, trying to convince himself a dent in the sofa cushion was where her head had rested. He sat down and put his own head there, but this simply provided a more painful vantage point from which to survey the emptiness of the room.

It'll get better, he told himself.

It didn't.

*   *   *

He took to walking the streets at night in an effort to get tired enough to sleep. London by night fascinated him. He walked along the pavements, looking at place-names: Marble Arch, Piccadilly, Charing Cross, Tottenham Court Road. All these places had trenches named after them. And, gradually, as he walked through the streets of the night city, that other city, the unimaginable labyrinth, grew around him, its sandbag walls bleached pale in the light of a flare, until some chance happening, a piece of paper blown across the pavement, a girl's laugh, brought him back to a knowledge of where he was.

*   *   *

He got a letter from Sarah and put it on the mantelpiece, under a small china figure of a windblown girl walking a dog, where he would see it as soon as he came through the door.

*   *   *

Often, on his night-time walks, he thought about Spragge, and the more he thought the more puzzled he became. The man's whole sweaty, rumpled, drink-sodden appearance suggested a down-and-out, a man blundering through life, and yet the effort required to watch the flat and follow him all the way to Kew revealed a considerable degree of persistence. It didn't make sense.

One obvious explanation was that he was working for Lode, but Prior distrusted the idea. The atmosphere in the Intelligence Unit was such that baseless suspicions were mistaken for reality at every turn. It was like a trick picture he'd seen once, in which staircases appeared to lead between the various floors of a building. Only very gradually did he realize that the perspective made no sense, that the elaborate staircases connected nothing with nothing.

*   *   *

His landlady, Mrs Rollaston, turned up on the

doorstep, cradling her bosom in her arms as women do when they feel threatened. 'I thought you'd like to know there's somebody coming to do the bins. I know I said Monday, but I just couldn't get anybody.'

She was obviously *continuing* a conversation.

Prior nodded, and smiled.

He could recall no occasion on which he'd spoken to Mrs Rollaston about the bins.

*   *   *

He needed to see Spragge, but the address on the file, as he discovered standing on a gritty, windswept pavement in Whitechapel, was out of date. The bloodless girl who peered up at him from the basement, a grizzling baby in her arms, said she'd lived there a year and no, she didn't know where the previous tenant had gone. The landlady might, though.

The landlady, traced to the snug bar of the local pub, confirmed the name had been Spragge. She didn't know where he was now. Did *he* know this was the very pub Mary Kelly had been drinking in the night the Ripper killed her? She'd known Mary Kelly as well as she knew her own sister, heart in one place, liver in another, intestines draped all over the floor, *in that very chair—*

He bought her a port and lemon and left her to her memories. Odd, he thought, that the fascination with the Ripper and his miserable *five* victims should persist, when half of Europe was at it.

He was losing more time. Not in huge chunks, but frequently, perhaps four or five times a day. In the evenings, unless he was seeing Rivers, he stayed at

203

home. He knew the flat was bad for him, both physically and mentally, but he was afraid to venture out because it seemed to give *him* more scope. Nonsense, of course. *He* could and did go out, though sometimes the only sign was the smell of fresh air on Prior's skin.

*   *   *

One morning Lode sent for him.

'I just thought I'd share the good news,' Lode said. 'Since there isn't much of it these days. They've caught MacDowell.'

Prior was knocked sick by the shock, but he managed to keep his face expressionless. 'Oh? When?'

'A few days ago. In Liverpool. Charles Greaves's house. They got Greaves too.'

'Hmm. Well, that *is* progress.'

'Good news, isn't it?'

Prior nodded.

'You know,' Lode said, watching him narrowly, 'I used to think I understood you. I used to think I had you taped.' He waited. 'Ah, well. Back to work.'

Prior wondered why Lode's endless patting and petting of his moustache should ever have struck him as a sign of vulnerability. It didn't seem so now.

The nights were bad. He was still taking sleeping draughts, sometimes repeating the dose when the first one failed to work. Rivers strenuously advised him against it, but he ignored the advice. He had to sleep.

That evening, fast asleep after the second draught, he was awakened by a knocking on the door. The bromide clung to him like glue. Even when he managed to get out of bed, he felt physically sick. For a moment, as he pulled on his breeches and shirt, he thought he might actually be sick. The knocking went on, then stopped.

Presumably whoever it was had got tired and gone away. Prior was about to fall back into bed when he remembered he'd left the door open. Of all the bloody stupid things to do. But it was the only way of getting some air into the place.

It was no use, he'd have to go and close it.

The passage was full of the smell of rotting cabbage. The area round the bins had not been cleaned, in spite of Mrs Rollaston's promise. Prior stumbled along, hitching up his braces as he went.

The door was open. He looked out. The sky was not the normal blue of a summer evening, but brownish, like caught butter. He went back inside and closed the door.

He was walking past the door of the living-room when he heard a movement.

Slowly, he pushed the half-open door wide. Spragge was sitting, stolidly, in the armchair, thick fingers relaxed on his splayed thighs. He looked up with a sheepish, rather silly expression on his face. Sheepish, but obstinate. 'Well?' he said. 'What do you want to see me about?'

'Do you always walk into people's houses uninvited?'

'I thought I heard you say come in.' He didn't bother to make the lie convincing. 'I knew you must be in because the door was open. You want to watch that. You could get burgled.' A glance round the room pointed out that there was nothing worth taking.

Prior was angry. Not because Spragge had walked in uninvited; it was deeper, less rational than that. He was angry because of the way Spragge's fingers curled on his thighs, innocent-looking fingers, the waxy pink of very cheap sausages.

'I'll get up and knock again if you like,' Spragge said, pulling a comical face.

'It doesn't matter,' Prior said, sitting down. 'What do you want?'

'What do *you* want?'

Prior looked blank.

'You're the one who's been chasing me.'

Spragge was drunk. Oh, he hid it well. There was just the merest hint of over-precision in his speech, a kind of truculence bubbling beneath the surface.

'What about a drink?' Prior suggested.

'Yeh, all right.'

Prior needed time to think, to work out how he was going to approach Spragge. He went into the kitchen where he kept the whisky. The trouble was he detested Spragge to the point where the necessary manipulation became distasteful. You didn't *manipulate* people like Spragge. You squashed them.

He poured a jug of water and, in the sudden silence after he'd turned off the tap, heard a movement, furtive, it seemed to him, in the next room. Rapidly, he crossed to the door.

Spragge was removing Sarah's letter from underneath the ornament on the mantelpiece. No, not removing it. *Putting it back.*

'Have you read that?' Prior burst into the room. He was remembering how explicit Sarah's references to their love-making had been. 'Have you read it?'

Spragge swallowed hard. 'It's the job.'

'You shouldn't've done that.'

'Aw, for God's sake,' Spragge said. 'Do you think she'd mind? I saw her in the Palm House, she

206

virtually had your dick out.'

Prior grasped Spragge lightly by the forearms and butted him in the face, his head coming into satisfying, cartilage-crunching contact with Spragge's nose. Spragge tried to pull away, then slumped forward, spouting blood, snorting, putting up an ineffectual shaking hand to stop the flow.

Prior tried to make him stand up, like a child trying to make a toy work. Spragge staggered backwards and fell against the standard lamp, which crashed over and landed on top of him. He lay there, holding his spread fingers over his shattered nose, trying to speak, and gurgling instead.

Disgusted, with himself as much as Spragge, Prior went into the kitchen, wrung out a tea-towel in cold water, came back, and handed it to Spragge. 'Here, put this over it.'

Wincing, tears streaming down his face, Spragge dabbed at his face with the wet cloth. 'Broken,' he managed to say. He gestured vaguely at the towel, which was drenched in blood. Prior took it away and brought another. He looked at the roll of fat above Spragge's trousers and contemplated landing a boot in his kidneys. But you couldn't, the man was pathetic. He threw the tea-towel at Spragge and sat down in the nearest chair, shaking with rage, unappeased. He wanted to *fight*. Instead of that he was farting about with tea-towels like Florence fucking Nightingale.

After a while Spragge started to cry. Prior stared at him with awed disgust and thought, my God, I'm not taking this. 'Come on,' he said, grabbing Spragge by the sleeve. '*Out.*'

'Can't walk.'

'I'll get you a taxi.'

207

Prior struggled into his boots and puttees, then returned to the living-room and dragged Spragge to his feet. Spragge lurched and stumbled to the door, half of his own volition, half dragged there by Prior. *Bastard*, Prior thought, pushing him up the steps, but the anger was ebbing now, leaving him lonely.

They staggered down the street, Spragge leaning heavily on Prior. Like two drunks. 'Do you realize how much trouble I'd get into if I was seen like this?' Prior asked.

The first two taxis went past. Spragge's face, in the brown air, looked dingy, but less obviously bloody than it had in the flat. He stood, swaying slightly, apart from the noise and heat, the passing crowds, the sweaty faces. He was visibly nursing his bitterness, carrying it around with him like a too full cup. 'Lode offered me a passage to South Africa. Did you know that? All expenses paid.'

'Will you go?'

'Might.' He looked round him, and the bitterness spilled. 'Fuck all here.'

Prior remembered there were things he needed to know. 'Did Lode tell you to follow me?'

'Yes.'

'Were you following me when I went to see Hettie Roper?'

'No, not there.'

Either Spragge was a better actor than he'd so far appeared, or he was telling the truth. Spragge started waving and shouting 'Taxi!'

It pulled up a few paces further on. 'I'll need money,' he said.

Prior dug in his breeches pockets. 'Here, take this.'

Spragge bent down and said, 'Marble Arch.' He wasn't going to give an address while Prior was within hearing.

'You must have been following me,' Prior said. 'It was you who told the police where to find MacDowell.'

Spragge looked up from the dim interior. 'Not me, guv.' His tone was ironical, indifferent. 'Lode says it was you.'

CHAPTER SIXTEEN

In the Empire Hospital Charles Manning surveyed the chess-board and gently, with the tip of his forefinger, knocked over the black king.

'You win,' he said. 'Again.'

Lucas grinned, and then pointed over Manning's shoulder to the figure of a man in army uniform, standing just inside the entrance to the ward.

*　　　*　　　*

Manning stood up. For a second there might have been a flicker of fear. Fear was too strong a word, perhaps, but Manning certainly wasn't at ease though he gave the usual, expensively acquired imitation of it, coming towards Prior, offering his hand. 'Well,' he said. 'This *is* a surprise.'

'How are you?'

'Getting better. Let's go along to my room.'

Manning chatted easily as they walked along the corridor. 'Remarkable chap, that. Do you know, he can't remember the names of any of the pieces? But, my God, he knows how to play.'

Manning's room was pleasant, with a bowl of roses on the bedside table, and a bright yellow and red covered book lying face down on the bed.

'A name you'll know,' Manning said, picking it up.

Prior read the title, *Counter-Attack*, and the name, Siegfried Sassoon.

'You must've been at Craiglockhart at the same

time,' Manning said.

'Ye-es. Though I don't know how much of a bond that is. Frankly.' Prior closed the book and put it on the bedside table beside a photograph of Manning's wife and children, the same photograph that had been on the grand piano at his house. 'He *hated* the place.'

'Did he?'

'Oh, yes, he made that perfectly clear. *And* the people. Nervous wrecks, lead-swingers and degenerates.'

'Well,' Manning said, waving Prior to a chair, 'as one nervous, lead-swinging degenerate to another ... how are you?'

'All right, I think. The Intelligence Unit's being closed down, so I don't quite know what's going to happen.'

Manning smiled. 'I suppose you want to stay in the Ministry?'

'Not particularly.'

'Oh? Well, that might be a bit more difficult. I've got a friend at the War Office—Charles Moncrieff—I don't know whether you know him? Anyway, one of his jobs is to select instructors for cadet battalions. I suppose that might be a possibility?'

Prior leant forward. 'Hang on a minute. I didn't come here to brown-nose you *or* your fucking friend at the War Office. What I was going to say—if you wouldn't mind *listening*—is that I want to talk to you about something.'

'What?'

'Who. A woman called Mrs Roper. Beattie Roper.'

Manning was looking puzzled. '*The* Mrs Roper? Poison-plot Roper?'

'Yes.' Prior got a file out of his briefcase. 'Except she didn't do it.'

Manning took the file from him. 'You want me to read it?'

'I've summarized it. It'll only take you a few minutes.'

Manning read with total concentration. When he finished he looked up. 'Can I keep this?'

'Yes, I've got a copy. I've got copies of the documents as well.'

'You mean you've made personal copies of Ministry files?' Manning pursed his lips. 'You certainly don't play by the rules, do you?'

'Neither do you.'

'We're in the same boat there, aren't we?' A hardening of tone. 'I would have thought we were in *exactly* the same boat.'

The merest hint of a glance at the photograph. 'Not quite.'

Manning got up and walked across to the window. For a while he said nothing. Then he turned and said, 'Why? Why on earth couldn't you just come in and say, "Look, I'm worried about this. Will you read the report?" *All right*, you've got the opening to do so because of ... There was no need for anything like that.'

Prior had a sudden chilling perception that Manning was right. 'Rubbish. Beattie Roper's a working-class woman from the back streets of Salford. You don't give a fuck about her. I don't mean you personally—*though that's true too*—I mean your class.'

Manning was looking interested now rather than angry. 'You really do think class determines everything, don't you?'

212

'Whether people are taken seriously or not? Yes.'

'But it's not a question of individuals, is it? All right, I don't know anything about women in the back streets of Salford. I don't pretend to. I don't want to. It doesn't mean I want to see them sent to prison on perjured evidence. Or anybody else for that matter.'

'Look, can we skip the moral outrage? When I came in here, you assumed I was after a cushy job. I didn't even get the first bloody sentence out. Are you seriously saying you would have made that assumption about a person of your own class?'

'Yes.'

'I don't believe you.'

'No, I would.'

'You get dozens of them, I suppose, begging for safe jobs?'

'Yes,' Manning said bleakly.

Prior looked at him. 'Golly. What fun.'

'Not really.'

They sat in silence, each registering the change in atmosphere, neither of them sure what it meant. 'You're right,' Manning said at last. 'It was an insulting assumption to make. I'm sorry.'

At that moment the door opened and Rivers came in.

'Charles, I—' He stopped abruptly when he saw Prior. 'Hello. I'm sorry, I didn't realize you had a visitor.' He smiled at Prior. 'I hope you're not tiring my patient?'

'He's wearing me out,' Prior snapped.

'What did you want to see me about?' Manning asked.

Rivers said, 'Nothing that can't wait.'

He went out and left them alone.

213

There was a short silence. 'I'm sorry too,' Prior said. 'You're right, of course. Class prejudice isn't any more admirable for being directed upwards.' Just more fucking justified. 'Do you think I should show that to her MP?'

'Oh, God, no, don't do that. Once they've denied it in the House, it'll be set in concrete. No, I'll have a word with Eddie Marsh. Only don't expect too much. I mean, it's perfectly clear even from your report she was sheltering deserters. *That*'s two years' hard labour. She's only done one.'

'She wasn't charged with that.'

Manning said, 'They're not going to let her out yet.'

'So what will they do?'

'Wait till the war's over. Let her go quietly.'

Prior shook his head. 'She won't last that long.'

*   *   *

That night, at nine o'clock, Prior went out for a drink. He came to himself in the small hours of the morning, fumbling to get his key into the lock. He had no recollection of the intervening five hours.

*   *   *

Rivers rubbed the corners of his eyes with an audible squidge. 'That's the longest, isn't it?'

'Yes. Just.'

'Any clues? I mean, had you been drinking?'

'Like a fish. I've still got the headache.'

Rivers replaced his glasses.

'One of the ... how shall I put it?' Prior breathed deeply. '*Inconveniences* of my present position is that

I do tend to end up with somebody else's hangover. Really rather frequently.'

'Not "somebody else's".'

Prior looked away. 'You've no idea how disgusting it is to examine one's own underpants for signs of "recent activity".'

Rivers looked down at the backs of his hands. 'I'm going to say something you probably won't like.'

The telephone began to ring in the next room.

Prior smiled. 'And I'm going to have to wait for it too.'

The call was from Captain Harris, telephoning to arrange the details of a flight they were to make tomorrow. Rivers jotted the time down, and took a few moments to collect his thoughts before returning to Prior.

Prior was standing by the mantelpiece, looking through a stack of field postcards. Well, that was all right, Rivers thought, closing the door. Field postcards contained *no* information about the sender except the fact that he was alive. Or had been at the time it was posted. 'His book's out, you know?' Prior said, holding a postcard up. 'Manning's got a copy.'

'Yes.'

Rivers sat down and waited for Prior to join him.

'I suppose this is the real challenge,' Prior said. 'For you. The ones who go back. They must be the ones you ask the questions about. I mean obviously all this face your emotions, own up to fear, let yourself feel grief ... works wonders. *Here.*' Prior came closer. Bent over him. 'But what about *there*? Do you think it helps *there*? Or do they just go mad quicker?'

'Nobody's ever done a follow-up. Electric shock treatment has a very high relapse rate. What mine is, I

215

just don't know. Obviously the patients who stay in touch are a self-selected group, and such evidence as they provide is anecdotal, and therefore almost useless.'

'My God, Rivers. You're a cold bugger.'

'You asked me a scientific question. You got a scientific answer.'

Prior sat down. 'Well dodged.'

Rivers took his glasses off. 'I'm really not trying to dodge anything. What I was going to say is I think perhaps you should think about coming into hospital. The—'

'No. You can't order me to.'

'No, that's true. I hoped you trusted me enough to take my advice.'

Prior shook his head. 'I just can't face it.'

Rivers nodded. 'Then we'll have to manage outside. Will you at least take some sick leave?'

Another jerk of the head. 'Not yet.'

*   *   *

Prior avoided thinking about the interview with Beattie Roper till he was crossing the prison yard. She'd been on hunger strike again, the wardress said, jangling her keys. And she'd had flu. No resistance. In sick bay all last week. He'd find her weak. The prison doctor had wanted to force-feed her, but the Home Office in its wisdom had decided that such methods were not to be used.

She was thinner than he remembered.

He stood just inside the door. She was lying on the bed, the light from the barred window casting a shadow across her face. The wardress stood against the wall, by the closed door.

'I need to see her alone.'

He expected an argument, but the wardress withdrew immediately.

'The voice of authority, Billy.'

Mucus clung to the corners of her lips when she spoke, as if her mouth were seldom opened.

He moved closer to the bed. 'I hear you've been ill.'

'Flu. Everybody's had it.'

He remained standing, as if he needed her permission to sit. She nodded towards the chair.

'I've been doing what I can,' he said. 'I'm afraid it doesn't amount to much. I was hoping Mac might be able to help, but—'

A chest movement that might have been a laugh. 'Not where he is. You know where they've sent him, don't you? Wandsworth.'

'You see, you did shelter deserters. They think you'd do it again.'

She hoisted herself up the bed. 'Bloody right 'n' all. I might look like a bloody scarecrow but *in here*'— she tapped the side of her head—'I'm the same.'

Outside the door the wardress coughed.

'You remember a lad called Brightmore?'

'No.'

'Go on, you do.'

He didn't, but he nodded.

'Lovely lad. They sent him to Cleethorpes. Twelve months' detention. 'Course he went on refusing to obey orders so he got twenty-eight days solitary and what they did they dug a hole, and it was flooded at the bottom and they put him in that. Couldn't sit down, couldn't lie down. Nothing to look at but clay walls. Somebody come to the top of the pit and told him his pals had been shipped off to France and shot, and if he didn't toe the line the same thing'd happen

217

to him. He thought his mind was going to give way. Then it started pissing down and the hole flooded and the soldiers who were guarding him were that sorry for him they took him out and let him sleep in a tent. They didn't half cop it when the CO found out. Next day he was back in the pit. If one of them soldiers hadn't given him a cigarette packet to write on, he'd've died in there. As it was they got a letter smuggled out—'

'And the officers who did it were court-martialled. Beattie, there's a million men in France up to their *dicks* in water. Who's going to get court-martialled for that?'

'Every bloody general in France if I had my way. You're not the only one who cares about them lads, what do you think this is about if it's not about *them*?' A pause. 'What I was *trying* to say was compared with a hole in the ground this is a fucking palace. And I'm lucky to be here.'

He looked at her, seeing her heart beat visibly under the thin shift. 'Have you seen Hettie?'

'Twice. Fact, she's due today. I gather we've got you to thank for that?'

'It's nothing.'

'No, it's not nothing, Billy. It's a helluva lot.' She hesitated. 'One thing I should tell you—I'm not saying *I* believe it, mind—our Hettie thinks it was a bit too much of a coincidence Mac getting picked up the way he was. She...' Beattie shook her head. 'She thinks you told them where to go.'

'That's not true.'

'No, I know it's not. It's all right, son, I'll talk to her.'

He put his hand on her bare arm and felt the bone. 'I've got to go,' he said.

218

He went to the door and knocked. 'I'll see you again,' he said, turning back to her.

She looked at him, but didn't answer.

Following the wardress across the yard, he was hardly aware of the massive walls with their rows of barred windows. He didn't see Hettie coming towards him, carrying a string bag, accompanied by another wardress, until they were almost level. Then he called her name and, reluctantly, she stopped.

The wardresses stood and watched.

Hettie came towards him. 'I'm surprised you've got the nerve to show your face.'

In spite of the words he bent towards her, expecting a greeting. She spat in his face.

The wardress grasped her arm. Wiping his cheek, slowly, not taking his eyes off Hettie, he said, 'It's all right. Let her go.'

Each with an escort, they moved off in opposite directions, toiling across the vast expanse of asphalt like beetles. Hettie turned before the building swallowed her and, in a voice that cracked with despair, she shouted, 'You bastard. *What about Mac?*'

Outside, Prior stared up at the building as the blood-and-bandages façade darkened in the light drizzle. Hettie's spit seemed to burn his skin. He raised his hand and wiped his cheek again, then turned and began walking rapidly towards the station. A refrain beat in his head. With every scuff and slurry of his boots on the gravel, he heard: the bastards have won. The bastards have won. The bastards...

219

PART THREE

CHAPTER SEVENTEEN

Rivers had cleared the afternoon to finish a report on military training for the Medical Research Council. For days now he'd had infantry-training manuals piled up on his desk, and he spent the first hour immersed in them, before going back to the last sentence he'd written.

> Many of those who pass unscathed through modern warfare do so because of the sluggishness of their imaginations, but if imagination is active and powerful, it is probably far better to allow it to play around the trials and dangers of warfare than to carry out a prolonged system of repression.

A tap on the door. Captain Bolden had attacked a nurse. Rivers did a disguised run along the corridor, saw the lift was in the basement and took the stairs three at a time. He found a group of nurses and two orderlies clustered round Bolden's door. Apparently he was refusing to let them in. From a babble of indignant chatter he managed to extract the information that Bolden had thrown a knife at Nurse Pratt. Not a very sharp knife, and it hadn't hit her, but still a knife. Nurse Pratt was one of the oldest and most experienced nurses on the ward. Unfortunately her experience had been gained on the locked wards of large Victorian lunatic asylums, where in any altercation between a member of staff and a patient the patient was automatically and indisputably wrong. One could see it so clearly from both points of view. Bolden resorted to violence quickly and easily, but then he had spent the past four years being trained to do exactly that. Nurse Pratt was being asked, for the first time in a working life of thirty years, to handle patients who were as accustomed to giving orders as to taking them.

Rivers handed his stick to an orderly and tapped on the door. 'Can I come in?'

A grunt, not definitely discouraging. Rivers opened the door and walked in. Bolden was standing by the window, still angry, sheepish, ashamed. Rivers, who was taller than Bolden, sat down, allowing Bolden to tower over him. Bolden was a very frightened man. 'Now then. What is it this time?'

'I told her the beef was inedible. She said I should think myself lucky to have it.'

'So you threw a knife?'

'I missed, didn't I?'

They talked for half an hour. Then Rivers stood up to go.

'I'll tell her I'm sorry,' Bolden said.

'Well, that would be a start. As long as you don't get irritated by her response.'

'I do try,' Bolden said, glowering at him.

'I know you do. And you're right about the beef. I couldn't eat it either.'

Rivers had a word with Sister Walters, hoping she could persuade Nurse Pratt to receive the apology graciously, and then thought he might as well have a word with Manning, since he was on the ward anyway. He set off towards Manning's room, then checked, remembering Manning was more likely to be on the neurological ward where he had struck up a firm friendship with Lucas and a couple of other chess fanatics. Manning was making good progress. He was almost ready to go home.

They *were* playing chess. Entirely silent and absorbed. He was standing beside them before they looked up.

Now that the discharge from Lucas's wound had stopped, his hair was growing back, and it covered the white scalp in a dark fuzz. Rather touching. He looked like some kind of incongruous, ungainly chick. 'How's it going?' Rivers asked, directing the question at Manning.

'I'm being trounced,' Manning said cheerfully. '19–17 in his favour.'

Lucas pointed to the board. '*20*–17,' he gurgled and grinned.

He certainly knew his numbers, Rivers thought, smiling as he walked away. In an unscreened bed further down the ward one of the pacifist orderlies was cleaning up an incontinent patient. Viggors's legs circled continuously in an involuntary stepping movement, and it really needed two people to change him, one to clean him up, the other to hold his legs. He was getting liquid excrement on his heels, and spreading it all over the bottom sheet. Martin, the orderly, was red-faced and flustered, Viggors white with rage and shame.

Rivers stopped by the bed. 'Have you heard of screens?' he asked.

Martin looked up. 'Wantage said he was going to get them.'

Wantage was lounging in the doorway of the staff-room, smoking a cigarette, clearly in no hurry to rescue a conchie orderly from an impossible position. His eyes widened. 'I was just—'

'I know exactly what you're doing. Screens round

that bed. *Now*. And get in there and help.' He called over his shoulder as he walked off. 'And put that cigarette out.'

Rivers was still shaking with anger when he got back to his desk. He made himself concentrate on the uncompleted sentence.

...if imagination is active and powerful, it is probably far better to allow it to play around the trials and dangers of warfare than to carry out a prolonged system of repression by which morbid energy may be stored so as to form a kind of dump ready to explode on the occurrence of some mental shock or bodily illness.

Exploding ammunition dumps had become a cliché, he supposed. Still, Bolden did a very good imitation of one. He wasn't doing too badly himself.

A tap on the door. '*No*,' Rivers said. 'Whatever it is, *no*.'

Miss Rogers smiled. 'There was a telephone call, while you were up on the ward. About a Captain Sassoon.'

Rivers was on his feet. 'What about him?'

'He's in the American Red Cross Hospital at Lancaster Gate with a head wound, they said. Would you go and see him?'

'How bad is it?'

'I don't know. They didn't say.'

*　　　*　　　*

In the taxi going to Lancaster Gate, Rivers's own words ran round and round in his head. *If imagination is active and powerful, it is probably far*

226

better to allow it to play around ... He looked out of the window, shaking his head as if to clear it. It wasn't even as if the advice were appropriate. He didn't need imagination, for Christ's sake. He was a neurologist. He knew exactly what shrapnel and bullets do to the brain.

The ward was a large room with ornate plasterwork, and tall windows opening on a view of Hyde Park. Two of the beds were empty. The others contained lightly wounded men, all looking reasonably cheerful. On a table in the centre of the ward a gramophone was playing a popular love song. *You made me love you.*

A nurse came bustling up to him. 'Who were you—'

'Captain Sassoon.'

'He's been moved to a single room. Didn't they tell you? Another two floors, I'm afraid, but I don't think he's allowed...' Her eye fell on his RAMC badges. 'Are you Dr Rivers?'

'Yes.'

'I think Dr Saunders is expecting you.'

Dr Saunders was waiting outside the door of his room, a small man with pouched cheeks, receding ginger hair and blue eyes ten years younger than the rest of his face. 'They sent you to the main ward,' he said, shaking hands.

Rivers followed him into the room. 'How bad is he?'

'The *wound*—not bad at all. In fact, I can show you.' He took an X-ray from a file on his desk and held it to the light. Sassoon's skull stared out at them. 'You see?' Saunders pointed to the intact bone. 'The bullet went right across there.' He indicated the place on his own head. 'What he's got is a rather neat

227

parting in the scalp.'

Rivers breathed out. 'Lucky man,' he said, as lightly as he could.

'I don't think *he* thinks so.'

They sat at opposite sides of the desk. 'I got a rather garbled message, I'm afraid,' Rivers said. 'I wasn't clear whether *you*'d asked me to see him or—'

'It was me. I saw your name on the file and I thought since you'd dealt with him before you might not mind seeing him again.' Saunders hesitated. 'I gather he was quite an unusual patient.'

Rivers looked down at his own signature at the end of the Craiglockhart report. 'He'd protested against the war. It was...' He took a deep breath. 'Convenient to say he'd broken down.'

'Convenient for whom?'

'The War Office. His friends. Ultimately for Sassoon.'

'And you persuaded him to go back?'

'He decided to go back. What's wrong?'

'He's ... He was all right when he arrived. Seemed to be. Then he had about eight visitors all at his bed at the one time. The hospital rules say *two*. But the nurse on duty was very young and apparently she felt she couldn't ask them to leave. She won't make *that* mistake again. Anyway, by the time they finally did leave he was in a terrible state. Very upset. And then he had a bad night—everybody had a bad night—and we decided to try a single room and no visitors.'

'Is he depressed?'

'No. Rather the reverse. Excitable. Can't stop talking. And now he's got nobody to talk *to*.'

Rivers smiled. 'Perhaps I'd better go along and provide an audience.'

Deep-carpeted corridors, gilt-framed pictures on the wall. He followed Saunders, remembering the corridors of Craiglockhart. Dark, draughty, smelling of cigarettes. But this was oppressive too, in its airless, cushioned luxury. He looked out of a window into a deep dark well between two buildings. A pigeon stood on a window-sill, one cracked pink foot curled round the edge of the abyss.

Saunders said, 'He seems to have a good patch in the afternoon. He might be asleep.' He opened the door softly and they went in.

Sassoon was asleep, his face pale and drawn beneath the cap of bandages. 'Shall I—' Saunders whispered, pointing to Sassoon.

'No, leave him. I'll wait.'

'I'll leave you to it, then,' Saunders said, and withdrew.

Rivers sat down by the bed. There was another bed in the room, but it was not made up. Flowers, fruit, chocolate, books were piled up on the bedside table. He did not intend to wake Siegfried, but gradually some recollection of whispered voices began to disturb the shuttered face. Siegfried moistened his lips and a second later opened his eyes. He focused them on Rivers, and for a moment there was joy, followed immediately by fear. He stretched out his hand and touched Rivers's sleeve. He's making sure I'm real, Rivers thought. A rather revealing gesture.

The hand slid down and touched the back of his hand. Siegfried swallowed, and started to sit up. 'I'm glad to see you,' he said, offering his hand. 'I thought for a mo—' He checked himself. 'They won't let you stay,' he said, smiling apologetically. 'I'm not

229

allowed to see anybody.'

'No, it's all right. They know I'm here.'

'I suppose it's because you're a doctor,' Siegfried said, settling back. 'They wouldn't let Lady Ottoline in, I heard Mrs Fisher talking to her in the corridor.'

His manner *was* different, Rivers thought. Talkative, restless, rapid speech, and he was looking directly at Rivers, something he almost never did, particularly at the beginning of a meeting. But he seemed perfectly rational, and the changes were within normal bounds. 'Why won't they let you see anybody?'

'It's because of Sunday, everybody came, Robert Ross, Meicklejon, Sitwell, oh God, Eddie Marsh, and they were all talking about the book and I got excited and—' He raised his hands to his forehead. 'FIZZLE. POP. I had a bad night, kept everybody awake, and they put me in here.'

'How was *last* night?'

Siegfried pulled a face. 'Bad. I keep thinking how big it is, the *war*, and how impossible it is to write about, and how useless it is to get angry, that's such a trivial reaction, it doesn't, it just doesn't do any sort of justice to the to the to the tragedy, you know you spend your entire life out there obsessed with this tiny little sector of the Front, I mean *thirty yards* of sandbags, that's the war, you've no conception of anything else, and now I think I can see all of it, vast armies, flares going up, *millions* of people, *millions, millions.*'

Rivers waited. 'You say you see it?'

'Oh, yes, it just unfolds.' A circling movement of his arms. 'And it's marvellous in a way, but it's terrible too and I get so frightened because you'd have to be Tolstoy.' He gripped Rivers's hand. 'I've

230

got to see Ross, I don't care about the others, but you've got to make them let me see him, he looks awful, that *bloody bloody bloody* trial. Do you know Lord Alfred Douglas called him "the leader of all the sodomites in London"? Only he said it in the witness-box, so Robbie can't sue.'

'Just as well, perhaps.'

'*And* he's been asked to resign from all his committees, I mean he offered, but it was accepted with alacrity. *I've got to see him.* Apart from anything else he brings me the reviews.'

'They're good, aren't they? I've been looking out for them.'

'*Most* of them.'

Rivers smiled. 'You can't write a controversial book *and* expect universal praise, Siegfried.'

'Can't I?'

They laughed, and for a moment everything seemed normal. Then Siegfried's face darkened. 'Do you know we actually sat in dug-outs in France and talked about that trial? The papers were full of it, I think it was the one thing that could have made me *glad* I was out there, I mean, for God's sake, the Germans on the Marne, five thousand prisoners taken and all you read in the papers is who's going to bed with whom and are they being blackmailed? *God.*'

'I'll see what I can do about Ross.'

'Do you think they'll listen to you?'

Rivers hesitated. 'I think they might.' Obviously Siegfried didn't know he'd been called in professionally. 'How's the head?'

A spasm of contempt. 'It's a scratch. I should never've let them send me back, do you know that's the last thing I said to my servant, "I'm coming

231

back." "Back in three weeks," I yelled at him as I was being driven away. And then I let myself be corrupted.'

'*Corrupted?* That's a harsh word, isn't it?'

'I should've refused to come back.'

'Siegfried, nobody would have listened to you if you had. Head injuries have to be taken seriously.'

'But don't you see, the timing was perfect? Did you see my poem in the *Nation*? "I Stood with the Dead". Well, there you are. Or there I was rather, perched on the top-most bough, carolling away. BANG! Oops! Sorry. Missed.'

'I'm glad it did.'

A bleak sideways glance from Siegfried. 'I'm not.' Silence.

'I feel amputated. I don't belong here. I keep looking at all this . . .' The waving hand took in fruit, flowers, chocolates. 'I just wish I could parcel it up and send it out to them. I did manage to send them a gramophone. Then I got . . . ill.'

'You know, what I don't understand,' Rivers said, 'is how you could possibly have been wounded there.'

'I was in No Man's Land.'

'No, I meant *under the helmet.*'

'I'd taken it off.' An awkward pause. 'We'd been out to lob some hand-grenades at a machine-gun, two of us, they were getting cheeky, you see, they'd brought it too far forward, and so we . . .' He smiled faintly. 'Re-established dominance. Anyway, we threw the grenades, I don't think we hit anybody—by which I mean there were no screams—and then we set off back and by this time it was getting light, and I was so *happy.*' His face blazed with exultation. 'Oh, God, Rivers, you wouldn't *believe* how happy. And I stood up and took the helmet off, and I turned to

232

look at the German lines. And that's when the bullet got me.'

Rivers was so angry he knew he had to get away. He walked across to the window and stared, unseeing, at the road, the railings, the distant glitter of the Serpentine under the summer sun. He had been lying to himself, he thought, pretending this was merely one more crisis in a busy working day. This anger stripped all pretence away from him. '*Why?*' he said, turning back to Siegfried.

'I wanted to see them.'

'You mean you wanted to get killed.'

'No.'

'You stand up in the middle of No Man's Land, in the morning, the sun rising, you take off your helmet, you turn to face the German lines, and you tell me you weren't trying to get killed.'

Siegfried shook his head. 'I've told you, I was happy.'

Rivers took a deep breath. He walked back to the bed, schooling himself to a display of professional gentleness. 'You were happy?'

'Yes, I was happy most of the time, I suppose mainly because I've succeeded in cutting off the part of me that hates it.' A faint smile. 'Except when writing poems for the *Nation*. I was ... There's a book you ought to read. I'll try to dig it out, it says something to the effect that a man who makes up his mind to die takes leave of a good many things, and is, in some sense, *dead already*. Well, I had made up my mind to die. What other solution was there for me? But making up your mind to die isn't the same as trying to get killed. Not that it made much difference.' He touched the bandage tentatively. 'I must say, I thought the standard of British sniping

233

was higher than this.'

'*British* sniping?'

'Yes, didn't they tell you? My own NCO. Mistook me for the German army, rushed out into No Man's Land shouting, "Come on, you fuckers," and shot me.' He laughed. 'God, I've never seen a man look so horrified.'

Rivers sat down by the bed. 'You'll never be closer.'

'I've *been* closer. Shell landed a foot away. Literally. Didn't explode.' Siegfried twitched suddenly, a movement Rivers had seen many thousands of times in other patients, too often surely for it to be shocking.

'You can't get shell-shock, can you?' Siegfried asked. 'From a shell that doesn't explode?'

Rivers looked down at his hands. 'I think that one probably did a fair amount of damage.'

Siegfried looked towards the window. 'You know, they're going on a raid soon, Jowett, five or six of the others, *my* men, Rivers, *my men*, men *I* trained and I'm not going to be there when they come back.'

'They're not *your* men now, Siegfried. They're somebody else's men. You've got to let go.'

'I can't.'

CHAPTER EIGHTEEN

Rivers had been invited to dinner with the Heads, and arrived to find the Haddons and Grafton Elliot Smith already there. No opportunity for private conversation with Henry or Ruth presented itself until the end of the evening, when Rivers contrived that he should be the last to leave. It was not unusual after a dinner with the Heads for him to stay behind enjoying their particular brand of unmalicious gossip, well aware that his own foibles and frailties would be dissected as soon as he left, and sure enough of their love for him not to mind.

Not that he was inclined to gossip tonight. As soon as they were alone, he told them about Siegfried, clarifying his own perception of the situation as he spoke.

'Excited, you say?' Henry asked.

'Yes.'

'Manic?'

'Oh, no, nowhere near. Though there was a hint of ... elation, I suppose, once or twice, particularly when he was talking about his feelings immediately before he was wounded. And the afternoons *are* his best time. Apparently the nights are bad. I've promised I'll go back. In fact, I ought to be going.' He stood up. 'I'm not *worried*. He'll be all right.'

'Does he regret going back?' Ruth asked.

'I don't know,' Rivers said. 'I haven't asked.'

After seeing Rivers off, Head came back into the living-room to find Ruth gazing reflectively into the fire.

'No, well, he wouldn't, would he?' she said, looking up.

'He might think there wasn't much point,' Henry said, sitting down on the other side of the fire.

A long, companionable silence. They were too replete with company and conversation to want to talk much, too comfortable to make the move for bed.

'He came to see me last year, you know,' Henry said. 'Almost a sort of consultation. He got himself into quite a state over Sassoon.'

'Yes, I know. I didn't realize he'd talked to you about it.'

Head hesitated. 'I think he suddenly realized he was using ... his professional skills, if you like, to defuse a situation that wasn't ... *medical*. There's really nothing else you can do if you're a doctor in the army in wartime. There's always the possibility of conflict between what the army needs and what the patient needs, but with Sassoon it was ... very sharp. I told him basically not to be silly.'

Ruth gave a surprised laugh. 'Poor Will.'

'No, I meant it.'

'I'm sure you did, but you wouldn't have said it to a patient.'

'I told him Sassoon was capable of making up his own mind, and that his influence probably wasn't as great as he thought it was. I thought he was being ... I don't know. Not vain—'

'Over-scrupulous?'

'Frankly, I thought he was being neurotic. But I've seen him with a lot of patients since then, and I'm not so sure. You know how you get out of date with people if you haven't seen them for a while? I think I

236

was out of date. Something happened to him in Scotland. Somehow or other he acquired this enormous power over young men, people generally perhaps, but particularly young men. It really is amazing, they'll do anything for him. Even get better.'

'Even go back to France?'

'Yes, I think so.'

Ruth shrugged slightly. 'I don't see the change. But then I suspect he's always shown a slightly different side to me anyway.' She smiled. 'I'm very fond of him, but—'

'He is of you.'

'I sometimes wonder why we even *like* each other, you know. When you think how it started. You going to Cambridge every weekend so he could stick pins in your arm. I never had a weekend with you the whole of the first year we were married.'

'It wasn't as bad as that. Anyway, you got on all right.'

'Do you think he still thinks Sassoon went back because of him?'

Head hesitated. 'I think he knows the extent of his influence.'

'Hmm,' Ruth said. 'Do you think he's in love with him?'

'He's a patient.'

Ruth smiled and shook her head. 'That's not an answer.'

Head looked at her. 'Yes, it is. It has to be.'

*   *   *

Siegfried was sitting up in bed, pyjama jacket off, face and chest gleaming with sweat. 'Is it hot, Rivers?' he

237

asked, as if their conversation had never been interrupted. 'Or is it just me?'

'Warm.'

'I'm *boiling*. I've been sitting here simmering like a kettle.'

Rivers sat down beside the bed.

'I've been writing to Graves. In verse. Do you want to read it?'

Rivers took the notepad and found himself reading an account of his visit that afternoon. The pain was so intense that for a moment he had to keep quite still. 'Is that how you see me?' he said at last. 'Somebody who's going to make you go back to France till you break down altogether?'

'Yes,' Sassoon said cheerfully. 'But that's all right, I want you to. You're my external conscience, Rivers, my father confessor. You can't let me down now, you've *got* to make me go back.'

Rivers read the poem again. 'You shouldn't send this.'

'Why not? It took me ages. Oh, I know what it is, you don't think I should say all that about the lovely soldier lads. Well, they are lovely. You think Graves is going to be shocked. Frankly, Rivers, I don't care; shocking Graves is one of my few remaining pleasures. I wrote to him—not to shock him—just an ordinary letter, only I made the mistake of talking with enthusiasm about training in one paragraph, and in the next paragraph I said what a bloody awful business the war was, and what do I get back? A lecture on consistency, oh, and some very pathetic reproaches about not terrifying your friends by pretending to be mad, I thought that was particularly rich. I've done *one* totally consistent, totally *sane* thing in my life, and that was to protest against the war. And who stopped me?'

Graves, Rivers thought. But not only Graves. It was true, he saw it now, perhaps more clearly than he had at the time, that whatever the *public* meaning of Siegfried's protest, its private meaning was derived from a striving for consistency, for singleness of being in a man whose internal divisions had been dangerously deepened by the war.

'You mustn't blame Graves. He did what—'

'I don't blame him, I'm just not prepared to be lectured by him. I survive out there by being two people, sometimes I even manage to be both of them in one evening. You know, I'll be sitting with Stiffy and Jowett—*Jowett is beautiful*—and I'll start talking about wanting to go and fight, and I'll get them all fired up and banging the table and saying, yes, enough of training, time to get stuck in to the real thing. And then I leave them and go to my room and think how young they are. Nineteen, Rivers. *Nineteen*. And they've no bloody idea. Oh, God, I hope they live.'

Suddenly, he started to cry. Wiping the back of his hand across his mouth, he sniffed and said, 'Sorry.'

'That's all right.'

'You know what finally put the kibosh on my Jekyll and Hyde performance, no, listen, this is funny. I got a new second in command. Pinto. Absolute jewel. But the first time I met him he was reading *Counter-Attack*, and he looked up and said, "Are you the same Sassoon?" My God, Rivers, what a bloody question. But of course I said, "Yes." What else could I say? And yet do you know I think that's when things started to unravel.' A marked change in tone. 'It was when I faced up to how bloody stupid it was.'

239

Rivers looked puzzled. 'What was?'

'My pathetic little formula for getting myself back to France.' He adopted a mincing, effeminate tone. '"I'm not going back to kill people. I'm only going back to look after some men."' His own voice. 'Why didn't you kick me in the head, Rivers? Why didn't you put me out of my misery?'

Rivers made himself answer. 'Because I was afraid if you started thinking about that, you wouldn't go back at all.'

He might as well not have spoken. 'You've only got to read the training manual. "A commander must demand the impossible and not think of sparing his men. Those who fall out must be left behind and must no more stop the pursuit than casualties stopped the assault." That's it. Expendable, interchangeable units. That's what I went back to "*look after*".' A pause. 'All I wanted was to see them through their first tour of duty and I couldn't even do that.'

'Pinto's there,' Rivers said tentatively.

'Oh, yes, and he's good. He's really good.'

Siegfried's face and neck were running with sweat. 'Shall I open the window?' Rivers asked.

'Please. They keep shutting it, I don't know why.'

Rivers went to open the window. Behind him, Siegfried said, 'I'm sorry you don't like my lovely soldier lads.'

'I didn't say I didn't *like* them. I said you shouldn't *send* them.'

'There was one in particular.'

'Jowett,' said Rivers.

'I wrote a poem about Jowett. Not that he'll ever know. He was asleep. He looked as if he were dead.' A silence. 'It's odd, isn't it, how one can feel fatherly towards somebody, I mean, *genuinely* fatherly, not exploiting the situation or even being tempted to, and yet there's this other current. And I don't think one invalidates the other. I think it's perfectly possible for them both to be genuine.'

'Yes,' said Rivers, with the merest hint of dryness, 'I imagine so.' He came back to the bed. 'You say things "started to unravel"?'

'Yes, because I'd always coped with the situation by blocking out the killing side, cutting it off, and then suddenly one's brought face to face with the fact that, no, actually there's only one person there and that person is a potential killer of Huns. That's what our CO used to call us. It had a very strange effect. I mean, I went out on patrol, that sort of thing, but I've always done that, I've never been able to sit in a trench, it's not courage, I just can't do it, but this time it was different because I wasn't going out to kill or even to test my nerve, though that did come into it. *I just wanted to see.* I wanted to see the other side. I used to spend a lot of time looking through the periscope. It was a cornfield. Farmland. Sometimes you'd see a column of smoke coming up from the German lines, but quite often you'd see nothing.' A pause, then he said casually, 'I went across once. Dropped down into the trench and walked along, and there were four Germans standing by a machine-gun. One of them turned round and saw me.'

'What happened?'

'Nothing. We just looked at each other. Then he decided he ought to tell his friends. And I decided it was time to leave.'

A tense silence.

'I suppose I should have killed him,' Siegfried said.

'He should certainly have killed you.'

'He had the excuse of surprise. You know, Rivers,

241

it's no good encouraging people to know themselves and ... face up to their emotions, because out there they're better off not having any. If people are going to have to kill, they need to be brought up to expect to have to do it. They need to be trained *not to care* because if you don't ...' Siegfried gripped Rivers's hand so tightly that his face clenched with the effort of concealing his pain. 'It's too cruel.'

Rivers had been with Siegfried for over an hour and so far nothing had been said that might not equally well have been dealt with at some more convenient time of day. But now, his excitement began to increase, words tripped him up, his mind stumbled along in the wake of his ideas, trying desperately to catch up. He spoke of the vastness of the war, of the impossibility of one mind encompassing it all. Again and again he spoke of the need to train boys to kill; from earliest childhood, he said, they must be taught to expect nothing else and they must never never be allowed to question what lies ahead. All this was mixed in with his anxieties about the raid Jowett and the others were going on. He spoke so vividly and with so much detail that at times he clearly believed himself to be in France.

There was no point arguing with any of this. It took Rivers three hours to calm him down and get him to sleep. Even after his breathing had become steady, Rivers went on sitting by the bed, afraid to move in case the withdrawal of his hand should cause him to wake. Long hairs on the back of Siegfried's forearm caught the light. Rivers looked at them, too exhausted to think clearly, remembering the experiments he and Head had done on the pilomotor reflex. Head's hairs had become erect every time he read a particular poem. The holy shiver, as the

Germans call it. For Head it was awakened by poetry; for Rivers, more than once, it had been the beauty of a scientific hypothesis, one that brought into unexpected harmony a whole range of disparate facts. What had intrigued Rivers most was that human beings should respond to the highest mental and spiritual achievements of their culture with the same reflex that raises the hairs on a dog's back. The epicritic grounded in the protopathic, the ultimate expression of the unity we persist in regarding as the condition of perfect health. Though why we think of it like that, God knows, since most of us survive by cultivating internal divisions.

Siegfried was now deeply asleep. Cautiously, Rivers withdrew his hand, flexing the fingers. It had grown colder and Siegfried had fallen asleep outside the covers. Rivers went to shut the window, and stood for a moment attempting to arrange the story he'd been told into a coherent pattern, but that wasn't possible, though the outline was clear enough. Siegfried had always coped with the war by being two people: the anti-war poet and pacifist; the bloodthirsty, efficient company commander. The dissociation couldn't be called pathological, since experience gained in one state was available to the other. Not just *available*: it was the serving officer's experience that furnished the raw material, the ammunition, if you liked, for the poems. More importantly, and perhaps more ambiguously, that experience of bloodshed supplied the moral authority for the pacifist's protest: a *soldier's* declaration. No wonder Pinto's innocent question had precipitated something of a crisis.

Though he would have broken down anyway this time, Rivers thought. He had gone back hating the

243

war, turning his face away from the reality of killing and maiming, and as soon as that reality was borne in upon him, he had found the situation unbearable. All of which might have been foreseen. Had been foreseen.

Night had turned the window into a black mirror. His face floated there, and behind it, Siegfried and the rumpled bed. If Siegfried's attempt at dissociation had failed, so had his own. He was finding it difficult to be both involved and objective, to turn steadily on Siegfried both sides of medicine's split face. But that was *his* problem. Siegfried need never be aware of it.

It was still dark. A light wind stirred the black trees in the park. He took his boots off and climbed on to the other bed, not expecting to be able to sleep, but thinking that at least he might rest. He closed his eyes. At first his thoughts whirred on, almost as active as Siegfried's and not much more coherent. For some reason the situation reminded him of sleeping on board the deck of a tramp steamer travelling between the islands of Melanesia. There, one slept in a covered cabin on deck, on a bench that left vertical stripes down one's back, surrounded by fellow passengers, and what a motley assemblage they were. He remembered a particular voyage when one of his companions had been a young Anglican priest, so determined to observe holy modesty in these difficult conditions that he'd washed the lower part of his body underneath the skirt of his cassock, while Rivers stripped off and had buckets of water thrown over him by the sailors who came up to swab the deck.

His other companion on that trip had been a trader who rejoiced in the name of Seamus O'Dowd, though he had no trace of an Irish accent. O'Dowd drank. In the smoky saloon after dinner, belching gin and dental decay into Rivers's face, he had boasted of his exploits as a blackbirder, for he'd started life kidnapping natives to work on the Queensland plantations. Now he simply cheated them. His most recent coup had been to convince them that the great Queen (nobody in the Condominion dared tell the natives Victoria was dead) found their genitals disgusting, and could not sleep easy in her bed at Windsor until they were covered by the long johns that Seamus had inadvertently bought as part of a job lot while even more drunk than usual.

They wore them on their heads, Rivers remembered. It had been a feature of the island in that first autumn of the war, naked young men wearing long johns elaborately folded on their heads. They looked beautiful. Meanwhile, in England, other young men had been rushing to don a less flattering garb.

Drifting between sleep and waking, Rivers remembered the smells of oil and copra, the cacophony of snores and whistles from the sleepers crammed into the small cabin on deck, the vibration of the engine that seemed to get into one's teeth, the strange, brilliant, ferocious southern stars. He couldn't for the life of him think what was producing this flood of nostalgia. Perhaps it was his own experience of duality that formed the link, for certainly in the years before the war he had experienced a splitting of personality as profound as any suffered by Siegfried. It had been not merely a matter of living two different lives, divided between the dons of Cambridge and the missionaries and headhunters of Melanesia, but of being a different person in the two places. It was his Melanesian self he

245

preferred, but his attempts to integrate that self into his way of life in England had produced nothing but frustration and misery. Perhaps, contrary to what was usually supposed, duality was the stable state; the attempt at integration, dangerous. Certainly Siegfried had found it so.

He raised himself on his elbow and looked at Siegfried, who was sleeping with his face turned to the window. Perhaps the burst of nostalgia was caused by nothing more mysterious than this: the attempt to sleep in a room where another person's breathing was audible. Sleeping in the same room as another person belonged with his Melanesian self. In England it simply didn't happen. But it was restful, the rise and fall of breath, like the wash of waves round the prow of the boat, and gradually, as the light thinned, he drifted off to sleep.

He woke to find Siegfried kneeling by his bed. The window was open, the curtains lifting in the breeze. A trickle of bird-song came into the room.

In a half-embarrassed way, Siegfried said, 'I seem to have talked an awful lot of rubbish last night.' He looked cold and exhausted, but calm. 'I suppose I had a fever?'

Rivers didn't reply.

'Anyway, I'm all right now.' Diffidently, he touched Rivers's sleeve. 'I don't know what I'd do without you.'

CHAPTER NINETEEN

A week later Rivers was sitting in his armchair in front of the fire, feeling physically tired in an almost sensuous way. This was a rare feeling with him, since most days produced a grating emotional exhaustion which was certainly not conducive to sleep. But he had been flying, which always tired him out physically, and he'd seen Siegfried a lot calmer and happier than he had recently been, though still very far from well.

Prior was the mystery. Prior had missed an appointment, something he'd never done before, and Rivers wasn't sure what he should do about it. There was little he *could* do except drop Prior a line expressing his continued willingness to help, but there had been some suggestion that Prior worried about the degree of his dependence. If he had decided to break off the association there was nothing Rivers could—or should—do about it. He wouldn't come now. He was over two hours late.

Rivers was just thinking he really must make the effort to do something when there was a tap on the door, and the maid came in. 'There's a Mr Prior to see you,' she said, sounding doubtful, for it was very late. 'Shall I tell him—'

'No, no. Ask him to come up.'

He felt very unfit to cope with this, whatever it was, but he buttoned his tunic and looked vaguely around for his boots. Prior seemed to be climbing the stairs very quickly, an easy, light tread quite unlike his usual step. His asthma had been very bad on his last visit. He had paused several times on the final flight of stairs and even then had entered the room almost too breathless to speak. The maid must have misheard the name, that or—

Prior came into the room, pausing just inside the door to look round.

'Are you all right?' Rivers asked.

'Yes. Fine.' He looked at the clock and seemed to become aware that the lateness of the hour required some explanation. 'I had to see you.'

Rivers waved him to a chair and went to close the door.

'Well,' he said, when Prior was settled. 'Your chest's a lot better.'

Prior breathed in. Testing. He looked hard at Rivers and nodded.

'You were going to go to the prison last time we spoke,' Rivers said. 'To see Mrs Roper. Did you go?'

Prior was shaking his head, though not, Rivers thought, in answer to the question. At last he said, in a markedly sibilant voice, 'I didn't think you would have *pretended*.'

'Pretended what?' Rivers asked. He waited, then prompted gently, 'What am I pretending?'

'That we've met before.'

Momentarily, Rivers closed his eyes. When he opened them again Prior was grinning. 'I thought of saying, "Dr Rivers, I presume?"'

'If we haven't met before, how did you know me?'

'I sit in.' Prior spread his hands. '*I sit in*. Well, let's face it, there's not a lot of choice, is there? I don't know how you put up with him. *I* couldn't. Are you *sure* it's a good idea to let him get away with it?'

'With what?'

'With being so cheeky.'

'The sick have a certain licence,' Rivers said dryly.

'Oh, and he *is* sick, isn't he?' Prior said earnestly, leaning forward. 'Do you know, I honestly believe he's getting *worse*?'

A long silence. Rivers clasped his hands under his chin. 'Do you think you could manage to say "I"?'

''Fraid not. No.'

The antagonism was unmistakable. Rivers was aware of having seen Prior in this mood before, in the early weeks at Craiglockhart. Exactly this. The same incongruous mixture of effeminacy and menace.

'You know, it's really quite simple,' Prior went on. 'Either we can sit here and have a totally barren argument about which pronouns we're going to use, or we can talk. I think it's more important to talk.'

'I agree.'

'Good. Do you mind if I smoke?'

'I never do mind, do I?'

Prior was patting his tunic pockets. 'I'll *kill* him,' he said smiling. 'Ah, no, it's all right.' He held up a packet of cigars. 'I've got him trained. He used to throw them away.'

'What would you like to talk about?'

A broad smile. 'I thought *you* might have some ideas.'

'You say you "sit in". Does that mean you know everything he knows?'

'Yes. But he doesn't know anything I know. Only it's ... it's not quite as neat as that. Sometimes I see things he can't see, even when he's there.'

'Things he doesn't notice?'

'Doesn't want to notice. Like for example he hates Spragge. I mean, he has perfectly good reasons for *disliking* him, but what he feels goes a long way

249

beyond that. And he knows that, and he doesn't know why, even though it's staring him in the face. Literally. Spragge's like his father.'

'Like his own—like Spragge's father?'

'No. Well, he may be. How would *I* know? Like *Billy's* father. I mean, it's a really striking resemblance, and he just doesn't see it.' Prior paused, puzzled by some quality in Rivers's silence. 'You see what I mean?'

'*His* father?'

'Yes.'

'Are you really saying he's not *your* father?'

'Of course he isn't. How could he be?'

'How could he not be? In the end one body begets another.'

Prior's expression hardened. 'I was born two years ago. In a shell-hole in France. I have no father.'

Rivers felt he needed time to think. A week would have been about right. He said, 'I met Mr Prior at Craiglockhart.'

'Yes, I know.'

'He mentioned hitting Billy. Was that a frequent occurrence?'

'No. Oddly enough.'

'How do you know?'

'I've told you. I know everything he knows.'

'So you have access to his memories?'

'Yes.'

'And you also have your own memories.'

'That's right.'

'Why "oddly"?'

A blank look.

'You said it was odd his father didn't beat him.'

'Just because when you look at the relationship you think there must have been something like that.

250

But there wasn't. Once his parents were having a row and he went downstairs and tried to get between them, and his father picked him up and threw him on the sofa. Only, being a bit the worse for wear, he missed the sofa and hit the wall.' Prior laughed. 'He never went down again.'

'So he just used to lie in bed and listen.'

'No, he used to get up and sit on the stairs.'

'What was he feeling?'

'I'm not good on feelings, Rivers. You'd better ask him.'

'Does that mean you don't know what he was feeling?'

'Angry. He used to do this.' Prior banged his clenched fist against the palm of the other hand. 'PIG PIG PIG PIG. And then he'd get frightened, I suppose he was frightened that if he got too angry he'd go downstairs. So he fixed his eyes on the barometer and blotted everything out.'

'Then what happened?'

'Nothing. He wasn't there.'

'Who was there?'

Prior shrugged his shoulders. 'I don't know. Somebody who didn't care.'

'Not you?'

'No, I *told* you—'

'You were born in a shell-hole.' A pause. 'Can you tell me about it?'

An elaborate shrug. 'There isn't much to tell. He was wounded. Not badly, but it hurt. He knew he had to go on. And he couldn't. So I came.'

Again that elusive impression of childishness. 'Why were *you* able to go on when he couldn't?'

'I'm better at it.'

'Better at...?'

'Fighting.'

'*Why* are you better?'

'Oh, for God's sake—'

'No, it *isn't* a stupid question. You're not taller, you're not stronger, you're not faster ... you're not better trained. How could you be? So why are you better?'

'I'm not frightened.'

'Everybody's frightened sometimes.'

'I'm not. And I don't feel pain.'

'I see. So you didn't feel the wound?'

'No.' Prior looked at Rivers, narrowing his eyes. 'You don't believe a bloody word of this, do you?'

Rivers couldn't bring himself to reply.

'*Look.*' Prior drew strongly on his cigar, until the tip glowed red, then, almost casually, stubbed it out in the palm of his left hand. He leant towards Rivers, smiling. 'This isn't acting, Rivers. Watch the pupils,' he said, pulling down the lid of one eye.

The room filled with the smell of burning skin.

'And now you can have your little blue-eyed boy back.'

A withdrawn, almost drugged look, like extreme shock or the beginning of orgasm. Then, abruptly, the features convulsed with pain, and Prior, teeth chattering uncontrollably, raised his shaking hand and rocked it against his chest.

* * *

'I haven't got any pain-killers,' Rivers said.'You'd better drink this.'

Prior took the brandy and held out his other hand for Rivers to complete the dressing. 'Aren't you going to tell me what happened?' he said.

252

'You burnt yourself.'

'Why?'

Rivers sighed. 'It was a dramatic gesture that went wrong.'

He'd decided not to tell Prior about the loss of normal sensation. It was a common symptom of hysterical disorders, but knowledge of it would only serve to reinforce Prior's belief that the alternating state of consciousness was a monster with whom he could have nothing in common.

'What was he like?' Prior asked.

'What were you like? Bloody-minded.'

'Violent?'

'Well, yes. *Obviously*,' Rivers said, indicating the burn.

'No, I meant—'

'Did you take a swing at me? No.' Rivers smiled. 'Sorry.'

'You make it sound as if it's something I *want*.'

Rivers was thinking deeply. 'I think that's true,' he said, knotting the ends of the bandage.

'*No*. Why should I want it? It's creating bloody havoc.'

'You know, Billy, the really interesting thing about tonight is that you turned up *in the other state*. I mean that while in the other state you still wanted to keep the appointment.'

'What did you call me?'

'Billy. Do you mind? I—'

'No, it's just that it's the first time. Did you know that? Sassoon was Siegfried. Anderson was Ralph. I noticed the other day you called Manning Charles. I was always "Prior". In moments of exasperation I was *Mister* Prior.'

'I'm sorry, I—' Oh, God, Rivers thought. Prior

253

was incapable of interpreting that as anything other than snobbery. And perhaps it had been. Partly. Though it had been more to do with his habit of sneering suggestiveness. 'I'd no idea you minded.'

'No, well, you're not very perceptive, are you? Anyway, it doesn't matter.' He stood up. 'I'd better be off.'

'You can't go now, the trains have stopped. And, in any case, you're in no state to be on your own. You'd better sleep here.'

Prior hesitated. 'All right.'

'I'll make up the bed.'

Rivers saw Prior settled for the night, then went to his own room, telling himself it would be fatal, at this late hour, to attempt any assessment of Prior's situation. That must wait till morning. But the effort of *not* thinking about Prior proved almost equally disastrous, for he drifted off into a half-dreaming state, the only condition, apart from feverish illness, in which he had normal powers of visualization. He tossed and turned, scarcely aware of his surroundings, while persistent images floated before him. France. Craters, a waste of mud, splintered trees. Once he woke and lay looking into the darkness, faintly amused that his identification with his patients should have reached the point where he dreamt *their* dreams rather than his own. He heard the church bell chime three, and then sank back into his half-sleep. This was a dreadful place. Nothing human could live here. Nothing human did. He was entirely alone, until, with a puckering of the surface, a belch of foul vapours, the mud began to move, to gather itself together, to rise and stand before him in the shape of a man. A man who turned and began striding towards England. He tried to call out, no, not that way, and the movement of his lips half woke him. But he sank down again, and again the mud gathered itself into the shape of a man, faster and faster until it seemed the whole night was full of such creatures, creatures composed of Flanders mud and nothing else, moving their grotesque limbs in the direction of home.

Sunlight was streaming into the room. Rivers lay thinking about the dream, then switched his thoughts to yesterday evening. In the fugue state (though it was more than that) Prior had claimed to feel no pain and no fear, to have been born in a shell-hole, to have no father. Presumably *no* relationships that pre-dated that abnormal birth.

To feel no pain and no fear in a situation that seemed to call for both was not impossible, or even abnormal. He'd been in such a state himself, once, while on his way to the Torres Straits, suffering from severe sunburn, severe enough to have burnt the skin on his legs black. He'd lain on the deck of a ketch, rolling from side to side as waves broke across the ship, in constant pain from the salt water that soaked into his burns, vomiting helplessly, unable to stand or even sit up. Then the ketch had dragged her anchor and they'd been in imminent danger of shipwreck, and for the whole of that time he'd moved freely, he hadn't vomited, he'd felt no pain and no fear. He had simply performed coolly and calmly the actions needed to avert danger, as they all had. After they'd landed, his legs had hurt like hell and he'd once more been unable to walk. He'd been carried up from the beach on a litter, and had spent the first few days seeing patients from his sick bed, shuffling from the patient to the dispensing cupboard and back again on his bottom. He smiled to himself, thinking Prior would like that story. Physician, heal thyself.

Other people had had similar experiences. Men had escaped from danger before now by running on broken legs. But Prior had created a state whose freedom from fear and pain was persistent, encapsulated, inaccessible to normal consciousness. Almost as if his mind had created a warrior double, a creature formed out of Flanders clay, as his dream had suggested. And he had brought it home with him.

Rivers, thinking over the previous evening, found that he retained one very powerful impression. In Prior's speech and behaviour there had been a persistent element of childishness. He'd said, *He was wounded. Not badly, but it hurt. He knew he had to go on. And he couldn't. So I came.* So I came. The simplicity of it. As if one were talking to a child who still believed in magic. And on the stairs. *What happened then? Nothing. He wasn't there.* It was like a toddler who believes himself to be invisible because he's closed his eyes. And that extraordinary claim: *I have no father.* Surely behind the adult voice, there was another, shrill, defiant, saying, *He's not my Dad?* At any rate it was a starting-point. He could think of no other.

*　　　*　　　*

Rivers had not thought Prior would appear for breakfast, but no sooner had he sat down himself than the door opened and Prior came in, looking dejected, and in obvious pain. 'How did you sleep?' Rivers asked.

'All right. Well, I got a couple of hours.'

'I've asked the girl to bring us some more.'

'It doesn't matter, I'm not hungry.'

'Well, at least have some coffee. You ought to have something.'

'Yes, thanks, but then I must be going.'

'I'd rather you stayed. For a few days. Until things are easier.'

'I wouldn't dream of imposing on you.'

'You wouldn't be "imposing".'

'All right,' Prior said at last. 'Thank you.'

The maid arrived with a second tray. Rivers was amused to see Prior devour the food with single-minded concentration, while he sipped milky coffee and read *The Times*. 'I've got an hour before I need go to the hospital,' he said, when Prior had finished. 'Do you feel well enough?'

When they were settled in chairs beside the desk, Rivers said, 'I'd like to go back quite a long way.'

Prior nodded. He looked too exhausted to be doing this.

'Do you remember the house you lived in when you were five?'

A faint smile. 'Yes.'

'Do you remember the top of the stairs?'

'Yes. It's no great feat, Rivers. Most people can.'

Rivers smiled. 'I walked into that one, didn't I? Do you remember what was there?'

'Bedrooms.'

'No, I mean on the landing.'

'Nothing, there wasn't … No, the barometer. That's right. The needle always pointed to stormy. I didn't think that was funny at the time.'

'Do you remember anything else about it?'

'No.'

'What did you do when your father came in drunk?'

'Put my head under the bedclothes.'

257

'Nothing else?'

'I went down once. He threw me against the wall.'

'Were you badly hurt?'

'Bruised. He was devastated. He cried.'

'And you never went down again?'

'No. I used to sit on the landing, going PIG PIG PIG PIG.' He made as if to pound his fist against the other palm, then remembered the burn.

'Where were you exactly? Leaning over the banisters?'

'No, I used to sit on the top step. If they started shouting I'd shuffle a bit further down.'

'And where was the barometer in relation to you?'

'On my left. I hope this is leading somewhere, Rivers.'

'I think it is.'

'It was a bit like a teddy-bear, I suppose. I mean it was a sort of companion.'

'Can you imagine yourself back there?'

'I've said I—'

'No, take your time.'

'All right.' Prior closed his eyes, then opened them again, looking puzzled.

'Yes?'

'Nothing. It used to catch the light. There was a street lamp...' He gestured vaguely over his shoulder. 'This is going to sound absolutely mad. I used to go into the shine on the glass.'

A long silence.

'When it got too bad. And I didn't want to be there.'

'Then what happened? Did you go back to bed?'

'I must've done, mustn't I? Look, if you're saying this dates back to then, you're wrong. The gaps started in France, they got better at Craiglockhart,

258

they started again a few months ago. It's nothing to do with bloody barometers.'

Silence.

'Say something, Rivers.'

'I think it has. I think when you were quite small you discovered a way of dealing with a very unpleasant situation. I think you found out how to put yourself into a kind of trance. A dissociated state. And then in France, under that *intolerable* pressure, you rediscovered it.'

Prior shook his head. 'You're saying it isn't something that happens. It's something I do.'

'Not deliberately.' He waited. 'Look, you know the sort of thing that happens. People lose their tempers, they burst into tears, they have nightmares. They behave like children, in many respects. All I'm suggesting is that you rediscovered a method of coping that served you well as a child. But which is—'

'I went into the shine on the glass.'

Rivers looked puzzled. 'Yes, you said.'

'No, in the pub, the first time it happened. The first time in England. I was watching the sunlight on a glass of beer.' He thought for a moment. 'And I was very angry because Jimmy was dead, and ... everybody was enjoying themselves. I started to imagine what it would be like if a tank came in and crushed them. And I suppose I got frightened. It was so vivid, you see. Almost as if it had happened.' A long pause. 'You say it's self-hypnosis.'

'I think it must be. Something like that.'

'So if I could do it and tell myself to remember in theory that would fill in the gaps. All the gaps, because I'd bring all the memories back with me.'

'I don't know if that's the right thing to do.'

'But in theory it would work.'

'If you could become sufficiently aware of the process, yes.'

Prior was lost in thought. '*Is* it just remembering?'

'I don't think I know what you mean.'

'If I remember is that enough to heal the split?'

'No, I don't think so. I think there has to be a moment of . . . recognition. Acceptance. There has to be a moment when you look in the mirror and say, yes, this too is myself.'

'That could be difficult.'

'Why should it be?'

Prior's lips twisted. 'I find some parts of me pretty bloody unacceptable even at the best of times.'

The sadism again. 'There was nothing I saw or heard last night that would lead me to believe anything . . . terrible might be happening.'

'Perhaps you're just not his type.'

'"*Mister* Prior."'

A reluctant smile. 'All right.'

Rivers stood up. 'I think we've got as far as we can for the moment. *Don't* spend the day brooding, will you? And don't get depressed. We've made a lot of progress. It'll do you much more good to have a break. Here, you'll need this.' Rivers went to his desk, opened the top drawer, and took out a key. 'I'll tell the servants to expect you.'

CHAPTER TWENTY

Prior woke with a cry and lay in the darkness, sweating, disorientated, unable to understand why the grey square of window was on his right, instead of opposite his bed as it should have been. He'd been with Rivers for over a fortnight and yet he still had these moments when he woke and couldn't remember where he was. Footsteps came padding to his door.

'Are you all right?' Rivers's voice.

'Come in.' Prior put the lamp on. 'I'm sorry I woke you.'

'You cried out. I couldn't think what it was.'

'Yes, I know, I'm sorry.'

They looked at each other. Prior smiled. 'Shades of Craiglockhart.'

'Yes,' Rivers said. 'We've done this often enough.'

'You were on duty then. Go on, get back to bed. You need the rest.'

'Will you be able to get back to sleep?'

'Oh, yes, I'll be all right.' He looked at Rivers's exhausted face. 'And *you* certainly should. Go on, go back to bed.'

The dream had been about Mac, Prior thought, as the door closed behind Rivers. He couldn't remember it clearly, only that it had been full of struggling animals and the smell of blood. Rivers seemed to think it was a good sign that his nightmares had moved away from the war, back into his childhood, but they were no less horrifying, and in any case they were still about the war, he knew they were. Rivers made him talk endlessly about his childhood, particularly his early childhood, the rows between his parents, his own fear, the evenings he'd spent at the top of the stairs, listening, words and blows burnt into him till he could bear it no longer, and decided not to be there. He could still not remember what happened in the childhood gaps, though now he remembered that there had been gaps, though only when he was quite small. Once, in sheer exasperation, he'd asked Rivers how he was getting on with his own gap, the darkness at the top of his own stairs, but Rivers had simply smiled and pressed on. One always thought of Rivers as a *gentle* man, but Prior sometimes wondered why one did. Relentless might have been a better word.

The nightmares, though, were not about the rows between his parents. The nightmares were about Mac. And that was strange because most of his memories of Mac were pleasant.

An expanse of gritty asphalt. A low building with wire cages over the windows. Smells of custard and sweaty socks. The singing lesson, Monday morning, straight after Assembly, with Horton prowling up and down the aisles, swishing his cane against his trouser leg, listening for wrong notes. His taste had run to sentimental ballads, 'The Lost Chord' a firm favourite. This was the time Mr Hailes was inculcating a terror of masturbation, with his lectures on Inflamed Organs and the exhaustion which followed from playing with them. Horton sat down at the piano and sang in his manly baritone:

I was seated one day at the organ
Weary and ill at ease.

262

Prior gave an incredulous yelp of laughter, one or two of the others sniggered, Mac guffawed. The piano faltered into silence. Horton stood up, summoned Mac to the front of the room and invited him to share the joke. 'Well?' said Horton. 'I'm sure we could all do with being amused.'

'I don't think you'd think it was funny, sir.'

Mac was savagely caned. Prior was let off. Horton had heard Prior laugh too, he was sure of it, but Prior, thanks to his mother's scrimping and saving, was always well turned out. Shirts ironed, shoes polished, he looked like the sort of boy who might get a scholarship, as indeed he did, thanks partly to Father Mackenzie's more robust approach to organ playing. *Bastard*, Prior thought, as Horton's arm swung.

Years later, after witnessing the brutalities of trench warfare, he still thought: *Bastard*.

At the time he had been determined on revenge. Angrier on Mac's behalf than he would ever have been on his own.

Horton was a man of regular habits. Precisely twenty minutes before the bell rang for the end of the dinner break, he could be seen trekking across the playground to the masters' lavatory. Not for him the newspaper the boys had to make do with. Bulging from one side of his jacket, like a single tit, was a roll of toilet-paper. He marched across the yard with precise military tread, almost unnoticed by the shouting and running boys. Humour in the playground was decidedly scatological, but Horton's clockwork shitting was too old a joke to laugh at.

One dinnertime, posting Mac where he could see the main entrance to the school, Prior went in on a recce. Next day he and Mac slipped into the lavatory and locked the door of one of the cubicles. Prior lit a match, applied it to the wick of a candle, shielded the flame with both hands until it burned brightly, and fixed it in its own wax to a square of plywood.

Prompt to the minute, Mr Horton entered. He was puzzled by the locked cubicle. 'Mr Barnes?'

Prior produced a baritone grunt of immense effort and Horton said no more. Not even that constipated grunt tempted them to giggle. Horton's beatings were no laughing matter. They waited in silence, feeling the rise and fall of each other's breath. Then, slowly, Prior lowered the candle into the water that ran beneath the lavatory seat. It was one long seat, really, though the cubicles divided it. The candle flickered briefly, but then the flame rose up again and burnt steadily. Prior urged it along the dark water, and it bobbed along, going much faster than he'd thought it would. Mac was already unbolting the door. They ran across the playground, to where a game of High Cockalorum was in progress (by arrangement) and hurled themselves on top of the heap of struggling boys.

Behind them, candle flame met arse. A howl of pain and incredulity, and Horton appeared, gazing wildly round him. No use him looking for signs of guilt. He inspired such terror that guilt was written plain on every one of the two hundred faces that turned towards him. In any case there was dignity to be considered. He limped across the playground and no more was heard.

Once he was safely out of sight, Prior and Mac went quietly round the corner to the forbidden area by the pile of coke and there they danced a solemn and entirely silent dance of triumph.

And why am I bothering to recall such an incident

in so much detail, Prior asked himself. Because every memory of friendship I come up with is a shield against Hettie's spit in my face, a way of saying of course I couldn't have done it. What surprised him now was how *innocent* he'd felt when Beattie first mentioned Hettie's belief that he'd betrayed Mac. 'I didn't do it,' he'd said automatically, with total assurance, for all the world as if he could answer for every minute of his waking life. Only on the train coming back to London had he forced himself to accept that it was *possible* he'd betrayed Mac. Or at any rate that it was impossible for him to deny it.

Since then he'd gained one fact from Rivers that filled him with fear. He now knew that in the fugue state he'd denied that his father was his father. If he was prepared to deny that—a simple biological fact after all—what chance did pre-war friendships have? Rivers had hesitated visibly when telling him what his other state had said, and yet Prior's reaction to it had been more complicated than simple rejection or denial. To say that one had been born in a shell-hole is to say something absurdly self-dramatizing. Even by my standards, Prior thought wryly. Yet if you asked anybody who'd fought in France whether he thought he was the same person he'd been before the war, the person his family still remembered, the overwhelming majority—no, not even that, *all of them, all of them* would say no. It was merely a matter of degree. And one did feel at times very powerfully that the only loyalties that actually mattered were loyalties forged there. Picard clay was a powerful glue. Might it not, applied to pre-war friendships with conscientious objectors, be an equally powerful solvent?

Not in *this* state, he reminded himself. In *this* state

265

he'd risked court martial for Beattie's sake, copying out documents that incriminated Spragge. But then Beattie was a woman, and couldn't fight. His other self might be less tolerant of healthy strapping young men spending the war years trying to disrupt the supply of ammunition on which other lives depended.

But *Mac*, he thought. Mac.

He did eventually drift off to sleep, and woke three hours later, to find the room full of sunshine. He peered sleepily at his watch, then reached for his dressing-gown. Rivers, already shaved and fully dressed, was sitting over the remains of breakfast. 'It seemed better to let you sleep,' he said. 'I'm afraid the coffee's cold.'

'Did you get back to sleep?'

'Yes.'

Lying hound, thought Prior. He drank the cold coffee as he shaved and dressed. Rivers was waiting by the desk. For a moment Prior felt rebellious, but then he looked at Rivers and saw how tired he was and thought, my God, if he can manage, it, I can. He sat down, and the familiar position, the light falling on to Rivers's face, made him aware that he'd taken a decision. 'I'm going to see Mac,' he said.

Silence. 'I think the reason I'm not making any progress is that ... there's a there's th-there's *oh, for Christ's sake*.' He threw back his head. 'There's a barrier, and I think it's something to do with him.'

'Finding out one fact about your behaviour over the past few weeks isn't going to change anything.'

'I think it might.'

Another long silence. Rivers shifted his position, 'Yes, I do see that.'

'And although I see the point, I mean, I see how

266

important it is to get to the root of it, I do need to be functioning *now*. Somehow going over what happened with my parents just makes me feel like a sort of lifelong hopeless neurotic. It makes me feel I'll never be able to *do* anything.'

'Oh, I shouldn't worry about that,' Rivers said. 'Half the world's work's done by hopeless neurotics.'

This was accompanied by an involuntary glance at his desk. Prior laughed aloud. 'Would you like me to help you with any of it?'

Rivers smiled. 'I was thinking of Darwin.'

'Like hell. Why don't you let me do that?' Prior asked, pointing to a stack of papers on the desk. 'You're just typing it out, aren't you? You're not altering it.'

'It's very kind of you, but you couldn't read the writing. That's why I have to type it. My secretary can't read it either.'

'Let's have a look. Do you mind?' Prior picked up a sheet of paper. 'Rivers, do you realize this is the graphic equivalent of a stammer? I mean, whatever it is you couldn't say, you certainly didn't intend to write it.'

Rivers pointed his index finger. 'You're getting better.'

Prior smiled. Without apparent effort, he read a sentence aloud: *Thus, a frequent factor in the production of war neurosis is the necessity of restraint of the expression of dislike or disrespect for those of superior rank.* 'There's no hope for me, then, is there? I wonder why you bother.' He pushed Rivers gently off the chair. 'Go on, you get on with something else.'

Rivers shook his head. 'Do you know, nobody's ever done that before.'

'I'm good at breaking codes.'

267

'Is that a boast?'

'No. Pure terror.'

*   *   *

As Rivers turned the corner, he saw a man leaving Sassoon's room. They met face to face in the narrow corridor, and stopped.

'Dr Rivers?'

'Yes.'

'Robert Ross.'

They shook hands. After a few pleasantries about the weather, Ross said, 'I don't know whether Siegfried's talked about the future at all?'

'I believe he has various plans. Obviously he's in no state to do anything very much at the moment.'

'Gosse has some idea he could be useful in war propaganda, you know. Apparently Siegfried told him his only qualification for the job was that he'd been wounded in the head.'

They laughed, united by their shared affection for Siegfried, then said goodbye. Rivers was left with the impression that Ross had wanted to tell him something, but had thought better of it.

Siegfried was sitting up in bed, a notepad on his knees. 'Was that you talking to Ross?'

'Yes.'

'He looks ill, doesn't he?'

He looked worse than 'ill'. He looked as if he were dying. 'It's difficult to tell when you don't know the person.'

'I shan't be seeing him next week. He's off to the country.'

Rivers sat down by the bed.

'I've been trying to write to Owen,' Sassoon said.

268

'You remember Owen? Little chap. Used to be in the breakfast-room selling the *Hydra*.'

'Yes, I remember. Brock's patient.'

'Well, he sent me a poem and I praised it to to the skies and now it's been passed round...' Siegfried pulled a face. 'Nobody else likes it. And now I look at it again *I*'m not sure either. The fact is...' he said, putting the pad on his bedside table, 'my judgement's gone. And not just for Owen's work. I thought *I*'d done one or two good things, but when I look at them again they're rubbish. In fact, I don't think I've done anything good since I left Craiglockhart.'

Rivers said carefully, 'You think that at the moment because you're depressed. Give yourself a rest.'

'Am I depressed?'

'You know you are.'

'I don't know what point there is in it anyway. What's an anti-war poet except a poet who's dependent on war? I thought a lot of things were simple, Rivers, and...' A pause. 'Eddie Marsh came to see me. He thinks he can find me a job at the Ministry of Munitions.'

'What do you think about that?'

'I don't know.'

Rivers nodded. 'Well, you've got plenty of time.'

'I don't even know whether I'm going back to France. Am I?'

'I shall do everything I can to prevent it. I don't think anybody expects you to go back this time.'

'I never regretted going back, you know. Not once.' He sat up suddenly, clasping his arms round his knees. 'You know what I'd really like to do? Go to Sheffield and work in a factory.'

'In a factory?'

269

'Yes, why not? I don't want to spend the rest of my life wrapped up in the sort of cocoon I was in before the war. I want to find out about ordinary people. Workers.'

'Why Sheffield?'

'Because it's close to Edward Carpenter.'

Silence.

'Why not?' Siegfried demanded. '*Why not?* I did everything anybody wanted me to do. Everything *you* wanted me to do. I gave in, I went back. Now why can't I do something that's right for *me*?'

'Because you're still in the army.'

'But you say yourself nobody expects—'

'That's a very different matter from a General Discharge. I see no grounds for that.'

'Does it rest with you?'

'Yes.' Rivers got up and walked to the window. He had hoped this time to be able to use his skills unambiguously for Siegfried's benefit. Instead, he was faced with the task of putting obstacles in the way of yet another hare-brained scheme, because this was another protest, smaller, more private, less hopeful, than his public declaration had been, but still a protest.

Behind him Siegfried said, 'There was a great jamboree in the park yesterday. Bands playing.'

Rivers turned to look at him. 'Of course, I was forgetting. August 4th.'

'They were unveiling some sort of shrine to the dead. Or giving thanks for the war, I'm not sure which. There's a Committee for War Memorials. One of the committees Robbie had to resign from. Can't have the Glorious Dead commemorated by a sodomite. Even if some of the Glorious Dead *were* sodomites.'

270

'You're very bitter.'

'And you're right, it's no good. You can *ride* anger.' Siegfried raised his hands in a horseman's gesture, forefingers splayed to take the reins. 'I don't know what you do with bitterness. Nothing, probably.'

Rivers caught and held a sigh. 'There's something I want to say. In my own defence, I suppose. If *at any time* you'd said to me, "I am a pacifist. I believe it's always and in all circumstances wrong to kill", I . . . I wouldn't have agreed with you, I'd've made you argue the case every step of the way, but in the end I'd've done everything in my power to help you get out of the army.'

'You don't need a defence. I told you, I never regretted going back.'

'But then you have to face the fact that you're *still* a soldier.' Rivers opened his mouth, looked down at Siegfried, and shut it again. 'You know, you really oughtn't to be lying in bed on a day like this. Why don't you get dressed? We could go out.'

Siegfried looked at his tunic, hanging on the back of the door. 'No, thanks, I'd rather not.'

'You haven't been dressed since you arrived.'

'I can't be bothered to dazzle the VADs.'

'*Dazzle?* Isn't that a bit conceited?'

'*Fact*, Rivers.' Siegfried smiled. 'One of life's minor ironies.'

Rivers walked across the room, took Siegfried's tunic from the peg and threw it on to the bed. 'Come on, Siegfried. Put it on. You can't spend the rest of your life in pyjamas.'

'I can't spend the rest of my life in that either.'

'No, but you have to spend the rest of the war in it.'

For a moment it looked as if Siegfried would

271

refuse. Then, slowly, he pushed back the covers and got out of bed. He looked terrible. White. Twitching. Exhausted.

'We needn't go far,' Rivers said.

Slowly, Sassoon started to put on the uniform.

*   *   *

It was easier for Prior to arrange a visit to Mac than he had expected. He still had Ministry of Munitions headed notepaper, having taken a pile with him when he cleared his desk. But probably even without it, the uniform, the wound stripe, the earnestly expressed wish to save an old friend from the shame of pacifism, would have been enough to get him an interview.

Mac was sitting on his plank bed, his head in his hands.

Prior said, 'Hello, Mac.'

The hands came down. Mac looked ... as people do look who've had repeated disagreements with detention camp guards.

'On your feet,' the guard said.

'No,' Prior said sharply. 'Leave us.'

The man looked startled, but obeyed. It was a relief when the door clanged shut behind him. Prior had been dreading a situation where Mac refused to salute him, and the guards spent the next half hour bouncing his head off the wall.

'Well,' Prior said.

No chair. No glass in the window. A smell of stale urine from the bucket, placed where it could be seen from the door. And behind him ... yes, of course. The eye.

'I didn't expect to see *you*,' Mac said. Neither his voice nor his manner was friendly, but he showed no

272

obvious rancour. Perhaps, like a soldier, he'd become accustomed to the giving and receiving of hard, impersonal knocks. There was no room for emotion in this.

'At least they've given you a blanket.'

Mac was naked underneath the blanket and the cell was cold even in summer.

'For your visit. It goes when you go.'

Prior sat down at the foot of the plank bed and looked around him.

'One of the main weapons, that,' said Mac conversationally. 'Marching you about the place naked. Especially since they don't give you any paper to wipe yourself with and the food in here's enough to give a brass monkey the shits.' He waited. 'The arsehole plays a major part in breaking people down, did you know that?'

'You look as if they've worked you over.'

'*Work?* Pleasure. One of them...' Mac raised his forearm. 'Hang your towel on it.'

'Is that over now?'

'The beatings? They're over when I give in.'

A uniform was lying, neatly folded, on the end of the bed.

'Can I ask you something, Billy? Do you talk about the war in the trenches? I don't mean day-to-day stuff, pass the ammunition, all that, I mean, "Why are we fighting?" "What is it all for?"'

'No. We're 'ere because we're 'ere.'

'Same in here.'

Prior looked puzzled. 'There's nobody to talk *to*.'

Mac smiled. 'Morse code on the pipes. I take it I can rely on you not to tell the CO?'

'Of course.'

'"Of course", Billy?'

273

'It wasn't me.'

Mac smiled and shook his head. 'Why come here if you're going to say that? Why come at all? I don't know. Do you just want to see what you've done?'

Prior opened his mouth for a second denial, and closed it again. 'I've got something for you,' he said, digging into his tunic pocket and bringing out two bars of chocolate. He watched Mac's pupils flare, then go dead. 'Yes, I know. It's contaminated. I've touched it.' He held the chocolate out, using his body to screen Mac from the eye. 'But you have to survive.'

Mac aligned himself exactly with Prior so that he could take the chocolate without being seen. 'That's true.'

'You'd better eat it. They'll search you.'

'They won't. That would mean doubting your integrity. An officer and a gentleman, no less. All the same I think I will have some.' He slit the paper with his fingernail, broke off a piece and started to eat. The movements of his mouth and throat were awkward. Hunger had turned eating into an act as private as bishop-bashing. Prior tried to look away, but there was nothing to look at. His eyes could only wander round the cell and return to Mac.

'Nine steps that way. Seven this. I do a lot of walking.'

'How long are you in for?'

'Solitary? Ninety days. If I reoffend—which *is* my intention—back in. Another ninety.'

Prior looked down at his hands. 'And no letters?'

'No.'

Mac managed a smile between mouthfuls. 'Why did you come, Billy?'

'To find out what you thought.'

'About you? What a self-centred little shit you are.'

'Yes.'

'I didn't believe it. The sergeant in Liverpool told me it was you, I mean, he mentioned your name. He was standing on my scrotum at the time, so, as you can imagine, it had a certain ring to it. I still didn't believe it, but the more I thought about it the more I thought, yes.' Mac was speaking intently, and yet almost indifferently, as if he didn't care whether Prior listened or not. Perhaps speaking at all was merely a way of salving his pride, of distracting Prior's attention while the all-important business of devouring the chocolate went on. 'And then I thought, he told you. Do you remember in the cattle shed I asked you what you'd have done if you'd found a deserter in Hettie's scullery and you said, "I'd turn him in. What else could I do?" And then I remembered a story I heard, about a man who found a snake half dead and nursed it back to life. He fed it, took care of it. And then he let it go. And the next time they met it bit him. And this was a very poisonous snake, he ... knew he was going to die. And with his last gasp, he said, "But why? I saved you, I fed you, I nursed you. Why did you bite me?" And the snake said, "But you knew I was a snake."'

A long silence. Prior moved at last. 'It's a good story.'

'It's a fucking marvellous story. Only ...'

Prior waited. 'Only what?'

'Now shall I be greedy, and eat it all?'

'Make sure of it. I would.'

'I probably hate you a lot less than you think. Not that I'd say we were bosom pals exactly, in fact if I meet you after the war I'll probably try to kill you ...' He smiled and shook his head. 'Was it all a lie about wanting to help Beattie?'

'No, it was all true.'

'You know what I'd like? I'd like you to look me straight in the eye, put on that phoney public school accent of yours, and say, yes I told the police where to find you, and I'm not ashamed of that. It was my duty.'

'I can't.'

Mac was watching him intently. 'Then I don't understand. I thought you'd finally worked out whose side you were on.'

'There was never any doubt about that,' Prior said, raising his sleeve. 'People who wear this. More or less with pride.' He stood up. 'I shan't say I'm sorry.'

Mac looked up at him. 'Don't. Chocolate's too precious to bring back.'

Prior knocked, and waited impatiently for the guard to appear. He realized the painted eye must be looking straight at his belt buckle. Surreptitiously, he put his finger into the hole until it touched cool glass. Towers's eye, he remembered, lying in the palm of his hand, had been warm.

The guard appeared and, with one backward glance, he followed him along the iron landing and down the stairs. He had the rest of the day to get through before he could talk to Rivers, but he was glad of that. It was right that the first confusion and pain should be borne alone. He did not doubt for a moment that Mac's story was true—Mac had no reason to lie. Though he still had no memory of doing it, he had betrayed Mac.

He remembered an occasion when he'd held out a shaking hand to Rivers, stuttering something totally incoherent about Towers's eye, how the memory of holding it in his hand had become a talisman, a reminder of where the deepest loyalties lie. That was

276

still true. And yet he could not justify what he had done to Mac. Even if his other self hated Mac for refusing to fight, for trying to bring the munitions factories to a halt, it remained true that in arranging to meet Mac he had in effect offered him a safe conduct—for Beattie's sake. Even leaving aside the childhood friendship, there had been a personal undertaking given in the present, trusted in the present, betrayed in the present. He could not, whether to satisfy Mac or console himself, say, 'I did my duty.' What had happened was altogether darker, more complex than that.

Drill was going on in the yard outside. Familiar shouts, the slurrying and stamping of boots, lines of regimented bodies moving as one. In the front rank a conchie was being 'persuaded' to take part. That is, he was being manhandled first into one position, then another. 'Marking time' consisted of being kicked on the ankles by the guards on either side. No attempt was made to hide what was happening. Presumably it was taken for granted that an officer would approve.

Prior watched for a while, then turned away.

CHAPTER TWENTY-ONE

A freshening breeze, blowing across the Serpentine, fumbled the roses, loosening red and yellow petals that lay on the dry soil or drifted across the paths. Rivers and Sassoon had been wandering along beside the lake for no more than fifteen minutes, but already Sassoon looked tired.

'I've been very good,' he said. 'The last few days. Out of bed and dressed before breakfast.'

'*Good.*'

Glutinous yellow sunlight, slanting between the trees, cast their shadows across the water.

'Do you remember me telling you about Richard Dadd?' Siegfried asked suddenly. 'Drowning his father in the Serpentine?'

'Yes,' Rivers said, and waited for more. When Siegfried didn't speak, he asked, 'Should I be hanging on to a tree?'

Siegfried smiled. 'No, not you.'

The deck-chairs beside the lake were empty, bellying in the wind, but on a sunny sheltered bank soldiers home on leave sat or lay entwined with their girls, the girls' summer dresses bright splashes against the khaki of their uniforms. A woman in a black uniform appeared on the ridge and began to make her way diagonally down the slope. As she advanced, a black beetle toiling across the grass, the lovers drew apart, and a girl close to the path tugged anxiously at the hem of her skirt.

'I've even been to the common room,' Siegfried

said. 'You know what the topic of conversation was? The changes you notice when you're home on leave and whether any of them are for the better. And somebody said, yes, every time you came home women's skirts were shorter. I'm afraid it's not much consolation to *me*.'

Rivers caught a sigh. Depression and bitterness had become Siegfried's settled state. If he seemed better than he had when he first arrived, it was mainly because depression—provided it hasn't reached the point of stupor—is more easily disguised than elation. He was actually very ill indeed.

'I must say I'll be glad to be out of London,' Siegfried went on. 'Have you heard any more about this convalescent home?'

'Oh, yes. They can take you.'

'It's ... I'm sorry, I've forgotten where you said it was.'

'Coldstream. Near Berwick-on-Tweed.'

'Is that anywhere near Scarborough? It's just Owen's stationed in Scarborough.'

'Well, it's not *near*, but you could probably get there and back in a day.' Rivers hesitated. 'There is one thing I think you ... might not like. There has to be a Medical Board first.'

'Yes.'

Siegfried sounded puzzled. This wasn't the first time he'd been in hospital: riding accident during training, trench fever, wounded, 'shell-shocked' at Craiglockhart, wounded again. He knew the routine backwards.

'At Craiglockhart,' Rivers said.

A stunned silence. '*No*. Why Craiglockhart?'

'Because you're my patient. Because I want to be on the Board.'

Siegfried couldn't take it in. 'I can't go back there.'

'I'm afraid you've got to. It's only for a few days, Siegfried.'

Siegfried shook his head. 'I can't. You don't know what you're asking.'

There was an empty bench a few yards further on. Rivers sat down and indicated that Siegfried should join him. 'Tell me, then.'

A silence during which Sassoon struggled visibly with himself.

'Why can't you?' Rivers prompted gently.

'Because it would mean admitting I'm one of them.'

Rivers felt a flare of anger, but brought it quickly under control. 'One of whom?'

Siegfried was silent. At last he said, 'You know what I mean.'

'Yes, I'm afraid I do. One of the degenerates, the loonies, the lead-swingers, the cowards.' He waited for a response, but Siegfried had turned his head away. 'You know, Siegfried, sometimes I ... reproach myself with having exercised too great an influence on you. At a time when you were vulnerable and ... perhaps needed to be left alone to come to your own decision in your way.' Rivers shook his head. 'Well, I shan't be doing *that* again. If you still think like that I haven't influenced you at all. I haven't managed to convey a single bloody thing. Not a bloody thing.' He looked out over the lake. The wind blew a dark ripple across the surface like goose pimples spreading across skin. 'Perhaps we'd better be getting back.'

'Not yet.'

'You have to go back to Craiglockhart. I'm sorry, I'll make it as short as I can, but you have to go.'

280

Siegfried nodded. He was sitting with his big hands clasped between his knees. 'All right. But you do see what I'm trying to say? I *know* you find it offensive, but . . . It's not just admitting I'm one of them *now*, it's admitting I always was. Don't you see?'

'Yes, and it's nonsense. One day I'm going to give you a copy of your admission report. "No physical or mental signs of any nervous disorder." If you're tormenting yourself with the idea that your protest was some kind of symptom, well, for God's sake, stop. It wasn't. It was an entirely valid, sane response to the situation we're all in.' He paused. '*Wrong*, of course.'

'When I was in France I used to think of it as breakdown. It was easier than—'

'Than remembering what you believed?'

'Yes.' Siegfried looked down at his hands. 'Now I just feel as if a trap's been sprung.' A slight laugh. 'Not by you, I don't mean by you. But it has, hasn't it? It's absolutely *full circle. Literally* back to the beginning. Only worse, because now I belong there.'

'Three days. I promise.'

Siegfried got up. 'All right.'

Rivers remained seated for a moment. He wanted to say, if there *is* a trap, I'm in it too, but he couldn't. 'Come on,' he said, standing up. 'Let's go back.'

*   *   *

The bomb site had been tidied up, Prior saw. Rubble cleared away, the pavements swept clean of white dust, the houses on either side of the gap shored up. A cold wind whistled through the gap, disturbing the trees, whipping up litter into whirlpools that ran along the gutters. The sun blazed in the windows of

281

the houses opposite the gap, turning the far side of the square into a wall of fire.

Prior was early for his appointment and dawdled along, noticing what on his previous visit, walking with Charles Manning through the spring dark, he had not noticed: that many of the elegant houses had dingy basements, like white teeth yellow round the gums.

He pressed the bell of Manning's house and turned slightly away, expecting to have to wait, but the door was opened almost immediately and by Manning himself, so quickly indeed that he must have been hovering in the hall. He might have appeared anxious, but his smile, his whole bearing, gave the impression of impulsive informality.

'It's all right, I've got it,' he said to somebody over his shoulder, and stood aside to let Prior in. 'I'm glad you could come. I thought of waiting till we were both back at work, but—'

'I'm not going back,' Prior said quickly.

'Ah.'

The living-room door stood open. No dust-sheets now.

'Oh, yes, come and see,' Manning said, noticing the direction of his glance.

They went in. A smell of furniture polish and roses.

'You found a builder, then,' Prior said, looking up at the door.

'Yes. I must say he didn't inspire a lot of confidence, but he seems to have done all right. As far as one can tell.' Manning patted the wall. 'I've got a sneaking suspicion the wallpaper might be holding the plaster up.'

They found themselves staring rather too long at the place where the crack had been, and glanced at each other, momentarily at a loss. 'Come and sit down,' Manning said.

A bowl of red and yellow roses stood in the fireplace where before there had been scrumpled newspaper dusted with soot. No mirror either—that had been moved. The whole room had been redecorated. So much was changed that the unyielding brocade of the sofa came as a shock. Prior flexed his shoulders, remembering. It was almost as if the body had an alternative store of memory in the nerve endings, for the sensation of being held stiffly erect induced a state of sensual awareness. He looked at Manning, and knew that he too was remembering.

'Would you like a drink?'

Manning went across to the sideboard. Prior, noticing a book lying face down on the floor near an armchair, reached across and picked it up. *Rex V. Pemberton Billing*. It was a complete transcript of the trial. What an extraordinary thing for Manning to be reading. Manning came back with the drinks. 'Is it good?' Prior asked, holding up the book.

'Fascinating,' Manning said. 'I realized while I was reading it wh-wh-what's actually h-happening. It's just that people are saturated with tragedy, they simply can't respond any more. So they've decided to play the rest of the war as farce.'

'I can't say I'd be prepared to fork out good money for this.'

'I didn't,' Manning said, sitting down. 'It was sent to me. By "a well-wisher".'

Prior raised his eyebrows. 'Really?'

'Oh, yes. I've had several little ... communications.'

'Captain Spencer came to see us, you know.'

'"Us"?'

283

'The Intelligence Unit. I think somebody must have told him the first question he'd be asked in court was whether he'd informed the appropriate authorities when he discovered the Great Conspiracy. So he was scurrying round London informing them.' Prior laughed.

'Did he mention any names?'

'Good Lord, yes.' Prior looked up and caught a fleeting expression of anxiety. 'Not you.'

'No, I didn't think that, I'm not important enough. Robert Ross?'

'Well, yes.'

Manning nodded. 'You say you're not going back?'

'There's nothing to go back *to*. I went in to check my pigeonhole and ... it was like the *Marie Celeste*. Files gone. Lode gone.'

'He's...'

'Teaching cadets. In Wales. No doubt that pleases him.'

'Why, is he Welsh?'

'I was being sarcastic. I shouldn't think it pleases him in the least. Spragge. I don't know whether you—'

'The informer?'

'That's right. He's gone—or going, I'm not sure which—to South Africa. *All expenses paid.*'

Manning hesitated. 'I ... don't think you should feel *nothing* useful came out of that. I showed Eddie Marsh your report and ... he was rather impressed actually. As I was. He thought it was ... very cogently argued. Very effective.'

'It may have been cogently argued. It certainly wasn't *effective*. She's still in prison.'

Manning smiled. 'The point is—'

284

The french windows were thrown open, and a chubby-cheeked child peered, blinking, into the dark interior. 'Daddy?'

'Not now, Robert,' Manning said, turning round. 'Ask Elsie.'

Manning's face softened as he watched the child close the door carefully behind him. His delight in his house and family was so obvious it seemed churlish to wonder if he ever regretted the empty rooms of early spring, the smells of soot and fallen plaster, the footsteps that had followed him upstairs to the maids' bedroom.

'The point is that being able to organize an array of complicated facts and present them succinctly is quite a rare ability. And just the sort of thing we're looking for in my line of work.'

'Which is . . .'

'Health and safety. To cut a long story short, I'm offering you a job.'

'Ah.'

'I think you might find it worth while. Since it's basically protecting the interests of the workers.'

Prior was in no hurry to reply. He had resigned himself, not entirely with reluctance, to going back to Scarborough, to resuming the boring, comfortless life of an army camp in England. At the same time he knew Manning's offer was one for which a great many men would have given an arm or a leg, and not merely in the meaningless way that expression was normally used. 'Is Rivers behind this?'

'No.'

Prior wasn't sure he believed him. 'I'm very grateful, Charles—don't think I don't appreciate it— but I'm afraid I can't accept.'

'Why not?'

285

'Sarah—that's my girlfriend—she's in the north. I'd be able to see quite a lot of her if I was in Scarborough. And—that's a big factor. And ... I'm not sure how much I want a cushy job.'

Manning hesitated. 'It does have one very big advantage. It's most unlikely you'd be sent back to France. Though I suppose that's not very likely anyway.'

'Oh, I don't know.'

'What rating are you?'

'A4.'

'That's a long way from the top.'

'With a Board in two weeks' time.'

'Rivers wouldn't let it happen.'

'Rivers has nothing to do with it. I was given my original rating on the basis of my asthma.'

'But he'd write to the Board if you asked him.'

'I know. In fact I think Rivers could be quite eloquent on the subject of my unfitness for France. The point is, he won't be asked.'

'How are you really?'

'A lot better.'

Manning toyed with his glass. 'What was the trouble exactly?'

Prior smiled, remained silent just long enough for Manning to feel embarrassed by the intrusiveness of the question, then answered it. 'Memory lapses. Black-outs, I suppose. They do seem to be over.'

'Do you know what you did during them?'

'Yes.' Prior smiled again. 'Nothing I don't have a tendency to do.'

Manning became aware that he was looking almost indecently curious, and quickly corrected his expression.

'How about you?' Prior said.

'Mending. It was much harder *work* than I thought it would be.'

'Rivers? Oh, yes.'

'I mean, he's an absolute slave-driver. And you can't grumble because you know he's driving himself even harder.'

A glance of amusement and shared affection. Then Manning said, 'You sound almost as if you want to go back.'

'Yes, I suppose I do, in a way. It's odd, isn't it? In spite of everything—I mean in spite of Not Believing in the War and Not Having Faith in Our Generals and all that, it still seems the only *clean* place to be.'

'Yes. My God, *yes*.'

They stared at each other, aware of a depth of understanding that the surface facts of their relationship scarcely accounted for.

'Not an option for me, I'm afraid,' Manning added, stretching out his leg. 'But I do know what you mean.'

'Do you think we're mad?'

'Both been in the loony bin.'

'You'd better not let Rivers hear you calling it that.'

'I wouldn't dare. The offer's open for the next few days, you know,' Manning said, putting down his glass. 'I shan't be seeing Marsh till—'

Prior smiled and shook his head. 'No. Thank you, but no.'

'You don't think you might regret it?'

Prior laughed. 'Charles, if I get sent back—if, if, if, if—I shall sit in a dug-out and look back to this afternoon, and I shall think, "You *bloody* fool."'

'Well,' Manning said, standing up. 'I tried.'

287

In the hall a maid came forward carrying Prior's cap and cane. Prior glanced at her: she was sallow-skinned, middle aged, about as old as his mother, he supposed. He stared at her uniform, remembering how he'd pressed his face into the armpits, smelling the careworn, sad smell. Manning was saying something, but he didn't hear what it was. He turned to him and said, 'Now I come to think of it, Spencer *did* mention other names.'

Manning said smoothly, 'Thank you, Alice. I'll see Mr Prior out.'

'Winston Churchill and Edward Marsh.'

Manning gave an astonished yelp. '*Churchill?*'

'Yes.'

'Then he *is* mad.'

'Yes, that's what I thought.' Prior walked to the door, then stopped. 'He said Churchill and Marsh spent an entire afternoon beating each other's buttocks with a plaited birch.'

'Yes.'

'What do you mean "yes"?'

'Churchill was Home Secretary at the time.'

'Oh, well, that explains everything.'

'It was a new kind of birch.' Manning looked impatient. 'I don't know the details, there'd been some sort of controversy about it. I think people were saying it was cruel. So *naturally* they—'

'Tried it out on each other.'

'Yes.' Manning's expression hardened. 'They were doing their duty.'

'What conclusion did they reach?'

'I think they both thought they'd had worse beatings at school.'

Prior nodded, glanced round to make sure they

288

were unobserved, then took hold of Manning's pudgy cheeks and chucked them. 'There'll always be an England,' he told him and ran, laughing, down the steps.

AUTHOR'S NOTE

The reader may find it useful to have a brief outline of the historical events that occurred in 1917–1918 on which this novel is based.

Beattie Roper's story is loosely based on the 'poison plot' of 1917. Alice Wheeldon, a second-hand clothes dealer living in the back streets of Derby, was accused and convicted of having conspired to murder Lloyd George, Arthur Henderson and other persons by poisoning. The poison, in the case of Lloyd George, was to be administered by a curare-tipped blowdart. The trial depositions are in the Public Record Office, Chancery Lane, and provide a fascinating insight into the lives of absolutist pacifists on the run, and the Ministry of Munitions agents who spied on them. Mrs Wheeldon was convicted on the unsupported evidence of such informers and sentenced to ten years' hard labour, despite her insistence that the poison she had procured was intended for the guard dogs at a detention centre. After the war she was released, but, weakened by prison diet, hard labour and repeated hunger strikes, died in 1919.

Friends of Alice Wheeldon by Sheila Rowbotham (Pluto Press, 1986) contains a useful essay: 'Rebel Networks in the First World War'.

In January 1918 the *Imperialist* (later the *Vigilante*), a newspaper owned and edited by the MP Noel Pemberton Billing, carried an article entitled 'The First 47,000'. It purported to be written by

Pemberton Billing himself, but in fact the author was a Captain Harold Spencer, who claimed that he had been a British Intelligence agent at the time when he saw and read the Black Book in the *cabinet noir* of 'a certain German Prince'.

In April this article was followed by a short paragraph entitled 'The Cult of the Clitoris', again purporting to be written by Pemberton Billing, and again written by Harold Spencer. This suggested that the list of subscribers to a private performance of Oscar Wilde's *Salome* might contain many names of the 47,000. Maud Allan, who was to dance the part of Salome, sued Pemberton Billing for libel, since the paragraph clearly implied she was a lesbian.

The trial was presided over by Lord Justice Darling. Pemberton Billing defended himself. Having been identified early in the proceedings as one of the 47,000, Darling lost control of the court.

The star defence witness was Harold Spencer. In addition to giving free rein to his obsession with women who had hypertrophied and diseased clitorises and therefore could be satisfied only by bull elephants, Spencer alleged that many members of the Asquith War Cabinet had been in the pay of the Germans, that Maud Allan was Asquith's wife's lover and a German agent, that many high-ranking officers in the British army were Germans, and that persons who had the courage and patriotism to point these facts out were marooned on desert islands where they had to subsist on iron rations from submarines.

Lord Alfred Douglas, another defence witness, seized the opportunity of pursuing his personal dispute with Robert Ross, Oscar Wilde's devoted friend and literary executor, identifying him as 'the leader of all the sodomites in London'.

After six days of chaos in the courtroom and hysteria in the newspapers, Pemberton Billing won the case and was carried shoulder-high through the cheering crowds that had gathered outside the Old Bailey.

Later that year Harold Spencer was certified insane.

Robert Ross died of heart failure, on 5 October, aged forty-nine.

Pemberton Billing went on to have a distinguished parliamentary career.

In 1917 Siegfried Sassoon (1886–1967), after protesting against the war, had been persuaded by his friend Robert Graves to accept a Medical Board, which decided that he was suffering from a mental breakdown and that he should be sent to Craiglockhart War Hospital, Edinburgh. There he came under the care of Dr W. H. R. Rivers, FRS (1864–1922), the distinguished neurologist and social anthropologist. At Craiglockhart, Sassoon reached the conclusion that, although his views on the war had not changed, it was nevertheless his duty to return to active service, where he could at least share the suffering of his men.

After a period in Palestine he returned to France on 9 May 1918. On 13 July, returning late from a patrol, he was wounded in the scalp by a rifle shot from one of his own NCOs; he was then sent back to England, to the American Women's Red Cross Hospital at Lancaster Gate. The fact that he was ill enough for Rivers to have found it necessary to sit up with him is recalled in a letter from Katharine Rivers to Ruth Head (unpublished letters of the Rivers family, Imperial War Museum).

Winston Churchill's and Edward Marsh's devotion to duty while at the Home Office is mentioned in *Edward Marsh, Patron of the Arts: A Biography* by Christopher Hassall (Longmans, 1959).

The LARGE PRINT HOME LIBRARY

If you have enjoyed this Large Print book and would like to build up your own collection of Large Print books and have them delivered direct to your door, please contact The Large Print Home Library.

The Large Print Home Library offers you a full service:

☆ **Created to support your local library**

☆ **Delivery direct to your door**

☆ **Easy-to-read type & attractively bound**

☆ **The very best authors**

☆ **Special low prices**

For further details either call Customer Services on 01225 443400 or write to us at:

The Large Print Home Library
FREEPOST (BA 1686/1)
Bath BA2 3SZ